LISTEN TO THE CAT!

ALSO BY LOUISE CLARK

The Nine Lives Cozy Mystery Series

The Cat Came Back

The Cat's Paw

Cat Got Your Tongue

Let Sleeping Cats Lie

Cat Among The Fishes

Cat in the Limelight

Fleece the Cat

Listen to the Cat!

When The Cat's Away

Forward in Time Series

Make Time For Love

Discover Time For Love

Hearts of Rebellion Series

Pretender's Game

Lover's Knot

Dangerous Desires

LISTEN TO THE CAT!

THE 9 LIVES COZY MYSTERY SERIES
BOOK EIGHT

LOUISE CLARK

Book and cover design by eBook Prep
www.ebookprep.com

May 2023
ISBN: 978-1-64457-311-2

ePublishing Works!
644 Shrewsbury Commons Ave
Ste 249
Shrewsbury PA 17361
United States of America

www.epublishingworks.com
Phone: 866-846-5123

CHAPTER 1

The tower rose tall and sleek from the jumble of low-rise buildings constructed when Vancouver was still young. Massive at its base, it was designed as a lanky pyramid, slowly narrowing until it reached its peak some thirty floors above the ground. Its structure was clad in reflective blue glass that gleamed in the April sunshine.

Christy Jamieson pulled her van into the parking lot. Eventually the area would become a residents' garden and leisure complex, complete with an outdoor swimming pool. Right now the lot was full of the personal cars of the construction crew, along with pickup trucks emblazoned with the logo of Ferguson Green Construction, the company building the massive structure. She found a spot some distance from the entrance and cut the engine. Sitting beside her in the passenger seat, her aunt-in-law, Ellen Jamieson, stared at the building in silence. Christy stared at it too, wondering if Ellen's silence boded well for the apartment viewing they were about to do, or if it would be yet another wasted appointment.

Christy opened her door, saying with forced cheerfulness, "Let's get to it."

Ellen didn't reply, but she did open the passenger door and climb out. Access to the interior was mid-structure, on the street side of the building, via an extra wide set of revolving glass doors, or through a set of double doors beside it. As they neared the entrance, Christy saw a woman's form through the dark glass. She was standing just inside, near the revolving door. "Miss Kippen beat us here."

"Of course she did." Ellen sounded grumpy.

Christy resisted the urge to sigh. She decided the question she'd asked herself before they exited the car had been answered—this viewing wasn't going to go well. She shrugged mentally. Ellen had been hunting for a new apartment since hers had been broken into almost a year and a half ago. Shelley Kippen, a diligent soul, had searched across Vancouver and through all its many regions for the perfect combination of location and living space. So far, she had shown Ellen units in repurposed buildings, condo communities, and traditional apartment complexes. The Seymour View Hotel and Tower was the first new build she'd suggested though. Christy was curious about it, and she suspected Ellen was too, even if she didn't want to admit it.

Miss Kippen greeted them with her usual enthusiasm. She was an attractive young woman with thick dark hair, wide blue eyes, and a warm smile. She was wearing a well-cut skirt suit, this one in power red, and pumps with three-inch heels. Her clothing was a stark contrast to the jeans, sweater, and half boots Christy had chosen because the Seymour View was still under construction. Ellen too was wearing slacks, but hers were a wool silk blend and beautifully tailored. Her blouse was silk and like Kippen, she was wearing dress shoes with narrow heels.

"Good morning, ladies! I'm so excited to show you this fantastic suite today!"

"Good morning." Ellen didn't precisely frown, but her expression was far from enthusiastic and her tone repressive. Ellen was an attractive woman, her shining blond hair only lightly shot through with silver, even though she was well over fifty. Like all the Jamiesons she had regular, even features. In Ellen, these were enhanced by wide blue eyes and a lush mouth. Those eyes could turn ice cold in an instant and her mouth could harden into a narrow, dangerous line that said she was not someone you wanted to mess with. Right now, the blue in her eyes was edging toward gray and her lips were compressed. Not good signs.

Kippen swallowed and for a moment her smile faltered, then she rallied, and her face lit with positive energy. Christy didn't know how she did it. A client like Ellen Jamieson would leave her inclined to bash her head against the nearest wall.

"As you know from the data I sent you, this building is nearing completion, with a residency date of September this year. The vendor has been preselling units, but many select ones remain. Today, I'll be showing you a representative suite on the twentieth floor. While we're there, I'll also provide floor plans for specific apartments, and we can discuss the similarities and differences with the show unit."

"I would prefer to see the residence I purchase. I can't commit to investing in something that is merely a design on a piece of paper," Ellen said imperiously.

Kippen nodded without hesitation. *She must be used to Ellen's fits and starts by now,* Christy thought.

"Structurally, the building is complete, while the interiors are not." Her expression positively glowed with enthusiasm. "That's the benefit of buying a new build like this. You can choose your interior finishes and, if you want, you can redesign the room layout." She nodded with considerable energy. "You can put your own stamp on your apartment without doing costly and time-consuming renovations."

"That does have some appeal," Ellen said grudgingly.

Christy personally thought living in a building for a while before considering renovations helped identify what worked and what needed to be changed, but that was her, not Ellen. Or Miss Kippen, it seemed.

The realtor gestured to the cavernous interior of the lobby, pointing as she spoke. "As you know, this building will be a combination of boutique hotel and serviced apartments. The registration desk for the hotel will be over there, and the elevators for the hotel floors will be there. The corridor leading to the residents' lobby and elevators is around that corner."

She handed Christy and Ellen hard hats since the site was still under construction. Ellen grimaced as Kippen plopped the bright yellow headgear into her hands. She carefully placed it on her head, gingerly adjusting it to ensure it caused the least damage to her styled hair.

Christy plopped hers on without concern. Her chin-length, red-brown hair was cut to look good with a minimal amount of work. She washed it, brushed it out, and let it dry naturally. If she needed a fancier look, she had her hairdresser do it. Today, she was in wash and wear mode. There wasn't much for the helmet to damage.

"If you'll follow me, Miss Jamieson, Mrs. Jamieson. I'll tell you about the plans for the hotel as we go."

Kippen chattered happily as they picked their way through the vast space. By the time they reached the corridor that led to the residents' elevators, Christy had a mental image of a hotel that would exude unabashed luxury and opulent wealth in its décor and design.

Not Ellen's style. She preferred quiet, understated luxury that didn't broadcast its cost or quality.

Miss Kippen stopped. Ahead of them, the corridor widened into an open space. To their right was a bank of elevators; to the left stairs leading up and down. There was also a doorway to the outside.

"This is the residents' lobby. Once construction is finished the stairs will have a locked door, of course. They lead up to the residences and down to the owners' parking. The doorway opens to a garden, exclusively for the use of the residents."

"It's a nice feature," Christy said.

Kippen nodded. "Yes, it is, isn't it? They put the garden on the ground level because there can't be a roof garden for this complex. Instead, the penthouse suite takes up the top two floors of the building's pinnacle."

Ellen ignored the garden, probably because it was currently the parking lot, so there was nothing to see or give her an idea of what the space would be like. "Shall we go up?"

"Of course!" Kippen pushed the call button. "There are four suites on each floor from eleven to twenty-four. The building narrows as we rise, so from twenty-five up to twenty-eight there are two suites to a floor, and they are two-story apartments. The penthouse is also two story, as I mentioned, and access is on level thirty."

The elevator arrived. Kippen continued to talk after they were all inside and the car was rising. "The display suite is a three-bedroom, four-bath unit, twenty-eight hundred square feet in size. The building doesn't have balconies, but a solarium is included as part of the family room."

The elevator stopped smoothly, and the doors slid open. Christy's first impression of the landing was favorable. The space was large and airy. The apartment doorways opened off the central area, so there was no long corridor to traverse to reach your own entryway once you left the elevator. The exit stairs were on the far side of the rectangular lobby.

"The display suite is 2004, opposite the elevator," Kippen said as she hurried toward it. Ellen marched with her as determined as Kippen to begin the actual viewing. Christy ambled behind, looking around. She was a spectator on this excursion. Ellen liked her to come with her to the viewings, and Christy was happy to do so. She liked looking at homes for sale. They made her appreciate her own cozy townhouse in Burnaby all the more.

"Oh," said Kippen. She and Ellen had stopped at the door to 2004. Frowning, she reached out a hand.

Joining the other two, Christy realized that the door wasn't properly closed. Though not quite ajar, it wasn't firmly on the latch and was obviously not locked. She looked questioningly at Ellen, who shrugged, then she turned her gaze to Shelley Kippen.

Still frowning, Kippen said, "Well. This is unusual. We are supposed to be the first viewing of the day." She glanced briefly at Ellen. "As I mentioned when I proposed you inspect this unit, the agency I work for is listing these apartments. The suite is open only by appointment, so we don't have an individual on-site. Between viewings, the door is supposed to be kept closed." She shook her head in disapproval. "This apartment isn't sold yet, but the agency owns the furnishings. I'm sure my boss would not be happy to know the display suite is being treated so casually."

Neither Christy nor Ellen replied. Ellen probably didn't care about the brokerage's potential loss and Christy thought the realtor was talking more to herself than to her clients.

Kippen sighed, drew in a deep breath, and nodded to herself. She glanced at Ellen. "Shall we go in?"

"Of course," Ellen said in her usual decisive way.

Pushing open the door, Kippen stepped inside followed by Ellen, then Christy. The entryway was a lovely open space, tiled in slate, and painted a soft dove gray. A large cupboard designed to accommodate outdoor clothing opened on one side, with the doorway to a two-piece powder room on the other. So far Christy was impressed.

"The apartment was designed with two wings leading off the open foyer," Kippen said. To their left was the bedroom wing; to the right the public rooms. She began by showing them the open concept living-dining room, then the large kitchen, with the family room and solarium beyond.

By the time they reached the kitchen, Ellen was starting to thaw. The views from the wall-to-wall windows were spectacular. The interior space was open and bright, while the fittings were luxurious, but understated. She looked positively excited as they trooped back to the foyer to view the bedroom wing.

"The first bedroom is the smallest and designed to be used either as a bedroom or a home office," Kippen said.

She showed them the storage facilities and the en suite bathroom before they moved on to the second bedroom, which was across the hall. It was larger than the first by a considerable degree. A small laundry room beside the first bedroom explained the difference in size between the two chambers.

At the end of the corridor, double doors proclaimed the entry to the master suite. One of the doors was partially open. Kippen pushed the door wider and stepped inside. Turning, she faced Ellen and Christy. "This is the pièce de résistance of these units," she said grandly. "The master suite includes a private sitting room, as well as a dressing room with custom shelving. The en suite bath has a shower stall, a soaker tub, and in-floor heating. As we enter, you will see the sitting room to your left, with the dressing room on the right. At the end of the small corridor, the bedroom itself opens up. Come with me, ladies. You will be impressed!" She turned and marched forward.

Christy grinned at Ellen, who raised her brows and shook her head. The apartment was undoubtedly well designed, but Ellen was no fan of dramatics.

Ellen wandered into the sitting room, while Christy poked her head into the dressing room, which was bigger than her daughter Noelle's bedroom in the Burnaby townhouse. The space had been fitted with banks of drawers, areas to hang dresses or gowns, others that were tiered for shirts or tops, and a whole section to store shoes. The layout reminded her of her closet in the Jamieson mansion. She was feeling a pleasant nostalgia, or perhaps an unhappy regret at the loss of the house that had been her home for nearly ten years, when she heard Kippen scream. Tensing, she hurried to the doorway.

On the other side of the hallway, Ellen appeared in the opening to the sitting room. She raised her brows. "What's going on?"

Christy didn't even have a chance to shrug before Shelley Kippen bolted from the bedroom area, still screaming lustily. She passed Ellen and Christy without acknowledging them. A few moments later, they heard her heels clatter on the slate floor in the foyer, then the door slammed and there was quiet.

"Well," said Ellen. "What do you suppose set her off?"

They stared at each other for a moment, then Christy said, "I guess we'd best find out."

Another moment passed before Ellen nodded. "I guess we should."

Neither woman moved. Then Christy cleared her throat and Ellen nodded again. They set off down the short corridor.

Christy steeled herself for something awful. She wasn't surprised when Ellen moved closer and took her hand in hers. Christy squeezed it in acknowledgement just before they walked into the bedroom.

The scene that met their gazes made Christy gasp and close her eyes. Ellen made a small sound of dismay and the hand holding Christy's tightened.

One wall of the bedroom was floor-to-ceiling glass, from which light poured into the open space. A large bureau with a mirror attached stretched along the adjacent wall. The piece was antique, and at one time valuable, but not anymore. The large, framed mirror now had a hole in the middle, made, it appeared, by a bullet. Cracks radiated out from the hole, and it looked like the glass would shatter if touched. The gleaming

walnut structure of the dresser itself was torn; the beautiful craftsman-
ship ripped apart by another bullet.

An enormous king-sized bed dominated the other side of the room. A
pearl gray silk duvet covered it and half a dozen fat pillows were
mounded against the headboard to suggest a luxurious place to recline
and relax. The man half on, half off the silken coverlet wasn't relaxing,
though. His chest was a mass of blood, and his arms were spread wide as
if he'd fallen backward and thrown them out to try to break his fall. Part
of his face had been torn away by what looked like a stray bullet and
feathers were escaping from holes in the overstuffed pillows, probably
also caused by a spray of bullets. Blood had dyed the soft gray coverlet a
dark crimson.

Christy thought she was going to be sick. "Let's get out of here."

Ellen nodded. Together, they hurried down the corridor and out of
the master suite. They followed Kippen to the apartment's entryway.
There, Ellen paused. Her hand on the door handle, she looked at Christy.
"I think this building is off my list."

CHAPTER 2

Christy grimaced as they exited the suite, but her expression changed to dismay when she caught sight of Shelley Kippen. The real estate agent was standing at the elevator sobbing as she repeatedly pressed the call button.

"Miss Kippen, what are you doing?" Ellen demanded loudly.

Kippen turned her head but continued her frantic pounding of the button. Tears had caused her mascara to run, leaving dark smudges around her eyes and on her cheeks. Her lips trembled and her voice wobbled. "We have to get out of here! Where is the stupid elevator? Why won't it come?" The last was said on a wail as she turned back to look at the control panel.

"If you've been pounding the button since you ran out of the apartment, you've probably scrambled the mechanism," Ellen said, exasperated.

If Kippen was dealing with the dreadful scene they'd just witnessed by acting out and letting her emotions run rampant, Ellen's coping mechanism was the opposite. She'd clamped down the horror and revulsion to deal with later. A Jamieson was never weak and needy in public.

Christy walked over to Miss Kippen. Very gently, she took the woman's hand and drew it away from the call panel. "Pushing the button won't make the elevator arrive any more quickly. Come over here and take a moment to breathe."

Kippen allowed herself to be drawn into the center of the area, close to where Ellen was standing. She took a deep shuddering breath, then released it slowly.

"That's it," Christy said. "Breathe in. Nothing awful is going to happen to us. Breathe out. Whoever hurt that poor man is long gone."

"That poor man is Clayton Green and a more smug, entitled, obnoxious creature I cannot imagine," Ellen said, her lip curling. "He was a bully and a womanizer. He will not be missed."

Shelley was staring at Ellen, her mouth agape, her tears forgotten. "I... I didn't like him either." She gulped and drew another deep breath. Letting it out in a whoosh, she said, "He made a pass at me once. I didn't know what to do. He was so old. It was gross."

Since Miss Kippen looked to be somewhere around Christy's age, which was her early thirties, and the man on the bed appeared to be closer to Ellen's fifty plus, it was Ellen's turn to be taken aback. She rallied quickly though. "My point exactly. The man was a wretched specimen. We're better off without him."

Christy didn't think Clayton Green deserved to die, womanizer or not, but it looked like Ellen and Shelley Kippen were bonding over their dislike of the man, so she left them to it. Stepping away, she pulled out her cell to call 911. The operator kept her on the line, asking questions and telling her to keep calm. Christy appreciated her concern, but she answered the questions somewhat absently, half her attention focused on Shelley Kippen and Ellen.

"I don't understand why he was here, in the apartment," Kippen was saying. "I logged the viewing time in the agency database. He must have known we'd be in the suite."

Ellen frowned thoughtfully. "Ruby Cronin is the listing agent for all his developments, isn't she?"

Kippen nodded. "Yes. She's been really successful since she started working with Mr. Green. Ruby Cronin Realty is one of the top agencies in Vancouver."

Christy watched Ellen's mouth tighten. "Ruby could easily have told Clayton I'd be viewing the suite this morning."

"She could have." Miss Kippen's eyes widened as she caught Ellen's inference.

Christy caught it too. Ellen was wondering if Clayton Green had decided to add his sales pitch to Kippen's. It was the kind of thing Ellen would expect. She obviously knew the developer, and smug and entitled or not, she assumed he'd do his best to ensure one of the suites in his prestigious address was sold to a Jamieson.

And if this Ruby Cronin knew Clayton would be there this morning, was she the killer? Had the woman decided to take advantage of Ellen's presence to somehow implicate Ellen in the man's death?

There was a flaw to that theory, though. Little as she wanted to, Christy envisioned the murder scene. Clayton Green wasn't dressed like an executive planning to woo a wealthy woman who was a stickler for etiquette. If he had been in the suite as a representative of his company, Christy would have expected him to be wearing an expensive suit, a crisply ironed dress shirt, and a silk tie. On his feet would be leather shoes, probably tied, not slip-on, and his socks would be a dark color to match the suit.

Instead, he was wearing a sport jacket with more casual chinos, and his shirt was a soft, checked cotton, open at the neck. This wasn't the costume of a man intent on negotiating a multi-million-dollar sale.

Kippen was apparently also wrestling with the problem of why Clayton Green had been in the display suite, but her imagination had skittered off in a completely different direction. "Do you think he was killed by accident?"

"By accident?" Ellen repeated, sounding confused.

Kippen nodded. "Yes. Could the killer have been targeting us, but Mr. Green interrupted him, or surprised him, or something like that, so he was killed instead?" By the end of this speech, Kippen had worked herself up into another state of panic. Her gaze darted in every direction, and she chewed her lower lip nervously.

Christy said to the 911 operator, "Do you know when the police will get here?"

"They're in the building now," the voice said. "They will be with you momentarily."

Christy thanked her and kept a wary eye on Shelley Kippen. She didn't want her rushing the elevator again, taking her anxiety out on the call button.

Christy's report of a dead body and bullet holes in the walls and mirror had brought two uniformed cops. After a quick word with her, the man and woman both went into the apartment. As soon as they were inside, Kippen bolted for the elevator. Christy hurried after and caught her arm before she could enter the car. "We should stay here. The police may need to question us."

Kippen looked around uneasily. "Can't they do it downstairs? I don't want to be here."

"It would look highly suspicious if we were to leave now," Ellen said.

Christy nodded. "We should stay."

Kippen sent an anguished look at the elevator, then her head drooped, and she nodded.

A few minutes later, one of the constables emerged from the apartment. He said, "We've radioed for a detective and crime scene techs. In the meantime, I need to ask you a few questions." He took their names, their addresses, and their reason for being in the apartment. Then he asked, "Did any of you know the deceased?"

Miss Kippen nodded, looking fearful. Ellen said calmly, "I did. We were both members of the Vancouver Beautification Committee."

The man nodded, writing the information in a notebook. He looked at Miss Kippen. "And you, miss? Did you know him?"

Christy hoped Shelley didn't blurt out he'd once made a pass at her, but she swallowed and said in a very small voice, "I'm a real estate agent. Mr. Green develops property. He's well-known in the industry."

The constable nodded again as he copied this down. He looked less suspicious about Kippen's answer than Ellen's. From Ellen's pursed lips, Christy figured that annoyed her.

He turned to Christy, who shrugged. "Never met the man."

"Did any of you touch anything?"

"Doorknobs," Christy said.

"I inspected the kitchen cupboards, the fridge, the stove, the dishwasher," Ellen said.

"Oh! Right. I opened the washing machine and dryer doors," Christy said.

"Bathroom taps," Ellen said.

"I flushed the toilet in the powder room," Shelley said.

The constable, who'd been busily writing down their activities, raised his brows at that. Kippen blushed. "I wanted to show the ladies there was good suction. We turned on the taps to check the water pressure. These are important things to test out when you're buying a home!"

The cop didn't acknowledge that. Instead, he said, "What about the crime scene? Touch anything in there?"

"I ran my hand over the back of one of the chairs in the sitting room," Ellen said.

Christy said, "I opened the drawers in the dressing room. I wanted to see if they were easy close or not."

Miss Kippen bit her lip. "I touched the door to the master suite. It was ajar. I pushed it wider."

"Did you touch the doorknob?"

She shook her head.

The constable nodded. He glanced from Ellen to Christy. "Either of you ladies touch the door?"

They both shook their heads.

"Good," he said. "Now—"

The quiet sound of the elevator rising heralded its arrival. The door slid open. A woman stepped out. Tall and lean, with sable hair tied into a knot at her nape, she had wide dark eyes, intelligent features, and a scar that ran down the side of her face. After a quick comprehensive look around, she focused on the three women in the center of the lobby. She sighed. "Mrs. Jamieson. Why am I not surprised?"

CHAPTER 3

The constable turned. Christy smiled and said, "Hi, Detective Patterson. I'm glad to see you."

Patterson snorted. "Mrs. Jamieson, you are the last person I wanted to see."

The detective was wearing dark trousers and a jacket over a white tailored cotton shirt. On her feet were well-worn leather half boots with flat soles. Her head was covered by a hardhat identical to the ones Christy, Ellen, and Shelley Kippen were wearing.

She stopped in front of them and put her hands on her hips, but it was the constable she addressed initially. "Where's the deceased?"

The uniform jerked his head toward the open apartment door. "In the master bedroom of the display suite."

Patterson nodded. She turned to Christy and the others. "Okay, this is what's going to happen. The officer will take me to the crime scene. When I've finished my inspection, I'll talk to each of you. In the meantime, stay put. If any strangers appear, don't chase them down. Don't talk to anybody. Do not, for any reason, leave this area until I've given you the okay. Understood?"

Ellen's lips tightened. "Really, Detective—"

Patterson raised her brows, her expression as haughty as any Ellen

18

could produce. "Understood?" she said again, her voice harder than before.

"Yes," Miss Kippen said in a small, faltering voice.

Ellen cast Kippen a disapproving look that added a frown to the pursed lips, but she didn't acknowledge Patterson's demand.

Patterson raised her eyebrows and focused on Christy, who sighed and said, "Yes, Detective, we understand."

Patterson nodded, gestured to the constable to follow, and strode toward the display suite. The constable hustled behind her. As they disappeared into the apartment, Christy could hear the officer filling Patterson in on the crime scene she was about to see.

Her gaze on the apartment door, Ellen said, "Rude woman."

"She's just doing her job," Christy said.

"We are not her minions," Ellen retorted, her voice rising.

We're all edgy, Christy thought. Ellen and Shelley Kippen perhaps more than she was, as they both knew the victim. "The police have protocols they have to follow. Remember when Sledge found Karen Beaumont's body during the gala at MacLagen House? We all had to wait hours before we were allowed to leave."

Ellen hmphed an acknowledgement of sorts. Shelley's eyes widened. "Sledge of SledgeHammer?"

Christy nodded.

"Oh my." Christy wondered if she and Ellen had gone up in the agent's estimation.

Miss Kippen frowned, her fangirl reaction to Sledge's name chased away by more immediate matters. "Do you find bodies often?"

"No," Christy said, though she had been involved in the investigations of several murders. But bodies? She shuddered. She'd seen Karen Beaumont at a distance, lying in a twisted position at the bottom of a steep set of concrete stairs. Karen's loss of life had been real and understandable, but somehow less personal for Christy than today's situation. This was the first time she'd been within touching distance of a murder victim, and she was having trouble detaching herself from it.

Her stomach, which had calmed down, started to churn. She wondered if Patterson would freak if she went into the powder room where Shelley Kippen had so thoughtfully demonstrated the flushing power of the toilet and used it to rid herself of the contents of her stomach. Probably. She put the back of her hand over her mouth and eyed the open doorway longingly.

The sensation of a hand on her back rubbing in a soothing circular motion had her glancing sharply at Ellen, who smiled sympathetically. Christy felt her stress easing. Two years ago, Ellen's comforting gesture would never have happened. Ellen was her late husband Frank's aunt and during her marriage Christy's relationship with her had never been warm. That was probably because Frank had resented his aunt, who raised him after his parents died. Frank's disappearance and death had forced Christy and Ellen onto a new path, however, and they'd become close and were growing closer.

Christy gave her a wan smile and nodded. Ellen smiled back. She let her hand fall as she resumed her usual reserved and somewhat acerbic expression.

Deep in her own angst, Shelley apparently didn't notice Christy's reaction to her questions about murder. She tapped her watch, her expression more dismayed than before. "I have an appointment in Kerrisdale in a half an hour. I have to show up! My clients will be waiting for me. They won't know what to do!"

In Vancouver's traffic, Kerrisdale was at least a half an hour's drive away at this time of day. Even if Kippen left now, she'd probably be late.

Ellen shrugged. "Phone them and reschedule. You do have their number, don't you?"

Kippen's eyes widened. "I do, but.... The detective said we weren't to talk to anyone."

"You aren't talking to them about the murder. You're notifying clients you can't make your appointment." Ellen sounded impatient.

Miss Kippen bit her lip, then she nodded. She crossed the area to a spot as far away from the apartment door as she could manage, turned her back on them, and took out her phone. Moments later she was speaking in a low voice, her body hunched as if that would help increase her privacy. Ellen looked at Christy and shook her head. Christy smiled and shrugged.

Kippen had just finished her phone call when the elevator doors opened and the crime scene techs carrying their various implements bustled into the foyer. Kippen whitened, then fanned herself as if their arrival had generated an emotional overload. Ellen and Christy watched them cross the lobby to the apartment. The technicians scrutinized all three women but didn't acknowledge them as they made their way to the apartment.

Time passed. Christy looked at her watch, surprised to see it was after one o'clock. The viewing had been scheduled for an hour, beginning at eleven. She'd expected to see the place, have lunch with Ellen to discuss its suitability, then be home well before she needed to pick her daughter Noelle up from school at three. Now it looked as if she, like Miss Kippen, would have to make some phone calls to reschedule her afternoon.

Ellen saw her glancing at her watch. "We'll give Patterson another half hour. If she hasn't interviewed us by then, we'll leave." At Christy's raised brows, she shrugged. "She has our address."

Christy laughed. "That she does."

Another ten minutes slipped by. Once again, the elevator doors opened, this time disgorging a uniformed officer. He strode confidently across the lobby, a man on a mission. Ignoring the three women as he passed, he disappeared inside the open doorway to the apartment.

"He seemed full of himself," Ellen said.

Christy smiled. "Perhaps he's discovered a clue he thinks will crack the case. Maybe we can all go home."

"I'd like that," Shelley said wistfully. "My feet hurt, and I'd like to use the ladies room."

Christy sent her a sympathetic smile, but Ellen studiously ignored her comment.

The constable must have brought useful information, because it wasn't long before Patterson emerged from the apartment, the man trailing behind her. She stopped in front of Christy and the others, while the constable continued to the elevator, then disappeared inside when the doors opened.

Patterson looked them over and said, "Thank you all for staying."

"Did we have a choice?" Ellen asked. She'd raised her eyebrows and

21

was looking down her nose in a way that could only be described as disdainful.

"Not really," Patterson said easily. Her mouth rose into a half smile. "Though I do appreciate it when witnesses are cooperative."

"We are not witnesses!" Ellen retorted. "We were simply in the wrong place at the wrong time."

"Fair enough," Patterson said, refusing to be riled by Ellen's hostility. "I do need to ask you some questions about your movements prior to finding the deceased, though."

"One of your minions has already taken those details. If that is all, we will be leaving," Ellen said.

"Minions?" Patterson said on what sounded like a chuckle. "Wow. I had no idea I was the minder of minions."

Ellen stiffened and her lips tightened.

Christy resisted the urge to roll her eyes. Ellen and Patterson didn't have the greatest relationship. How could they when Patterson had once arrested Ellen for murder? Christy had proved Ellen's innocence, but for Ellen the shock had been profound. She might tolerate Patterson, but she would never willingly make life easy for the detective. Patterson, for her part, wasn't about to be intimidated by Ellen, especially when she was assessing a crime scene.

"Why don't we get the questions over and done with?" Christy checked her watch again. "I need to be back in Burnaby in just over an hour to pick up Noelle."

Patterson shot her a long look that said Christy's timeline wasn't going to influence her anymore than Ellen's imperiousness would. Christy raised her brows. Patterson smiled faintly. "All right. My *minion* tells me you ladies arrived at eleven o'clock to view the display suite."

"That is correct," Ellen said. Christy and Miss Kippen nodded agreement.

"During the viewing you touched various surfaces throughout the unit, until you reached the master suite where you saw the body of the deceased, one Clayton Green. You then exited the suite and called 911." More nods of agreement. "I'll need your fingerprints for elimination purposes."

Miss Kippen made a quick sound of dismay. Christy said, "Surely not, Detective. We only opened doors and cabinets in the kitchen and bathrooms. None of us touched anything in the master suite."

"Miss Kippen opened the door to the suite," Patterson countered.

"No! I pushed it with the flat of my hand. It was already ajar when we arrived," Kippen said, shaking her head emphatically.

"Nevertheless—"

"I will talk to Trevor," Ellen said, using a he'll-sort-this-mess-out-and-put-you-in-your-place tone of voice.

Trevor was Trevor Robinson McCullagh the third, a retired lawyer and a dear (becoming dearer all the time) friend of Ellen's.

"Come down to the station tomorrow. I'll let them know to expect you," Patterson said, completely ignoring Ellen, who narrowed her eyes.

Patterson turned to Miss Kippen. "You said you knew the deceased. How?"

Kippen put her hand to her lips. "I thought I explained to the policeman."

"Tell me anyway."

She shrugged. "I don't know him. I mean, I've met him, but we're not friends or anything. He's an important developer. Anyone who sells real estate in Vancouver knows him."

Patterson nodded. "So you go to networking events for people in your industry and see him there."

Relieved, Kippen smiled and nodded. "Yes. Yes, that's it, exactly."

"Ever had any personal interactions with him?"

"P...personal?" Kippen shot a desperate, frightened look at Christy and Ellen.

Patterson caught it and took note. She stared hard at Miss Kippen and let the silence draw out.

"It was years ago. At an awards gala. He had too much to drink. His wife was there!"

Patterson raised her brows, but when she spoke her voice was gentler than before. "What did he do?"

Biting her lip, Kippen looked down at the floor. "I was on my way to the ladies. I guess he was going to the men's room? Since we were both heading in the same direction we started to talk. There was a little alcove, and no one was around. He pulled me in. Pushed me against the wall. Kissed me." She stopped. Sighed. "I was wearing an evening gown with a low-cut bodice. He shoved his hand down it and pushed his leg between mine. I struggled and—" She shrugged. "He was drunk enough that I was able to push him away and escape. I went back to the ballroom."

"Did you tell anyone what he'd done?" Patterson asked.

"Ruby Cronin. She was another agent then and we worked for the same company. She's a broker now and has her own firm."

"Vile man," Ellen said. "He loved to pretend to be charming and debonair, but that was all on the surface. He had a bad reputation."

"You knew him from the Vancouver Beautification Committee?"

Ellen nodded. "That's right."

"What does the Vancouver Beautification Committee do and what was Green's part in it?"

"The committee is tasked with ensuring that Vancouver's neighborhoods remain attractive living spaces and to find ways to accommodate modernization without losing ambiance. We review requests for redevelopment, or repurposing parks and other green space, from the point of view of how the change will influence the immediate community. We also work with the historical society to help incorporate the preservation of significant buildings into the city's redevelopment plans. Often that is particularly relevant in areas that are run down and need restoration."

"Lots of those," Patterson muttered.

"Indeed," Ellen said.

"What was Green's role on the committee?"

"As Miss Kippen said, Mr. Green was one of Vancouver's most prolific developers. He represented the building community. In addition to providing us with his input on the benefits of new construction, he also had his vice president of Management Processes act as the committee's secretary."

Patterson blinked, then her mouth quirked up into a cynical smile. "I imagine the vice president was happy to practice his shorthand for a bunch of talking heads."

Ellen drew herself up taller. "He recorded the meetings, then had his secretary type up the minutes."

"I'll bet he did. So..." Patterson drew out the word. "You sound like you didn't like Clayton Green anymore than Miss Kippen did."

"My main experience with him was in the committee's meeting room in the basement of the city library building. I met him socially only at Jeff Darling's annual Christmas party."

"Jeff Darling, the city councilor?"

"Yes. The event is for a mix of people who work with him, or who are important constituents or contributors."

Patterson nodded. "Okay. I get that. What about the committee? You said he was there on behalf of the building community. I take it that other people on the committee represented different interests?"

"That's correct."

"Were there any conflicts between members? Personal or relating to the work you were doing?"

"Interpersonal strife? No." Ellen hesitated. "There is an issue of some contention at the moment."

Patterson waited, letting the silence spin out.

At last Ellen said, "There is a parcel of land in the West End, near Stanley Park. Part of a neighborhood with older, low-rise apartment buildings. An application has been made to the city to raze the buildings and redevelop the area into a complex like this one, a combination of hotel and apartments, with retail as well. The complex would dominate the landscape, completely changing the area. To get the project approved the city would need to change the zoning. We've been tasked with studying the effects and benefits the development would have on the neighborhood and surrounding regions. Some of us, Clayton among them, believe the project should be approved, while others do not. The debate has been quite heated at times."

"And?" Patterson asked when Ellen paused.

"There's a time constraint," she said finally, choosing her words carefully. "An investment company has optioned land and buildings in the area subject to redevelopment being approved. Clayton's company has an ongoing professional relationship with them and they were pushing him for a decision. So, Clayton was pressing us."

"Hence, the heat in the debate," Patterson said dryly.

Ellen nodded.

Patterson made a note on her phone before she turned to Christy. "You didn't know the man?"

Christy shook her head.

Patterson nodded. "I need to know the whereabouts for each of you between ten a.m. and eleven."

"That's specific, Detective," Christy said.

"Mr. Green entered the building shortly before ten o'clock. That was the last time he was seen alive."

"Ellen and I were at home, then in the van driving here," Christy said. Ellen nodded agreement.

"You were both together. Miss Kippen?"

"I was at my office. It's ten minutes away at the corner of Granville and Georgia. I left the office at ten forty-five and walked here. I arrived a few minutes before the ladies did."

"Okay. Thanks for your help."

Kippen's eyes widened hopefully. "We can go?"

Patterson nodded.

"Thank God," Ellen said.

CHAPTER 4

Quinn Armstrong—neighbor, investigative journalist, and the man who was rapidly claiming Christy's heart—was sitting on Christy's porch steps, waiting for them, when Christy and Ellen arrived home. He shared a townhouse with his father Roy two doors down from Christy's.

Roy was an award-winning novelist, but he'd lost his wife, the love of his life, three years before and wasn't doing well on his own. Quinn, at loose ends himself, had returned home to help his father through the rough spot. Then Christy moved in down the street and staying at the Burnaby townhouse seemed like a good idea to Quinn.

He had his phone in his hand and had apparently been reading it before he looked up at the sound of the car engine. Christy saw him stand as she turned into her driveway. He was waiting for them at the end of her short walk when she and Ellen emerged from the carport.

"Are you okay?" He scrutinized them both, concern on his frowning features. In his early thirties, he was a tall, lean man with thick dark hair that tended to fall over his forehead and long-lashed blue eyes. His face was narrow rather than round with a sensual mouth and strong chin.

Flooded with relief and very glad to see him, Christy nodded.

Ellen said, "It was dreadful! That poor man, even if he was horrible."

She shuddered. "And then to be interrogated by that police person." Another dramatic shiver. "I will not be purchasing a unit in that building."

There was amusement in Quinn's blue eyes as he listened to this, and he nodded at Ellen's final pronouncement. "I'm not surprised."

Ellen gave a brisk nod and stepped away. At the bottom of the steps, she paused and turned back. Christy had moved closer to Quinn, and he had his arm around her waist.

Ellen said, "You should both be prepared. It is quite likely I will consume more than my usual amount of wine this evening." After another quick nod and a deep breath, she continued up the stairs. Unlocking the front door, she entered the house.

"That bad?" Quinn asked Christy as the door quietly shut behind Ellen.

Christy nodded. "That bad."

Quinn drew her close and wrapped his arms around her. Christy slipped hers around his waist and hugged him tight as she buried her face in his strong shoulder. Held securely, she let his strength seep into her and was comforted.

After a minute Quinn murmured, "We can reschedule tonight." Quinn's cousin, the daughter of his late mother's sister, had come to stay for a few days. Roy had called this morning to invite Ellen, Christy, and Noelle over for dinner that evening to meet her.

Christy pulled away. She looked up at him. "No. I think Ellen and I would enjoy the distraction." She smiled. "You heard Ellen. It will give her a chance to cut loose."

"I'm not sure I'm ready for that," Quinn said.

Christy laughed. "Neither am I." She glanced at her watch. "I have to get going. School will be out in a few minutes, and I need to pick up Noelle."

"Want some company?"

"I'd love it. I'll just drop my purse inside, then we can go."

They walked the short distance to the school together. Christy had called Quinn before they left downtown and told him of the murder. Now she filled him in on the details. She ended saying, "It was horrible for me to witness, but I've never met the man. Even if she didn't like him, it was so much worse for Ellen." She gave herself a little shake. "Enough about this morning. Tell me about your cousin. How long is she visiting?"

"A good question," said Quinn. His tone was wry.

Christy glanced at him, her brows raised in question.

"She's licking her wounds after a major fight with her husband." Quinn sighed. "So, the duration of her stay is open ended." The expression on his face said he wasn't happy about that.

"Oh, dear. I suppose that means she's overwrought and being difficult."

"You could say that," Quinn muttered. He grimaced. "When she arrived yesterday afternoon, she was numb, I think. She rang the doorbell and said her husband had kicked her out and she needed a place to stay." He shook his head. "As if we were a close-knit family and there was nothing surprising about one of our members showing up without notice. But we're not!"

He paused to draw a deep steadying breath. "Dad took her in, and we talked a little before she went to bed. Then this morning she said her husband would be out, so she was going home to pick up some things." He shook his head. "I don't know what occurred while she was out. When she told us her plan she was quite calm, but when she came back—something must have happened while she was gone, because she was upset and we could see she'd been crying."

"She may have misjudged her timing and had a nasty run in with her husband," Christy suggested.

Quinn nodded. "Yeah. That's probably it. Dad asked her if she wanted to talk about whatever was bothering her, but she refused. She pulled herself together this afternoon. She says she's looking forward to tonight."

They'd reached the school. "Good," Christy said. "Sounds like she needs the distraction as much as Ellen and I do. Let's get Noelle, then we can go home and prep."

It turned out Noelle was looking forward to the party too. All the way home she chattered to Quinn about his cousin. How old was she? What did she look like? What did she do? Did she have any kids? Was she here

29

for long? The questions went on and on. Quinn answered each as best he could and sometimes laughingly admitted he had no idea what the answer was, which only made Noelle ask the same question in a different way.

Getting ready for the evening meant Noelle doing homework at the kitchen table while Christy put together a salad and Ellen baked a chocolate cake as their contributions to the dinner. Noelle plowed her way through math practice and a grammar exercise as the cake cooked and cooled. By the time it was ready to be iced, she was anxious to help. The frosting was a rich chocolate buttercream. Ellen organized the ingredients, but let Noelle put them together, then ice the cake. The process was messy and there were places where the icing was thicker than others, but everyone was pleased with the results. Then there was just enough time to clean up the kitchen and change clothes before they had to leave.

Noelle carried the precious cake over to Quinn's, her teeth worrying her bottom lip the whole way as she carefully held the cake plate steady before her. Ellen followed holding a bag with two bottles of wine. She also carried Stormy the Cat, a large boned gray tabby who tended to wind his way around people's feet when they had their hands full. Neither of the adults wanted Noelle to fall, so like it or not, Stormy made the short journey held tightly against Ellen's side. Christy brought up the rear with her salad.

Christy expected Quinn to answer the door at the Armstrong house, but it was Trevor, middle-aged, silver-haired, looking handsome, but comfortable, in tan chinos and a golf shirt, who opened it for them. He exclaimed over the beauty of the cake and told Noelle he wasn't going to bother with dinner. He just wanted cake. That made her giggle, but when he offered to carry it up the stairs for her, she bit her bottom lip again until he suggested he'd give it back to her at the top so she could carry it into the kitchen. She brightened at that and nodded. Trevor took the cake, winked at Ellen and Christy, and led the procession up the stairs.

Or he was going to lead it up. Released from Ellen's hold, Stormy bolted past him, beating him to the top where he stopped and cleaned a paw, just to show who got there first really didn't matter at all. Did it?

The cake reached the kitchen intact, Noelle bearing it triumphantly before her. Christy had grabbed Stormy as the cake was being transferred back to Noelle, so she didn't have to worry about her daughter tripping. She held him until she saw Noelle was safely in the kitchen, then set him down. He rushed into the action, his thumping paws indicating his annoyance.

As Christy followed the rest into the kitchen, she saw that Quinn was sitting at the table talking to a willowy woman who must be his cousin. She had long dark hair a shade or two lighter than Quinn's and her face, like his, was long rather than wide. Her eyes were blue, though not as deep a blue as his, and her lashes were long and black.

Roy was at the oven, checking the temperature of a roast. He was tall and lean, like his son, and wore his silver-shot hair long and tied in a tail at the back of his neck. He was dressed in his favorite apparel of jeans and a checked shirt. As they wandered into the kitchen, he straightened and turned to his guests. His gaze landed on Noelle and the cake, and he grinned. "Your handiwork, Noelle?"

She nodded, then added honestly, "I did the icing. Aunt Ellen baked the cake."

"And I tossed a salad," Christy said. She put down the bowl, then hovered by Noelle to help if needed as her daughter placed the cake carefully onto the counter.

"Looks yummy," Quinn's cousin said.

"It does, doesn't it?" Christy said. She smiled at the other woman.

Quinn stood. "Christy, Noelle, and Ellen Jamieson meet my cousin, Jodie Webster. Jodie's mom was my mom's sister."

There was a chorus of nice-to-meet-yous, then Ellen unloaded the bottles of wine. Roy offered everyone drinks and promised dinner would be ready in a half an hour. They all took a place around the table, including the cat who sat on Christy's lap peering over the top, green eyes wide, inspecting everything.

Jodie blinked, then frowned. "I didn't realize you had a cat, Uncle Roy."

"Not our cat," Roy said. "He lives at Christy's place."

Jodie turned puzzled eyes to Christy. "You bring your cat to dinner parties." Her tone of voice said this was not only a very weird thing to do, but that Jodie didn't approve.

Christy laughed. "If I didn't bring him, I'd never hear the end of it."

Roy and Trevor laughed too. Quinn rolled his eyes heavenward. Ellen said, "That cat."

Her expression still puzzled, Jodie turned to Ellen with a nod, apparently having decided she'd found a kindred spirit. "We've met before."

"Jeff Darling's Christmas party," Ellen said, nodding. "You're married to Lloyd Webster." Like Jeff, Lloyd was a member of the Vancouver Beautification Committee, along with Ellen.

Jodie sighed, looked into her glass of chardonnay, then downed half the wine in one gulp. She held the glass up in a parody of a toast. "For my sins."

Roy looked over from his spot in front of the oven and frowned. Noelle said, "Why?"

Everyone froze.

"Why?" Jodie repeated, looking wary.

Noelle nodded. "You drank wine, then said for my sins. Why?"

The cat put his paws on the table. *It's an expression, kiddo. I don't think Quinn's cousin likes her husband.* He stared at Jodie with unblinking green eyes.

She blushed and looked at Quinn in an accusatory way. "I do like him. We've just had a fight. I thought you understood."

Quinn groaned. Trevor looked at Ellen with raised brows. Roy said, "Pay no attention to Frank." He went back to checking potatoes boiling on the stovetop.

Jodie looked around the kitchen. She'd been introduced to everyone there. Well, not everyone. "Who's Frank?"

I am.

"He's my daddy," Noelle said.

Jodie looked even more bewildered as she gazed around the group. Quinn sighed. Christy felt like sighing too, but she said, "Frank is my late husband. He and the cat are roommates."

Jodie blinked. She looked at Stormy, who stared back, then at Quinn, who shrugged. Finally, her gaze reached Christy. At that point she erupted. "Are you crazy?"

"No," Christy said crisply. "You can resist all you want, but the voice in your head won't go away. Deal with it as you will."

I'm persistent, that's true. Think of it this way. Not everyone can hear me, so you're one of the lucky ones. Like everyone in this room, in fact. Except Quinn. He's deaf to me."

Jodie downed the rest of her glass of wine, then turned to Quinn. "Why?"

Quinn, who was about to take a swig from the beer bottle he was holding, frowned. "Why what?"

Jodie's voice rose. "Why can't you hear Frank?"

"Oh, for heaven's sake." He plunked the bottle on the table and glared at the cat. "Because Frank is dead, and the cat is just a cat."

A lot he knows. The voice was smug. Frank liked needling Quinn.

Jodie looked at Quinn for a moment longer, then her gaze traveled to everyone else. She shook her head. "This is weird." She pushed her glass forward. "Can someone give me a refill?"

Trevor poured. "It is odd until you get used to it." He passed the glass back to Jodie. "My recommendation? Don't fight it. The cat has a lot to give if you let him."

Trevor's well-meaning advice didn't seem to make Jodie any more comfortable. She shot him a sideways look, consumed a considerable amount of her topped up wine, then drew a deep breath. She looked at Quinn. "I'm with you. A cat is just a cat." She nodded briefly. "There is no voice in my head. It's been a long, hard day. That's all."

What! You won't listen to me? You don't want to hear me?

Noelle went over to the table. After putting her glass of cola down she stroked the cat. "It's okay. We love you." Stormy nestled his head close and purred.

Christy drew a deep breath. "So, Jodie, have you lived in Vancouver long?"

"I was born here, but my parents moved to the Yukon when I was little. I came back to go to university. That's where I met Lloyd. I stayed and we got married."

And now you have to hide away at your cousin's house because you had a big fight and he kicked you out.

Jodie colored.

Christy looked at Ellen. This evening was going to be a complete disaster if Frank was going to take pot shots at Jodie all night. Ellen shrugged, but she did her best to keep the conversation rolling. "I seem to remember Lloyd talking about you assisting him on one of his campaigns to help the homeless down on the East Side."

Jodie nodded, her expression brightening. "Lloyd's a good man," she said, her expression earnest. "He believes in fairness and equality—"

Is there such a thing?

"What do you mean, Daddy?"

Christy turned the cat's head until their gazes locked. "Enough. You and Noelle can have a conversation about equality when we get home. For now, be good."

Spoilsport.

Christy nodded. "You bet. I'm serious, Frank."

The cat wiggled out of her hold and jumped down, then he walked over to his dish, which Roy had set up since the cat had begun using the Armstrong house as his second home. The bowl was empty. He sniffed disdainfully, then looked up.

When's dinner? I'm hungry.

CHAPTER 5

Roy Armstrong paced from his kitchen table past the cooking area to the door that led to his living room. There he turned around and made his way back to the table, where he did an about-face and headed back to the doorway. His long hair was disheveled, strands coming loose from the tie at the back of his neck. He hunched into his checked shirt and had his hands in the pockets of his worn jeans.

It was the day after the dinner to welcome Jodie. On the food level, the party had been a success. Everyone enjoyed the roast and the delicious cake. There'd been an edge to the evening, though, with strong emotions swirling beneath the pleasant conversation. That stress had been caused by Jodie, he thought rather grimly, as he turned at the table to head back to the door.

He didn't like to pace. He never paced, but he was doing it today because he was consumed by nervous energy that wasn't his own. It permeated the house and Jodie wasn't even up yet. He was so edgy he couldn't concentrate, so he was pacing. Back and forth. Back and forth.

This morning Quinn had commented on Jodie's obvious tension the night before. He then had the good sense to go off to a meeting with a source for the new book he was working on. Well, it wasn't exactly good sense, since the appointment had been made earlier in the month, before

Jodie had descended on their home and turned it into a cauldron of anxious energy. Still, he was out doing something productive while Roy was stuck here, pacing his kitchen, wishing he could blow the negative energy to the farthest reaches of the universe.

Open the door, old man.

Roy stopped. Over the winter, when the days were cold, he'd provided a home away from home for the cat if both Christy and Ellen were out. Then he'd left his front door partly open, so the cat could come and go as he pleased. The temperature was warmer now, so the cat could stay outside until Christy got home from the Jamieson Trust offices where she managed the family affairs. Ever since he'd stopped leaving his door open, Frank made a point of showing up several times a day asking for him to open it. It was going from irritating to annoying, especially this morning when he was already jittery.

He didn't have to open the door. He thought about that for a moment and realized he was too jumpy to sit down and work. At least if he let the cat in, he'd have someone to talk to.

"Uncle Roy? What's for breakfast?" Her expression gloomy, her dark hair tangled, Jodie slouched into the kitchen. A black cloud of unresolved emotions trailed along behind her.

Roy pointed to the fridge. "Leftovers from last night. Bacon. Eggs. Cereal in the cupboard. I have to go open the door."

Jodie frowned. "Why? I didn't hear the doorbell."

"The cat wants in."

"Oh, please! Not the talking cat business again."

"Yup." As Roy made his way down to the front door, he reflected that Jodie Webster was a very easy person to dislike. That made him feel guilty because she was his beloved wife Vivian's only niece. He reached the small front foyer. He should like her. He wanted to like her...

He pulled open the front door.

The cat wasn't alone. Standing there, her hand raised to ring the doorbell, was Detective Patterson.

She just arrived. I didn't bring her. The cat sashayed into the foyer, then dashed up the stairs.

"Mr. Armstrong," Patterson said. She was dressed in her usual plain-clothes uniform of dark pants, white shirt, and dark jacket. Her long dark hair was bound in a knot at her neck.

Roy recovered from his surprise. "Detective Patterson." He opened the door wider. "This is unexpected. Why have you dropped by?"

Patterson stepped into the house. Roy closed the door behind her and gestured for her to go up the stairs to the living room.

Patterson didn't move. "I understand Jodie Webster is staying with you."

Roy nodded.

"Is she here? I'd like to speak to her."

Frowning, Roy said, "She's in the kitchen, having breakfast. What's going on?"

Probably something to do with the murder.

"Would you ask her to come down here, please?"

Murder? What murder? No one had told him about a murder. And how could Jodie be involved in a murder? Seriously annoyed, Roy contemplated the detective. "I could, if I knew what this was about."

Irritation flashed in Patterson's eyes. "It's a private matter, Mr. Armstrong."

Roy blinked and smiled in a fatuous way that he hoped would get under the detective's skin. He liked Patterson, but Jodie was family, even if she was exasperating family. "Come back in a couple of hours. That way Jodie will have finished her breakfast and Trevor will have arrived."

Patterson's jaw flexed and her mouth tightened into a hard line. "This isn't a joking matter, Mr. Armstrong."

Roy raised his brows. "I wasn't joking, Detective Patterson."

"Stupid cat," said Jodie's voice. From the direction of the sound, she was in the living room. "Uncle Roy? Why did you let this awful beast in?" And coming closer, apparently. Any moment now she'd be at the top of the stairs.

"Mrs. Webster, I'm Detective Patterson from the Vancouver Police Department. I'd like to speak to you." Patterson was looking over Roy's shoulder as she spoke. Jodie must have reached the top of the stairs.

Roy slowly turned and yes, indeed, there was Jodie holding a rather smug looking cat to her chest against the T-shirt she wore with baggy jogging pants. Roy wasn't sure why Frank had fetched her from the safety of the kitchen, but he could guess. Last night Jodie refused to acknowledge his voice and he was annoyed with her. Frank figured Patterson would make her uncomfortable, and he'd be there to enjoy her unease.

"Speak to me about what?" Jodie asked, putting the cat down. Stormy crouched beside her, paws tucked under his body, Sphinx-like.

Patterson looked at Roy. "If you wouldn't mind leaving us, Mr. Armstrong?"

Roy opened his mouth to say no way.

Might as well. We won't find out what Patterson wants until you're gone. Don't worry. I've got this.

Roy thought about the cat's involvement in other investigations. Frank liked to brag that he'd solved those mysteries. He hadn't, but he had influenced the outcomes. Closing his mouth, Roy shrugged and went up the stairs. As he passed Jodie, he poked her in the arm. "When the detective asks you a question, you say no comment and tell her you want to see your lawyer."

"Mr. Armstrong!"

Jodie's eyes widened. "I don't have a lawyer."

"Yes, you do. I'm phoning him now." Roy went into the kitchen where his phone was charging and called Trevor who promised to come as soon as he could. Roy disconnected, quietly returning to the living room, where voices drifted up from the front foyer.

"All right, it's true! I had an affair with Clay. That's why I'm here, camping out at my uncle's, instead of home with my husband." That was Jodie, sounding agitated, her tone strident.

Hey! Give the old man a break. He's offered you sanctuary. Don't dis him because you're upset.

"I'd like you to come down to the station with me to answer some questions, Mrs. Webster," Patterson said calmly, apparently unaffected by Jodie's rising emotions.

"What? No! Why?"

It's obvious. She thinks you killed Clayton Green.

"If you'd come with me, please."

"No!"

Roy couldn't tell if Jodie was refusing Patterson's request or denying the cat's observation. Either way, he should probably intervene.

Good answer. Now say you want your lawyer and tell her to go away.

"I won't say anything until my lawyer is with me." Jodie sounded panicked now, as if she was hovering on the edge of a precipice and she was afraid of heights.

Roy ambled to the top of the stairs. "Trevor's on his way. It would probably be best if you wait in your car until he arrives, Detective."

Patterson shot him a frustrated look. "Tell Mr. McCullagh to have Mrs. Webster at the station by one this afternoon."

Roy nodded amicably. "Will do."

Patterson shot Jodie one last searching look, before she opened the door and left. It closed behind her with a quiet click.

Jodie looked up at Roy, her eyes wide, her lips slightly parted as if she wanted to say something but couldn't quite manage it. Roy and the cat stared back.

You are in so much trouble.

Apparently, Jodie agreed. "What am I going to do?" She stared at Roy, her eyes beseeching him to promise he'd sort it all out.

While he wasn't immune to her obvious fear, Roy was a man who believed in doing—learning all the facts then taking a stand and defending your position. So, he raised his eyebrows and said, "When Trevor gets here, you're going to answer his questions truthfully and in detail so he can figure out how best to defend you. Then you're going to listen to his advice and follow it to the letter. Don't assume you know better. Trevor's the expert here, not you."

Couldn't have said it better myself.

Jodie glanced from Roy to the cat, then back to Roy, panic in her eyes. "What if that policewoman arrests me?"

Ignoring the cat, Roy answered Jodie instead. "Then Trevor will get you bail and make sure you have a strong defense."

Jodie wrapped her arms around herself and moaned. "I can't do this."

I don't think you have a choice.

Jodie moaned again, more loudly this time.

"You're not helping," Roy said to the cat. To Jodie he said, "Come up to the kitchen and have some breakfast."

More moaning—then, spoken on a wail, "How can I eat when I'm about to be accused of murder?"

"You haven't been accused of anything and you might not be. Don't rush your fences, girl. Take them when you're ready." Impatience added a bite to Roy's voice. He wanted to be sympathetic, but Jodie's whimpering was fraying his nerves. He much preferred Christy's pluckiness and Ellen's haughtiness.

A key sounded in the lock and the front door opened. Dressed in a dark business suit, with white shirt and dark tie, Quinn was tugging at the knot in his tie as he stepped across the threshold. He paused as he noticed the agitated Jodie halfway down the stairs and his annoyed father at the top. "What's going on?"

Relief coursed through Roy. Jodie responded more positively to Quinn than she did to him. Maybe he could persuade her to stop bemoaning the situation and do something. Anything.

Jodie started to cry.

Quinn's eyes opened wide, and he looked at his father with an expression of horror that mirrored Roy's own.

The cat hopped down the stairs to Jodie, then butted her leg. *Stop crying. You're upsetting the old man. He wants to help you.*

Jodie might not want to acknowledge she could hear the cat, but she did stop crying. She plodded slowly up the steps, followed by the cat and Quinn. Roy escaped to the kitchen before the little cavalcade reached the top of the stairs.

There he discovered a box of cereal on the counter, along with a four-liter jug of milk. A mug filled to the brim with milky coffee was nearby. Roy sat down at the table. If Jodie still wanted some of that cereal, she could get her own.

She drifted into the kitchen, paused to pick up her coffee mug, then joined Roy at the table. The cat hopped up onto a chair. Quinn went over to the coffee maker to brew himself a cup.

"I didn't expect you back for another hour or so," Roy said to him.

"I was supposed to meet with Fred Jarvis' parliamentary assistant, but he called to cancel when I was halfway there." Fred Jarvis had been a cabinet minister in the provincial legislature. His murder was the subject of Quinn's next true crime mystery. "I didn't have anything else going on downtown, so I turned around and came home."

Quinn was staring at the coffee maker with great intensity. Roy figured he wished he'd found some reason to stay away, at least until Jodie's current crisis was resolved.

Quinn's coffee finished brewing. He brought it to the table and shooed the cat from the chair before he sat down. Frank made a rude comment as Stormy hopped up onto the table.

Quinn frowned at the cat, but said to Jodie, "From your tears and my father's dismay, I'm guessing you've had bad news. From Lloyd?"

Jodie sniffed and shook her head. "No, it's the cops."

"The cops?"

"There's been a murder," Roy said, his eyes narrowing in an accusatory way. "Did you know about it?"

Quinn nodded. "Christy told me. She found the body along with Ellen and that real estate agent, Miss Kippen."

"How come everyone knew but me?" Roy demanded, feeling aggrieved.

"Christy didn't want to talk about it last night." Quinn paused, hesitated, then added, "From the way she described the scene, it must have been pretty shocking."

"She saw Clayton?" Jodie said. "Oh! How awful."

Quinn nodded. He was watching Jodie and Roy could see he'd clicked over into investigative mode. Now they'd start getting somewhere. Quinn was a damn fine journalist, he thought with considerable parental pride.

"Yes, she did. How do you know him?"

There was no inflection in Quinn's voice, no criticism or judgment, just a simple request for information. Still, Jodie's gaze skittered from his face to Roy's. She even looked at the cat, whose response had just the hint of amusement in it. *Spit it out. You know you're dying to tell us everything.*

Jodie colored. "I...Clay..." She broke off.

"Clay?"

41

Her color deepened. "Clayton Green. He's a developer. He builds high-rises."

Quinn nodded. "He's behind the hotel and apartment complex Ellen went to see yesterday."

Jodie nodded. She didn't offer anything further.

"You're friends with...Clay?" The little pause emphasized that Quinn's question wasn't simply about friendship, but what kind of friendship Green and Jodie had had.

Lovers more like.

Jodie flushed bright red and she refused to look at the cat. Quinn raised his brows and looked at his father. Roy shrugged. "Frank is of the opinion that Jodie and this Green fellow were in a romantic relationship."

Quinn looked at Jodie.

"All right, yes. I was having an affair with Clay."

"That's what your fight with Lloyd was about."

Quinn made it a statement, not a question, but Jodie nodded, her eyes downcast, and said, "Yes."

"How long has it been going on?" Roy asked. He couldn't quite achieve the impartial calm of Quinn's questions.

Jodie cast him a quick, guilty look. "Months."

"When did Lloyd find out?" Quinn asked.

"On Wednesday." Jodie sounded exhausted. She sniffed. "That's why we fought."

Quinn considered her for a moment. "You said something about cops being the reason you were crying. Why was that?"

She worried her bottom lip. "The detective wants to arrest me."

"For the murder," Quinn said, sounding skeptical.

She nodded.

"Why?"

"What do you mean, why?" Jodie's voice rose. "Because she thinks I killed him, of course!"

"She?" Quinn said.

"Patterson," Roy replied. "I told you before, Jodie. Patterson doesn't want to arrest you. She wants to ask you some questions. She can't arrest you without proof."

"More importantly she won't," Quinn added. "You've lucked out. Patterson's smart and she's thorough. She doesn't take the easy way out and arrest the first person who looks guilty."

Jodie looked at him with eyes wet with unshed tears. "Really?"

The doorbell rang.

"That'll be Trevor," Roy said.

Finally! I think she's about to cry again.

That dried Jodie's tears in a way sympathy could not. Annoyance flashed in her eyes as she glared at the cat, but she didn't acknowledge his comment.

Roy went down to answer the door and came back with Trevor. Like Quinn, he was dressed in a dark suit, pale shirt, and a silk tie. They filled him in on the morning's activities and the information Jodie had given them about her relationship with the dead man.

When they were finished Trevor said briskly, "Family and lovers are the first people the cops look at in a murder investigation. Patterson will already know you were in a relationship with the deceased. She'll ask you where you were at the time of the death. If you have an alibi, she'll want to check it, and, if it holds up, that will end it."

Jodie frowned. "I don't know when Clay was killed."

Trevor looked to Roy and Quinn. "Any ideas?"

"Yesterday morning before eleven o'clock," Quinn said.

Trevor turned to Jodie. "You were here yesterday, correct?"

"Yes, but..." She stopped, moistened her lips, chewed the bottom one uneasily. "Well, you see, I..."

Trevor said nothing. He waited, observing her unease, letting it grow.

"I...I went home."

Again, Trevor waited silently. When she didn't say anything more, he said, "Patterson will ask you why and when and if anyone saw you there."

"I..." She shook her head. "No one saw me."

She looked around the table, a little desperately Roy thought. He had a bad feeling about this.

"I wanted to pick up some clothes and I thought..." She broke off, dragged in a deep breath. "I hoped Lloyd would be home and we could talk."

"But he wasn't." Trevor was watching her narrowly, his expression skeptical.

Jodie looked down and shook her head. She said in a small voice, "No."

After a moment Trevor said, "If no one saw you, it's your word alone that you were at your home. That means you'll continue to be a suspect. Patterson will also look at motive. You were having an affair with the dead man and the night before the murder you fought with your husband over it. That you left the family home indicates the fight was serious. How serious?"

"I...He..." She caught her lip between her teeth again and grimaced. "He was angry."

Trevor raised his brows. "Divorce angry?"

Jodie opened her mouth, drew a breath to speak, then closed it and nodded instead.

"That gives you motive, but it also gives Lloyd motive," Trevor said. "I can work with that. Is there anything else I need to know?"

Jodie gulped and shook her head. Her eyes were huge, her expression terrified.

"All right," Trevor said. He glanced at his watch. "We have a couple of hours before I have to get you downtown. Change into more professional clothes, then have something to eat. This will be a long afternoon."

CHAPTER 6

Quinn slid his cup into the coffee brewer, then listened to it gurgle as the water boiled. Though he was staring at the machine, he was focused on his father. Roy was sitting at his usual place at the kitchen table. His laptop was open in front of him, and he was staring at the screen.

Occasionally, he'd manipulate the trackpad with one finger. He looked intent, as if he was engrossed in his work. Quinn knew he was actually playing computer solitaire. Roy couldn't settle any more than he could as they waited to hear how Jodie's interview with Patterson had gone.

The gurgle ended, replaced by the hiss of boiling water forced through the single-use coffee pod. Quinn waited moodily for the stream to end and the coffee to be ready. Earlier he'd ditched the business attire he'd worn for his meeting with the government official and changed into jeans and a long-sleeved sweater. He'd had a sense that the wait to find out Jodie's fate would be a long one. He'd been right.

The telephone rang, making them both jump. Roy looked up, his eyes wide. Quinn reached for the handset. "Hello?"

"Is Roy there?" a female voice asked.

"May I ask who's calling?"

"Quinn? Is that you? It's your Aunt Evelyn."

"Oh, hi, Aunt Evelyn." Across the room he could see his father making horizontal slashing motions with his hands. In case Quinn didn't get the message, he stopped gesturing. After typing something on the laptop, he fiddled with the controls, then turned it so Quinn could see the screen. In large, seventy-two-point font he'd written, I'm not here!

On the phone, Evelyn was saying, "How are you? I haven't seen you in ages. I read your book, though. It was wonderful."

Quinn did his own bit of gesturing, making a thumbs up sign for his father, who looked relieved. "Thanks Aunt Evelyn. Yes, it has been a while." They chatted for a minute or two about unimportant stuff the way people who are separated by more than just distance do. Finally, Quinn said, "Dad's not around, Aunt Evelyn. Can I give him a message? Is there something I can help you with?"

"That's sweet, honey, but no. I'm trying to contact Jodie. I've been calling her cell for the last hour, and she hasn't answered. I'm worried about her."

"Ah," said Quinn, who had no idea what to say. How did you tell your aunt, who has known you in a vague way since you were in diapers, that her daughter was implicated in the murder of her lover and was even now being questioned by the police?

Evelyn apparently thought Quinn's non-answer was Quinn covering for his cousin. "I know about the fight, Quinn. I talked to Lloyd before I called you. He was very forthcoming."

Unlike you lay there, unspoken. "I see," Quinn said. Before he disclosed anything about the current situation, he wanted to know what Lloyd had said, so he sent out a verbal probe. "Was Lloyd upset?"

"Upset?" Evelyn said. "The man was volcanic! He told me he and Jodie had split, that her crime was beyond anything he could ever forgive."

Crime was a big word. Quinn wondered if Lloyd had used it deliberately and if he knew more than he should of yesterday's events. "I'm sorry to hear that."

"So am I. Lloyd isn't a bad man, but he does tend to pontificate, particularly about his causes. I don't know what to make of this and when I asked, he refused to give me any details! Can you imagine that?"

Quinn could. His aunt Evelyn was the CEO of a mining company located in Whitehorse, up in the Yukon. She tended to be demanding and yes, bossy—when she wanted answers, she expected to get them. Her son-in-law, Lloyd Webster, was a dedicated social warrior. He organized demonstrations and enjoyed suing the companies he was targeting. If that didn't work, he destroyed their reputations on social media. He was very adept at framing information, so his position was always the virtuous one.

As an investigative reporter, Quinn had tangled with him a time or two as he fought to unearth the core issues behind a story. Lloyd believed passionately in what he did, but he wasn't always truthful, and he wasn't above doing his own cover up.

"Why did you call us, Aunt Evelyn?"

"Lloyd thought Jodie might come to you for help."

Quinn wondered how much he should reveal to his aunt. He met his father's eyes across the room. Roy shook his head and shrugged. Quinn figured he'd been following along and had at least a grasp of the conversation. After running the fingers of his free hand through his hair, Quinn said, "Jodie is staying with us."

"Staying with—" Anger simmered in her voice. "He threw her out of the house I provided the down payment for and cosigned the mortgage on? The one Jodie has been paying the monthly mortgage payments on for all these years?"

"Ummm...Yes?"

"That freeloader! Who does he think puts food on his table? Not him, with his do-gooder institute and worthy causes. No, it's my daughter who not only has a full-time, regular people job, but she also raised both his kids after he got her pregnant when she was only nineteen!"

"Ahhhh..."

"I have to go, Quinn. I need to have a word or two with my useless son-in-law."

There was a click, then a dial tone. Quinn slowly hung up the phone.

"You handled that well," Roy said approvingly.

Quinn removed his cup from the brewer and took a gulp. After talking to his aunt, he needed the boost. "Lloyd's in big trouble."

Roy cocked a brow. "Evelyn's after him?"

Quinn came over to the table and sat down. He nodded. "Did you know Aunt Evelyn helped finance Jodie and Lloyd's house?"

"I'm not surprised. It's a big old place in Kerrisdale. Nice neighborhood. Lloyd pretends he's one of the working class, but he likes his comforts and at heart he's a snob. He wanted his kids to go to a school with a reputation for high achievers and involved parents. No inner-city apartment and problem kids holding his own back for him."

Quinn nodded. That fit. Lloyd Webster liked to think he was a tireless worker for the urban poor and that his efforts were instrumental in making their lives better. In reality, he picked causes he could easily win, but which weren't perhaps as earth-shatteringly important as he pretended they were.

"I'm afraid I let Aunt Evelyn think Lloyd kicked Jodie out," Quinn said. He leaned back in his chair, holding his cup between both hands.

"Well done. Evelyn will have fun eviscerating Lloyd and he'll have a wonderful time abusing her as a corporate pig." Roy grinned. "And neither of them will bother us."

Quinn drank his coffee. Roy played computer solitaire. Time passed. No one called. There were no texts or emails. Quinn finished his coffee. Restlessly, he took his mug over to the sink where he rinsed it. Then he stood, still holding the mug, staring at the clock on the stove. It was almost two-thirty. Jodie had been at the station for an hour and a half. This wasn't good.

"I'm going to see Christy." He popped the mug into the dishwasher. "Call me if you hear anything."

Roy looked gloomy, but he nodded. "Okay."

Quinn found Christy about to walk over to the school to pick up Noelle. She was wearing jeans and a teal blue sweater that hugged her torso and looked great on her. He couldn't help but smile when he saw her.

She smiled back and said, "Want to come with me to the school?"

He did. As they walked, holding hands after a long kiss that satisfied them both, he told her about his aborted meeting, Patterson and Jodie, and Trevor's concerns.

Christy shook her head in disbelief. "Jodie was having an affair with Clayton Green? Really? Ellen said he was a horrible person. Why on earth would Jodie get involved with a man like that?"

Quinn shrugged. "That I can't tell you, but it doesn't look good for Jodie."

Christy leaned against him. "If she needs our help, I'm happy to give it."

Quinn looked down at her. She smiled back and his heart lurched. Her support was quick and freely given. He wondered how he'd got so lucky. "I hope I'm wrong. I hope Patterson grills Jodie but eliminates her as a suspect."

"You hope, but you don't expect," Christy said.

She knew him too well. He sighed. "Having an affair—this isn't Jodie. She's steady, solid, plodding, even. She's an accountant. She digs through people's books, makes sure all their expenses are in order and does their financial reports and taxes. For some reason she went off the rails with this Clayton Green guy, but I don't know why. That makes me wonder what else she's done."

Christy shuddered. "From the mess the room was in, it looked like whoever shot Green did it randomly, like they weren't used to handling a gun or they were full of anger." She shot a frowning look at Quinn. "Do you think Jodie is capable of violence? Could she murder another person?"

Quinn squeezed her hand in a reassuring way as she spoke, but when she finished, he said, "The Jodie I knew growing up wouldn't be, but I haven't seen her much since she married Lloyd and had her kids. If she did kill Green, she must have had a good reason to do it."

"Let's wait and see what her situation is before we start to worry. Once we hear what happened we can plan out what we need to do," Christy said.

Quinn nodded. "Yeah."

They reached the school. The classroom doors were still closed, the kids inside impatiently waiting for dismissal. Christy shot Quinn a mischievous look. "We'll invite everyone over for dinner and do one of our planning sessions. Jodie will be exonerated in no time."

He laughed. "Patterson is probably shaking in her boots."

Christy laughed too and agreed, then the bell rang, the doors were flung open, and kids danced boisterously through the portals. Blond pigtails flying, Noelle found Christy and threw herself exuberantly against her, hugging her energetically while announcing she had no homework for the weekend. Then she hugged Quinn too, making him feel like he'd just won the lottery.

They walked home, one of Noelle's hands in Christy's, one in Quinn's. Quinn pushed Jodie Webster's plight aside and concentrated on the two females who had become so important in his life.

CHAPTER 7

Christy tried to keep Saturday as a day for Noelle. That meant time for them to do things together, or for Noelle to invite her friends to visit. Today was a combination. Noelle asked Mary Petrofsky over for the afternoon and a sleepover and the two girls helped Christy and Ellen prep for the planning session that evening.

The day was a spectacular success. Christy decided to serve a hearty beef stew for dinner. She cut up the meat, but the two girls carefully chopped carrots, onions, celery, and peppers. Together, they made the sauce, and it was the girls who programmed the oven, while Christy shoved the casserole dish inside.

After the stew was in the oven, Ellen made a batch of dinner rolls, which she set aside to rise. When the dough was ready, she let Noelle and Mary punch it down, which both girls enjoyed immensely. She then instructed them on how to roll and shape the dough into buns, which were set aside for the second rise. They'd be baked later so they'd still be warm when dinner was served. Then they all cleaned up the kitchen and set the table before Noelle and Mary departed for the basement play-room. Christy and Ellen went up to change for dinner.

While she inspected her cupboard to decide which top to wear, Christy thought about the problem they would be tackling this evening.

She knew nothing about Clayton Green beyond that he was a property developer, and his company was responsible for building the apartment-hotel complex where he'd been killed. Ellen had been on the beautification committee with him, so she obviously knew more, but how much?

She pulled out a tailored silk blouse in a gorgeous green somewhere between emerald and forest and held it up against her. The color brought out the red highlights in her short dark hair and somehow added a luminescence to her skin. She smiled at her reflection and nodded. She laid the blouse on the bed, then went in search of slacks to match to it.

She chose a pair of charcoal gray trousers, slim cut and plain tailored like the blouse. As she took them over to the bed, she reflected that the crime scene must have provided the police with a great deal of forensic evidence. Their little band of amateur sleuths couldn't compete with that kind of information. What they were good at and where they could contribute, was to find out about the victim and get the people involved to talk to them. It seemed to her, then, that their challenge was to figure out who Clayton Green was.

She'd planned dinner for six-thirty, but invited everyone to come a couple of hours earlier. The first to arrive was Quinn, a little after four, and Christy had only just finished getting ready. She raised her brows when she opened the door. Quinn looked great, dressed in jeans that hugged his slim hips and a navy sweater that showed off his trim torso. His expression, however, was somewhere between harassed and grim.

Christy took note of that expression as she invited him in with a gesture. "Hi. What's the matter?"

He stepped inside. She was closing the door when he said, "Jodie is exhausting. She veers from believing she's going to jail for life to contempt that Patterson is stupid enough to include her as a suspect."

"Panic to bravado," Christy said thoughtfully as she headed up the stairs. Quinn followed. Halfway up she stopped, slowly turned, took the bottles of wine he was carrying, and put them on the step. Then she kissed him.

She didn't like to kiss him in the tiny landing, because Noelle could have looked up at any time, and she didn't want to kiss him in the middle of the living room, in case Ellen came down the stairs. Both knew she and

Quinn were in a relationship, but to Christy it seemed kinder not to show either the romantic, physical part of her growing feelings for him.

"That was nice," Quinn murmured when she pulled away.

She smiled, pleased to see that the tension had eased from his features. "Yes, it was. Come upstairs and get settled."

She suited action to words and Quinn followed, picking up the wine bottles as he went. He took them into the kitchen. "Something smells good."

"Beef stew," Christy said. She smiled mischievously. "Be sure to notice how well the vegetables are cut."

He laughed. "Noelle's work?"

Christy nodded. "And Mary Petrofsky's. She's here for a sleepover."

She poured them each a glass of wine and they went into the living room to sit.

"Trevor arrived just before I left. He and Dad were trying to talk Jodie down, but I don't know which is worse—her upset or her scornful. Trevor brought an appetizer for dinner. Dad made a salad." Quinn laughed. "Jodie instructed him on how to toss it and what salad dressing to use. I thought he was going to dump a whole bowl of lettuce on her head."

Christy sipped her wine. "She's probably terrified. It's a horrible feeling to have the police looking into your life because they suspect you of a crime." She resisted the urge to shiver. She'd been a suspect when Frank disappeared, and she remembered the sense of aloneness liberally mixed with fear. She'd lived with it for several weeks before it became obvious she'd done nothing wrong. Now the memories provided her with empathy for Jodie, but she also sympathized with Quinn and Roy. Jodie wasn't handling the pressure well and they were bearing the brunt.

"I suppose making a salad is something she can control." Quinn's tone said he was dubious about the truth of that statement.

Christy laughed. "Or maybe it was your dad she was trying to control. He can be...erratic sometimes."

Quinn laughed too. "Sometimes? But, yeah, you could be right. Speaking of erratic, Sledge texted me today. He's in town and he's got big news he wants to share. He wanted to get together tonight. I explained what was going on and suggested he join us. He can't make dinner, but he's coming after. He said he'd bring dessert."

"That's great!" Christy tapped her chin. "I wonder what's up." A laugh gurgled in her throat. Leaning forward, she said in a low conspiratorial voice, "Do you think he's met someone in LA? One of the contestants on his show, perhaps? Oh!" Her eyes widened and her mouth quivered into a delighted smile. "Do you think he might bring her tonight to introduce her to us?"

With a quiet chuckle, Quinn held up his hand. "Whoa! You're moving too fast. If Sledge had met someone important enough to introduce to us, he would have talked to his dad first and Trevor would be bursting with the news. He didn't say anything when he arrived, though, so..." He laughed at Christy's crestfallen look.

As he finished speaking Ellen came down the stairs wearing a boat necked dress with a wide skirt that swirled around her trim legs. "What didn't Trevor mention?"

Christy made a little face and told her. Ellen laughed. "Quinn's right. Trevor couldn't keep something like that to himself."

With a sigh, Christy said, "Okay. I wonder what his big secret is, then."

Ellen laughed again. "We'll have to wait. In the meantime, I'm going to check my rolls." She disappeared into the kitchen as the doorbell rang.

Stormy the Cat who had been in the playroom with the girls, was on the landing when Christy went down to answer the bell.

Is the meeting about to begin?

The voice spoke as Christy opened the door.

Roy, who was standing on the threshold holding his bowl of salad and wearing his standard jeans and checked shirt, said, "Soon, Cat."

Standing just behind him, Jodie pressed her lips firmly together and ignored both cat and uncle.

They trooped into Christy's foyer, then up the stairs, Roy in the lead. As Trevor passed Christy, he held up a white box. Like Ellen, he was dressed to impress in expensive slacks and chocolate brown shirt. Smiling, he said, "I ordered appys from Chef Rita."

Christy thanked him and closed the door. Upstairs, Trevor and Roy deposited their burdens in the kitchen. Christy shooed them out to find seats in the living room, then she plated the appetizers while Ellen took drink orders. When everyone had a plate and a glass, Christy sat beside Quinn on the sofa and said, "Shall we begin?"

Jodie sniffed. "I've done nothing wrong."

Sure, sure. Wink, wink.

"Frank!" Christy said.

"Not helping, man," Roy said, shaking his head.

The cat, who had inserted himself between Quinn and Christy on the sofa, licked one paw. *She can hear, but she won't listen!*

"That doesn't mean you have the right to be rude. This is serious, Frank. Jodie's been through a lot. Give her some space." Christy did her best to keep her tone even, but she heard irritation seep through.

Ellen was frowning as she stared at Jodie. "My nephew is right. You've behaved badly. Clayton Green was married. You're married." She shook her head. "Worse than that, your husband loathed everything Clayton stood for. Consider how he must feel knowing you were in a relationship with his adversary?"

Well said, Aunt Ellen.

Jodie said hotly, "Lloyd cares more about his causes than he does about me! I thought if I flirted with Clay at the Christmas party last year that Lloyd would get mad. That he'd see me for me, but no, he said nothing. Clay was sweet to me. He made me feel like a woman again, not just the major financial provider, and the family caregiver. Then Lloyd found out and he was so upset! I told Clay we'd have to end it and..." She broke off with a sob. "He laughed. He laughed and dusted his hands together and said his work was done!"

Her sobs grew and for a moment they were the only sound. Then Quinn said, "He used you to get at Lloyd."

Hiccupping, Jodie nodded.

"Good thing you didn't tell Patterson that," Trevor said.

When Jodie started to cry Christy went into the kitchen. She came back with a box of tissues, which she handed to Jodie. Nodding her thanks, Jodie pulled out a handful, which she used to dab her eyes and blow her nose.

So that makes Jodie and Lloyd suspects. Who else have we got?

Ellen had her leather binder open, her fountain pens neatly aligned on the coffee table in front of her. Holding one aloft, she said, "If Jodie and Lloyd are suspects, that means the murder was personal."

"It certainly looked personal, don't you think?" Christy said. She pursed her lips and shook her head. "The room was a mess. Green was a mess. Whoever killed him not only wasn't used to handling a gun, but he or she didn't care how much damage was inflicted."

"I didn't kill him," Jodie said.

"Could it have been some nut with a beef against his developments?" Roy asked.

"The cops don't think so," Trevor said. "They figure Green knew the person who killed him." He hesitated, glancing at Jodie before he continued. "The location of the murder is suggestive. The suite was where Green and Jodie had their liaisons."

"If he had an affair with Jodie to get at Lloyd, maybe he was doing the same thing with someone else," Roy suggested.

He raised his brows and looked hopefully at Trevor, who shrugged. "Could be."

Ellen, making notes using a pen filled with bright red ink, said, "Lloyd is a member of the Vancouver Beautification Committee and it was at the Christmas party Jeff Darling threw that Jodie and Clayton flirted. Two other women are on the committee. Maybe he was involved with one—or both!—of them."

"A personal relationship doesn't have to be a sexual one," Quinn said. "Maybe a business deal went sour. Or he cheated an associate who wanted revenge."

Then there's the mob.

"Good heavens," Christy said. "If organized crime is involved, we don't want to be."

"No indeed," Quinn said, rather grimly.

Trevor was shaking his head. "Unlikely. The crime scene calls attention to itself. An organized crime hit would have been more efficient, under the radar, so to speak."

"So, what have we got? A sexual relationship with a person or persons unknown or possibly someone angry over sharp dealing in his business practices." Roy looked around at the group. They all nodded. "Where do we start, then?"

A timer buzzer went off in the kitchen. Ellen closed her binder, placing it on the coffee table with her pens. As she stood, she said, "With the members of the beautification committee. Before we can decide why he was killed, we need to find out more about Clayton."

"Good suggestion," Trevor said, smiling approvingly.

Ellen smiled back. "That buzzer was my reminder that my dinner rolls need to go into the oven. I suggest we adjourn this discussion until after dinner."

Works for me.

"Good idea," Christy said. "Can I refill anyone's glass?"

CHAPTER 8

Noelle and Mary Petrofsky saved dinner from slipping into Jodie's dark, gloomy mood by gleefully itemizing every stroke they'd used to cut the vegetables, then describing, with a child's point of view, the absolutely hilarious process of making bread. Christy encouraged them, helped along by Quinn.

The cat made comments that stressed Jodie, mainly because she refused to acknowledge she'd heard them, which everyone did their best to ignore. Wine was drunk, food eaten, and compliments made to Christy, Ellen, and the girls. The men cleared the table, then Noelle and Mary carefully put the dishes into the dishwasher. Rather sulkily, Jodie excused herself to visit the bathroom.

When the doorbell rang, Quinn went to answer. Christy heard his voice and Sledge's mingling, then Sledge appeared in the kitchen doorway bearing two enormous white pastry boxes. Quinn followed, carrying a third.

"Good grief," Christy said as he put his burden onto the counter. "There's enough sweets here to put us all into a diabetic coma."

A founding member of the supergroup SledgeHammer, Sledge was every inch the glamorous rock star from his shaggy dark blond hair, through his ripped jeans and multi-colored sequined shirt. He grinned and leaned in to give her a hug and a kiss on the cheek. "I went to my favorite bakery. Their desserts are so good, I couldn't decide what I should buy, so I just asked for a bit of everything."

Quinn added his white box to the others on the counter. He popped open the lid. Inside was an eclectic collection of petits fours as well as slices of several types of cheesecake. "Wow. This looks amazing."

Roy had snooped into another of the boxes. His contained an array of cake slices. Christy's brows rose. "I never knew there were so many types of chocolate cake."

"There's lemon cake," Roy said. He sounded as if he'd just found the Holy Grail after a long hard search.

"Two types," Sledge said helpfully. "There's one that's a lemon sponge with lemon curd filling and the other is lemon and blueberry."

Roy's eyes lit up. "Really? That one's mine."

Trevor laughed. "I'll have a piece of cheesecake."

"I would like a piece of chocolate cake," Noelle said.

She sounded prim and proper, very Jamieson, Christy thought, but her eyes gleamed and she was practically drooling with anticipation. "Okay. What would you like, Mary?"

"Chocolate cake." She nodded, dark braids bobbing, as if to reinforce the decision.

I'll have chocolate cake too.

"Cats don't eat cake," Christy said. They'd had this conversation before, but one of the things Frank missed most about being human was sugar. Christy passed him bits of human food, like chunks of beef from tonight's stew chopped small, but she wouldn't feed him sweet sauces or desserts. Being Frank, that didn't stop him from asking—or bitching about it when she turned him down.

This cat does.

"He does not," Christy retorted, more interested in investigating the contents of the third box than bickering with the cat.

At this point Jodie walked into the room and said, "What's this?"

"Yummy dessert," Noelle said. She beamed and pointed to Sledge. "He brought it."

Sledge grinned back. "Thanks, kid."

Her brows knit together into a frown; Jodie stared at him. "Aren't you that guy on the TV show?"

Sledge blinked. He looked a bit lost and Christy guessed he wasn't yet completely used to being known as a TV personality, rather than Sledge of SledgeHammer, rock icon.

Quinn poked him in the ribs with his elbow. "Looks like you're on your way to stardom, my friend. Not quite there, though, since your audience can't remember your name. You'll have to work a little harder."

Sledge didn't reply, but he rolled his eyes skyward. Quinn's jibe grounded him though. He shot his trademark rock star grin at Jodie. "You could say that." He held out his hand. "I'm Sledge."

Jodie stared at it, then at him. Then she smiled, apparently unable to resist that seductive grin, and took his hand. "I'm Jodie."

In a blink he went from famous personality to concerned friend. "Ah, the lady in trouble we're here to defend."

Jodie softened even more. Her eyes opened wider, her lips trembled and she nodded. "It's been rough."

Frank spoiled the moment. *Oh, please. If you didn't kill the guy, we'll get you off. Quit the melodrama.*

Sledges brows shot up. "A bit harsh, don't you think, Cat?"

"You can hear him too?" Jodie blurted out.

"Sure. We all can." He grinned and with a gesture added, "Except Quinn. He doesn't believe the cat can talk."

Quinn shot him a long level look but didn't reply. He was helping Christy organize plates and cutlery for the desserts and mugs for after dinner coffee.

"I don't believe, either. At least, I didn't believe...But...How can such a thing be possible?"

"It's not," Quinn said. He dished out a big wedge of chocolate cake for Noelle, then followed with one for Mary Petrofsky.

"Sure it is." Sledge helped by passing plates to the other adults. Roy dived in to scoop up the lemon blueberry slice. Noelle and Mary scooted over to the table to gobble up their cake. Christy poured milk into glasses, which she handed to Ellen, who in turn passed them to the girls.

Roy tucked into his lemon cake. "Yum." His eyes were half closed and he appeared to be communing with some higher deity. "Gotta go with the flow. All things are possible if you open your mind."

Sledge grinned and jerked his head to indicate Roy. "It's one of those cosmic things."

Roy nodded, still mostly absorbed in his ecstatic enjoyment of the lemon blueberry cake.

"Give it up," Quinn said. He'd gone for a mille-feuille bar and was currently licking whipped cream from his fingers.

Jodie's gaze was darting from one to the other and she was biting her bottom lip again. Christy intervened. "Jodie, would you like a dessert? There's a variety of cheesecakes, some petits fours, cake slices, cupcakes, and pies."

"Pies?" Jodie said, looking relieved.

With a twinkle, Sledge cheerfully listed the varieties. "Pecan, Boston cream, key lime, blueberry, apple—"

"Blueberry pie?" said Roy. His fork hovered over the lemon blueberry cake on his plate.

Christy laughed. "Jodie gets first pick, but otherwise, the blueberry pie is yours."

At that Jodie laughed, for the first time that evening. It opened up her features and put a gleam in her eyes. She suddenly looked years younger and much more approachable. "I wouldn't take the blueberry pie away from Uncle Roy. He's always been a fan. When I was a kid and Aunt Vivian and Uncle Roy visited, my mom would bake a blueberry pie, just for him."

"Your mom makes great blueberry pie," Roy said.

"She does. I'll have the pecan pie, please, Christy."

While the adults were talking Noelle and Mary finished their cake and milk. Noelle, with Mary trailing behind, brought their plates to Christy. "Mom, can we be excused? We'd like to go downstairs and play."

Christy smiled. "Yup. Dishes in the dishwasher, then off you go. I'll be down later when it's time to get ready for bed."

"Thanks, Mom!" The dishes went into the dishwasher with speed, but also meticulous efficiency as Christy had taught Noelle. Then the two girls disappeared, off to their own private world.

There were a few more minutes of general conversation while Trevor, Ellen and Christy chose their desserts, then they all settled at the table, plates of treats and mugs of coffee before them.

"Fill me in on what's been happening," Sledge said.

Trevor did, with an economic description that provided the details but not a lot of the emotional side effects.

"Ellen thinks the killer might be one of the members of her committee?" Sledge said when his father had finished.

"I think we need a better understanding of who Clayton Green was and the members of my committee may be able to help us with that," Ellen replied.

Sledge nodded.

"I didn't kill Clay," Jodie said. She sounded worried again.

Sledge raised his brows. "Of course you didn't."

Jodie visibly relaxed. She nodded and smiled.

Now we've got that straightened out, who talks to whom?

Sledge rolled his eyes and shook his shaggy head.

Ellen tapped the sheet of paper in front of her. "We're agreed, Jodie, that you did not kill Clayton Green, but your husband, Lloyd, has reason to be angry with him on a personal level and perhaps on a business one."

"I'll talk to him," Jodie said. Her expression indicated she wasn't looking forward to the interview.

"Not a good idea," said Trevor.

Jodie's mouth hardened and her chin jutted out. "I need to see him."

Trevor shook his head. "Bad idea. You need to stay out of this, Jodie."

"I agree," Ellen said.

Looking mutinous, Jodie glared at Ellen, who ignored her. "Christy and I will talk to him. I disagree with Lloyd on many issues, but we have never been confrontational."

Amazement lightened Jodie's features and opened her eyes wide. "You don't know Lloyd well, do you?"

Ellen frowned. "I don't understand that comment."

She's saying this Lloyd guy thinks you're rich and privileged, but he's too chicken to say it to your face, so he bitches to his wife about you instead.

Jodie bit her lip and nodded.

Ellen narrowed her eyes. "Does he indeed? Even more reason for me to speak to him, then."

Christy heard something that sounded like a snort of laughter, then, *Go for it, Aunt Ellen. Grind the little twerp into dust.*

Quinn sighed and said, "Look, I agree with Trevor that it's not a good idea for Jodie to discuss the murder with Lloyd. Why don't Dad and I talk to him instead?"

"Could work," Roy said. His eyes lit with amusement. "Let him think that if he plays nice you'll write an article on his favorite cause."

Quinn's mouth twisted into an expression of distaste. "He's tried to get me to write a puff piece about his causes more than once and I've shut him down. I doubt he'll buy into a vague assurance I'll support him."

The expression in Jodie's eyes deepened into mischief as she nodded. "You're right about that. He says you're a mouthpiece of the oppressive socio-economic forces that are destroying this country."

For a second Quinn looked the way he might if he'd been punched in the solar plexus. His breath caught and his eyes widened. Then he shook his head. "Sounds like Lloyd."

Roy said, "Quinn? My Quinn? The most principled journalist in this country?" He surged to his feet as he pounded his fist on the table, making the plates jump. "Who does he think he is?"

"Dad," said Quinn.

Sledge laughed. "Sounds like this Lloyd dude eats conspiracy theories for breakfast along with his cereal." He studied Jodie. "He must be a lot to put up with."

"You have no idea," Jodie said. Her shoulders slumped and the fun leached out of her. "That's why I ended up with Clay. Lloyd cares more about his causes than he does about me and the kids. Clay—well, he made me feel special. Like I had value, like he cared about me for me." With a little shrug she looked around the group. "That's why I couldn't kill him. Why would I?"

Christy thought that if Jodie had discovered that Clayton Green didn't value her just for herself, she could have decided to do him in. She didn't say that though. For the moment she was willing to let Jodie's statement stand. Instead, she asked, "Is Lloyd possessive? Would he be angry at Clayton because you were lovers?"

Jodie shook her head and said, "No, of course not," but her expression said she wondered if it could be true.

Roy had resumed his seat, but he was still fuming. "I've known Lloyd for fifteen years. Quinn and Vivian and I went to your wedding. We've exchanged Christmas visits and done family picnics. He's always been polite and friendly." He waved his hand in an emphatic way. "Heck, I used him as a source when I wrote that novel on the plight of homeless people in Vancouver. His input helped shape that book."

Jodie sighed. "He said the book was shallow and that you were so wrapped up in your own privilege you could never understand." When Roy's jaw dropped, she hastily added, "I'm sorry, Uncle Roy, I know that book became a bestseller—"

"It won awards," Roy said. He narrowed his eyes, prepared to demand further explanations.

Quinn said, "Maybe you aren't the best person to talk to him, Dad."

The cat hopped up onto the table then trotted over to rub his cheek on Roy's. *I'll go, but I'll need a human to come with me.*

"You?"

The cat turned away from Roy to stare at Jodie. Christy could swear she saw a gleam of satisfaction in the wide green eyes. *Don't be surprised. I do good work. It was me who forced Jackson Hargreaves to tell the truth when we were seeking Karen Beaumont's killer.*

"I helped," Roy said.

You did. You took me to him. The cat rubbed against Roy again.

Roy scratched him behind the ears as he grumbled, "Nothing but a glorified chauffeur."

"If the cat is offering to get involved, I'm not taking him to visit Lloyd," Quinn said.

No one asked you to.

"Why doesn't Trevor go?" Christy asked, before Quinn ended up in a battle of words with a voice he couldn't hear.

I could work with that.

"You're a McCullagh of McCullagh, McCullagh and Walker," Jodie said.

Trevor nodded. "What of it?"

"Lloyd had a run in with one of your hot-shot associates a few years ago."

"Let me guess," Quinn said. "Was her name Mallory Tait?"

Jodie scrunched up her face and stared at the ceiling as she recollected. "I think so. Lloyd said she was a real shark. He didn't like her because he lost. If a lawyer whose last name is McCullagh shows up, he'll slam the door in your face."

Sledge laughed. "Guess that leaves me to partner up with you, Cat."

Works for me.

Jodie bit her lip.

Amused, Sledge said, "What? The guy has something against me, too?"

She nodded.

He laughed again. "Okay. Lay it on me. I can take it."

She nibbled her lip some more before she said, "You're part of Sledge-Hammer, right?"

Sledge nodded.

"Lloyd worked with Sydney Haynes for many years. He thinks you're a self-indulgent lazy libertine."

The amusement of moments before disappeared from Sledge's expression. Sydney Haynes had known Sledge before SledgeHammer became a superstar band and he was bitter about Sledge's success and his own failure. His anger had led to a rupture that could never heal between the two men.

Ellen said, "Sydney Haynes caused me a considerable amount of trouble. Did Lloyd ever speak of that to you?"

Jodie shook her head.

"Then I will have visit Lloyd. The cat may come with me." She held up her hand and shook her head when Roy opened his mouth to speak. "I have the advantage. When two-faced people like him are confronted with their duplicity they seek to minimize it. That I will not allow. I intend to make him squirm."

"Umm...It might not be that easy," said Jodie.

Christy sighed. "I'd better come too."

All right! A family party. Let's do it!

With Jodie's impulsive desire to confront her husband harnessed for the moment, they turned their minds to figuring out how to find out more about Clayton Green. Ellen firmly stated she would interview the members of the committee. Christy wanted to check in on Shelley Kippen and offered to help Ellen with the other interviews. Quinn decided he'd look into Green's private and business side, starting with his wife.

The planning session broke up soon after. Roy, Trevor, and Ellen took Jodie back to the Armstrong house, along with the piece of blueberry pie. Christy settled Noelle and Mary in the tent they'd erected in the basement and told them they had a half an hour, then it was lights out.

The cat followed Noelle and Mary into the tent and settled in. Christy knew he'd be asleep before the girls were.

When the house was quiet, she joined the men in the kitchen and sank down into a chair with a sigh. "Jodie Webster is a handful," she said. A plate of dessert treats was still in the center of the table, left from earlier in the evening. She noticed that inroads had been made on it since she'd left to organize the kids. Beside it was a bottle of cognac, a brand with a worldwide reputation of being the best. She raised her brows.

Sledge, who held a very pedestrian glass tumbler filled with the precious liquid, grinned at her. "I stashed it in the car. Quinn tipped me off that Noelle would be here tonight, so I decided to bring it out after she'd settled in to watch TV or play. Then I met—" He broke off, frowning. "You're right. That Jodie is hard to deal with."

Christy laughed. "So, you saved the good stuff until after she'd gone."

Sledge shrugged and grinned.

Quinn had acquired a glass for Christy while they talked. Now he put it on the table and held up the bottle. "Would you like some?"

Christy nodded. He poured and she took a sip. The fine liquor burned in the most pleasant way as it slid down her throat. She reached out and selected a small cake from the platter of treats. "I'm ready to take a break from worrying about who killed Clayton Green for a while." She smiled

mischievously at Sledge. "Quinn told me you had news. I've been speculating like crazy ever since. I thought you were going to announce you
have a new girlfriend you want us to meet. Quinn thinks I'm completely
wrong." She raised a brow. "Who's right?"

Sledge laughed and took a sip of cognac. "Sorry. It's Quinn."

Christy pouted. "Rats. I was so sure."

"We should've bet on it. I'd have made a bundle," Quinn said.

Sledge acknowledged that with an amused twitch of his mobile
mouth. "It's SledgeHammer news. Hammer and I have laid down the new
album and Mitch has been hounding us to get a new manager." He
shrugged. "He's right. If we want to move forward, we need someone to
make the arrangements. Vince's assistant has been covering the day-to-
day stuff, but she's not ready for the big time. Mitch sent us some recom-
mendations for new companies, including one he has a financial stake in.
We finally narrowed it down to two."

Vince Nunez was SledgeHammer's former manager. He'd been
murdered at a party at Sledge's house the year before. Mitch Crosier
owned the company that distributed SledgeHammer's records and he
tended to busy himself in the affairs of his top bands.

Sledge's mouth twisted into a rather cynical smile. "Mitch's offering
was one of the ones we discarded. I thought he'd be pissed about that,
but..." Shrugging, Sledge sipped cognac. "He took it okay. We're interviewing the two finalists this week. That's why I'm back in Vancouver."

Quinn moved his glass in a restless way over the tabletop. "What are
the next steps?"

Sledge shrugged. "A tour to support the new album, videos for the
songs, interviews."

"Frank will want to be part of it." Christy found another small cake
from the platter and popped it into her mouth.

Quinn shook his head. "The cat won't like the noise."

Sledge laughed. "We'll figure something out. Mitch wants Marenda
Riddle to do the videos. I'll get Kim to brainstorm with her on how to fit
the cat into the scenes."

Since Kim Crosier, Mitch's wife, was another of those who could hear
Frank, Christy figured this was the best plan to ensure Frank was involved

in the making of the videos. Kim and Frank were pals. She'd be delighted to include him. Marenda Riddle, a well-known producer and director of TV and videos was a close friend of Kim's, but she was one of those who were deaf to the cat.

"Mitch also thinks a primetime special on network TV is a good idea and he says I should go back on the singing show next year, if they invite me." Here Sledge paused to shrug again. "Everything will be moving faster and be more complex. SledgeHammer needs management that can not only keep up, but be five steps ahead."

"You have two options. What makes you think either one will work out?" Quinn asked.

"One is a Toronto company that represents a lot of Canadian acts. We talked to them back before we went with Vince. They're good and the guy who would be representing us is a go-getter. I like his fire and his energy. I think we'd be a good fit. The second one—"

When he stopped speaking and shook his head, Christy said, "But?"

He sighed. "Yeah, but. They're a branch of a well-established American firm, but new in Canada, and looking for clients." He drank some brandy and stared at nothing in particular. "The head of the Canadian operation is a woman. She'd run the team representing us. She's based in Toronto, but we'd have a Vancouver manager who was our local rep. Hammer and I would also each have a personal assistant to sort out our individual commitments. Those three people would be based here in Vancouver."

"Sounds very slick," Christy said.

Sledge nodded. "Yeah, but I'm not sure the Toronto woman has the chops to do the job."

Quinn leaned forward, inspecting the dessert tray. "Why?"

Sledge shrugged. "It's a gut feeling."

As Quinn ate the last of the cakes, Christy raised her brows in a challenge. "And maybe a bit of sexism going on?"

Sledge met her gaze. "It's a tough business, especially when you reach our level."

"Women can be tough too."

Quinn laughed and glanced at Christy. "Yup. Very true."

Sledge laughed too. "Yeah, you're right. I'll keep an open mind when we interview her, I promise."

Having made her point, Christy smiled. "Fair enough."

"When do you make the decision?" Quinn asked.

"We do the interviews this week, then I have to go back to LA for the show. That gives Hammer and me a chance to think about the decision. We expect to make an announcement a week or so later." He grinned. "We'll reveal it at a party. You guys are invited."

"Frank will be delighted," Christy said.

Sledge grinned. "So will Kim. I'm going to get her to organize it. I think the cat is her favorite guest."

Christy smiled at him. "I'm already looking forward to this. Now, we just have to get the murder sorted before then, and we can all relax."

Quinn and Sledge both nodded. Neither mentioned that if they didn't, there was every likelihood that Jodie Webster would be sitting in a jail cell charged with the murder of Clayton Green.

CHAPTER 9

Jodie picked the time—and the place—of the meeting with her husband, Lloyd. Christy quickly realized that was a mistake, since the time was five-thirty in the afternoon and not only was Lloyd at home, but so were Jodie's two kids. This was not going to be an easy question and answer session with a quick getaway.

It was going to be an emotional maelstrom.

And the cat was no help, remarking, *Well, this is fun. What a touching family reunion,* as Jodie and Lloyd squared off against one another and the daughter of the house cried.

It all began with some little white lies.

As they discussed options on Sunday morning, Christy thought they should arrange to meet Lloyd the next day, around mid-morning. The location would be in a neutral place, like a coffee shop or a restaurant. Jodie nixed that. She said Lloyd believed coffee was produced by oppressed workers in third world economies. Tea, in his opinion, was just as bad. Restaurants didn't pay their workers a fair wage and forced them to toil in degrading working conditions.

Ellen suggested they go to his office and ask to meet with him. Since he was on the beautification committee with her, she saw no reason why he would be unwilling to see them. Jodie said that as soon as he realized why they were there he'd refuse to speak to them. She then said she was coming with them and when Christy protested, she pouted and promised she'd go on her own if they wouldn't take her.

Reluctantly, Christy and Ellen agreed to include her in the meeting. That made Jodie smile, rather smugly, Christy thought. She then produced a house key and told them they could let themselves in and wait for Lloyd if he wasn't already at home.

That led to a discussion about timing. Christy thought that if they were going to the family home they should arrive there early in the morning, after the kids had left for school, but before Lloyd went to work. Jodie insisted they should go in the afternoon, after Lloyd returned home. Both kids, she promised, had extra-curricular activities on Monday afternoon and would only return about six. If she, Ellen, and Christy arrived around five-fifteen or five-thirty, they'd be able to ask Lloyd what he'd been up to on the morning of Clay's death, then leave.

The cat thought it was a bad idea.

He was right.

When they arrived at the designated time they found a small, eco-friendly car parked in the driveway. Jodie slid open the van door moments after Christy parked. "That's Lloyd's car. Come on, let's go." She hopped out without waiting for Christy or Ellen.

Jodie and Lloyd Webster lived on a nice street in Kerrisdale in a hundred-year-old house full of charm and character. A large cedar hedge sheltered the property, and an old apple tree, its gnarled branches packed with pink flowers, poked above, providing a cheerful contrast to the green hedge. As they headed up the walk, Christy noticed the lawn was lush and healthy, and had been recently mowed, but the flower borders were just dark earth and straggly plantings from last year. Jodie caught the direction of Christy's gaze. Her mouth tightened. "I'm the gardener. Lloyd keeps the lawn looking nice." She dug her keys out of her purse and strode to the door.

And that's where the problems started. The key didn't work.

Jodie took it out of the lock. Checked the key chain to make sure it was the right key and tried again. Even though she aggressively wiggled the key back and forth nothing happened.

Stormy's head poked out of the tote Christy carried. *Lock's been changed.* The voice sounded bored, as if this was a well duh moment and of course Lloyd would have quickly acted to secure his house from his probably soon to be ex.

Jodie sent a fuming look at the cat and rattled the key harder. Ellen looked at Christy with raised brows. Christy shrugged and reached for the doorbell.

Before she could press it, the door flew open.

A girl wearing jeans and a sweatshirt stood on the threshold. Her hair was a long silky fall of dark brown loose waves. It framed a pale oval face with big eyes and a mouth that was now open in an O of surprise. "Mom!"

Great. The kids were home.

"Nancy, sweetheart!" Jodie leaned in, the key ring forgotten in the lock, and hugged her daughter.

"Dad says you've abandoned us," Nancy said, as she hugged Jodie back.

"That's not true. I'd never abandon you," Jodie said. She stepped back and looked over her daughter's shoulder. "Is he home? We'll soon sort this out."

What's going on? Is she planning on moving back in?

"Good question," Christy muttered.

Jodie flushed as she pulled the useless key from the lock and ignored both the cat and Christy.

Nancy did not. She peered at Christy and Ellen, then frowned. "Who are these people, Mom? And why do they have a cat with them?"

"They're Jamiesons and Ellen is on a committee with your father. The cat is her mascot."

The answer appeased Nancy, who said, "Oh," and stepped backward so they could enter.

Frank, however, was not pleased. *The cat is no one's lackey. He is his own person. There is no need to be rude!*

Jodie ignored this and Nancy apparently didn't hear. They all stepped into the house.

"Dad's in the kitchen," Nancy said.

Jodie led the way down a short hall, her back straight, her steps firm. Nancy bounced after her like an eager puppy. Christy and Ellen trailed along behind, not wanting to be in the firing line when the first volleys were exchanged.

The kitchen was a big room, full of light from large windows that made up most of the back wall. Counters lined the wall, with a sink in the middle, so the person working there would have a view of the good-sized garden beyond. An enormous island stood in the middle of the room with an extended top to be used as a breakfast bar. A man of average height with thinning dark hair and thick black glasses stood at the island chopping vegetables. He was still wearing dress trousers from a suit combination, and a blue dress shirt, but he'd ditched his tie. This must be Lloyd Webster, currently the acting family cook.

As Jodie entered, he looked up. "What are you doing here?" His tone was unwelcoming.

"My key didn't work!" Jodie brandished her key ring.

Lloyd looked down and addressed the carrot he was chopping. "I changed the locks."

Ha! Did I call it, or what?

Lloyd frowned. Jodie shouted, "You had no right!"

"Of course I had a right. I threw you out. We're getting a divorce."

"Daaaaaad!" Nancy wailed.

Horror washed over his features. "Nancy? I didn't see you. I didn't know you were there. I'm sorry, honey. You weren't meant to hear that."

Who did he think let Jodie in? What a moron.

Lloyd frowned again and glanced around, in an uneasy way.

Jodie turned to her daughter and hugged her. "It's all right, sweetheart. Dad's just in a temper. Once he gets over being mad, we'll talk and everything will be okay."

"Honestly, Jodie. Will you get over the drama and stop blaming me for this mess? I'm not mad, I won't get over it, and I want you gone. That's why I changed the locks."

"When you gave us the new keys you said it was because you'd lost yours and a burglar could get into the house!" Nancy cried. Her expression was reproachful.

"You lied to our children? Shame on you, Lloyd."

Shame on both of you. Nothing you're saying is helping the kid to cope.

Disapproval resonated in the voice. Jodie glanced uneasily at Christy and Lloyd looked chastened. Then he noticed where Jodie was looking, and his gaze sharpened. "Ellen Jamieson? What are you doing here?" He frowned at Christy. "Aren't you Christy Jamieson?"

Christy nodded.

Lloyd visibly pulled himself together. He smiled apologetically and said, "I'm sorry. We haven't been introduced. It's a pleasure to meet you."

Christy stared at him. She had no idea what to say to a man who spoke to his wife with cold censure one moment then smiled and acted as if none of the last few minutes had ever happened and he was just delighted with the opportunity to get acquainted.

Her hesitation didn't matter because Jodie took over. "Can it, Lloyd. Ellen knows you think she's too rich and privileged to know what's up. Christy's fortune is as big as Ellen's so she's not going to believe your nonsense."

Bigger.

Lloyd frowned. So did Jodie. "What?"

My fortune is bigger than Aunt Ellen's. Let's get that straight right now.

Christy tapped the cat's head and said, "Stop."

No way. This is too much fun. He can hear me, just like she can, but he pretends he can't, just like she does. What is wrong with these people?

Having heard this complaint before, Jodie simply lifted her shoulder and made a dismissive sound in her throat. Lloyd stared at Christy and the cat, his mouth half open as if he intended to say something, but it wouldn't come out. He swallowed hard and cleared his throat before he said, "I think you should go."

Why? We only just got here. The voice was amused now, enjoying Lloyd's dismay. Taunting him.

Lloyd reddened. "Just go."

Nancy pulled away from her mother. "Dad, what's going on? You're acting weird."

Your dad's being rude to his guests, kid. That's all.

Lloyd's lips hardened into a straight, angry line. "Nancy, don't you have homework to do?"

Nancy's eyes widened. "Dad!"

"Well?" he said curtly.

Nancy burst into tears and ran back down the hallway to another part of the house.

"Honestly, Lloyd. Look what you've done. Did you have to?"

Ellen's cool tones cut through the swirl of angry emotions. "If you will answer a few questions, we'll happily leave."

Lloyd frowned. "About what?"

Clayton Green. What else?

"Clay—" Lloyd closed his mouth firmly, cutting off his question and his acknowledgement that yes, he was responding to a disembodied voice in his mind.

Ellen smiled thinly. "You found out Jodie was having an affair with Clayton Green only a few days ago. Is that true?"

Lloyd narrowed his eyes. "That's my business."

"I'll take that as an affirmative," Ellen said briskly. "Are you aware that Clayton Green was murdered?"

Lloyd seemed to close in on himself as he nodded bleakly.

"Where were you on the morning of the murder?"

"Like I told the cops when they came to interrogate me, I was at the office. Now, I've answered all the questions I'm going to. Go."

Liar.

A flush reddened his cheeks. "Now see here—"

"I agree," Ellen said. When Lloyd's brows snapped together, she smiled in a way that expressed power, not pleasure. "You shift your gaze when you're spinning a tall tale and I saw you do it just now. Tell me when you arrived at your office."

His gaze wavered and he swallowed uneasily. "Okay, give me a minute to think." He closed his eyes as if he was looking inward, searching his memory for the exact details of that morning.

Cut the theatrics and spit out the truth. We're waiting.

Lloyd's eyes popped open, and he screwed his mouth into an angry pout. "All right. I was still at home, okay?"

Were you now? Can you prove that?

"No! We ran late. The kids..." He looked over at Jodie. "They've been late to school every morning! They won't get up. They won't get ready. They miss the school bus. You should have been here."

Jodie's mouth dropped open. "I should have—you kicked me out."

Save the bickering for later.

Jodie glared at the cat. Lloyd's jaw hardened and his eyes blazed.

Ellen said, "Are you telling us your children are your alibi for the morning?"

Pretty cold, dragging your kids into your sordid lies.

"I'm not dragging the kids into anything! I had to drive them to school so they wouldn't be late. I've already had a call from the vice principal lecturing me on punctuality. They couldn't be late again, so I didn't even shower. I stuffed them both into the car and let them out at the school grounds just before the bell. Then I had to come home and get ready for my day. Except, I remembered I had a call with an important contributor at ten and I wouldn't get to the office in time, so I took it here."

"The name?" Ellen said.

Straightening, he said, "That's confidential."

That's your alibi, doofus. What's the name of this important donor?

Lloyd was pursing his lips again, looking stubborn. Christy said gently, "It will be easier if you tell us. Then we can go and leave you to pick up the pieces with your daughter."

I won't stop until we get a name.

Christy nodded.

"There is no name!" The words burst out, sharp with anger, tinged with despair. "His secretary sent a text saying something came up and he'd have to postpone the call. So, I went to the office."

Ellen raised her brows. "Interesting. When did you arrive?"

"Just after eleven."

"When did you leave the house?" Christy asked.

"About ten-thirty. Look, I've told you what you want to know. Can you go?"

Tut, tut. You were doing so well. We ask the questions. You answer them. Got it?

"I'm almost finished," Ellen said briskly. "I believe, from your somewhat garbled responses, that you were with your children until just before eight-thirty when you dropped them at their school." She waited until he'd nodded before continuing. "From that point, you were in your car returning to this house, where you performed your morning routine until ten, after which you waited for a telephone call that never came. You left the house at ten-thirty and were in transit until five or ten minutes after eleven. Am I correct?"

His jaw still clenched, his eyes angry, Lloyd nodded.

"Good," Ellen said. She glanced at Christy, her brows raised.

"I think we have all we need," she said.

Ellen nodded. "Then we will bid you good day.

See? That wasn't so hard, was it?

A taunt was clear in the voice. Lloyd flushed.

"Jodie?" Christy said. "Are you coming?"

Jodie's eyes were narrowed as she scrutinized her husband. "No. I think I need to stay and tend to my kids. Would you tell Roy I won't be back tonight?"

Christy glanced at Ellen, who shrugged. "Okay. We'll see you later."

Jodie nodded jerkily.

"I don't want you to stay," Lloyd said.

"What you want doesn't matter."

"Oh, yeah?"

They were set to have a right royal verbal brawl. Christy bit her lip. She wanted to go, but she didn't want to leave these two angry people to do their worst.

Do either of you care about your kids? Stifle the bitchiness and put them first. Tear each other apart some other place, some other day.

They both stopped. Lloyd had the grace to look sheepish. Jodie's lips tightened, but she nodded in a jerky way and said, "Kids first. Nancy is pretty upset, Lloyd."

"All right. Truce for tonight. But just for tonight."

Truce whenever you two are with your kids, dumbo. Why is it so hard to get through to you?

77

Imperious, Ellen fixed Lloyd with a cold stare. "I'm glad you have decided to prioritize your children, Lloyd, Jodie. Christy, shall we go?"

Yeah, let's split this scene. We've done all we can and I'm hungry. Hey! I did good work today. Does that mean I get canned tuna tonight?

"In your dreams," Christy muttered and headed for the door and escape.

CHAPTER 10

With the seasons changing, Christy decided she and Noelle were due for a trip to the local mall to update Noelle's wardrobe. After the way she'd spent her afternoon the previous day, she welcomed the normalcy of shopping with her daughter and the warmth of time spent together.

When they reached a chain store that featured medium-priced clothing, Christy ushered them all inside. "Noelle, look around and see if you can find anything you like. Aunt Ellen and I will look too. Then you can try on what we've found."

"Okay, Mom." Noelle knew the drill. This was the third store they'd been in and they already had several items in carrier bags. She scampered off to check out the tops.

Ellen peered at a nearby rack of dresses and pulled one out. She'd decided to come along even though she usually shopped at high-end boutiques found on stylish downtown streets. She made a derogatory sound in her throat. "This garment is of poor quality." Her reaction wasn't surprising. While Christy and Noelle were dressed casually—Christy in jeans and a sweater, Noelle in leggings and a cotton blouse—Ellen wore a silk dress that was clearly not off the rack.

Nor was this the first time she'd made the comment. Christy

answered her with the same argument she'd used every other time, although she varied the words she chose. "These are the kind of clothes Noelle's friends wear. I don't want her to feel out of place when she goes to a birthday party or on a play date. Besides, a dress like this is practical. I can throw it in the washing machine and dryer and if there are stains on it, I can use harsh cleaners to get them out without ruining a delicate fabric. Noelle will outgrow her summer clothes before it's time to wear them again next year so it won't matter if the garment is a little ragged, or faded out, when fall comes around."

As before, Ellen made a noncommittal sound in her throat as she put the dress back in the rack. She continued to browse with brows raised in a disapproving way. Christy found a cute little dress, a pair of cotton shorts, and a brightly patterned blouse before Noelle came up, her arms loaded with tops and pants. Not surprisingly, Ellen had picked out nothing.

"Wow. What a great selection," Christy said. "Let's go find a salesperson and see about trying these on."

Ellen's phone rang. She fumbled in her purse and pulled it out. When she saw who was calling, she frowned." That's odd."

"Not someone you expected?" Christy asked as she pointed to the sales counter and urged Noelle toward it.

"No." She accepted the call. "Yes. Ellen Jamieson speaking."

Christy left her to it while she and Noelle found a salesperson, then headed to the change rooms. When they emerged fifteen minutes later, Ellen was nowhere in sight. Assuming she'd left the store to conclude her conversation, Christy purchased three of the items, then ushered Noelle from the store.

They found Ellen sitting on a nearby bench, her phone nowhere in sight, her expression puzzled. She stood when she saw Christy and Noelle and smiled. "Where to next?"

Christy looked down at Noelle. "What about it, kiddo? More shopping or have you had enough?"

Noelle took a moment to consider this. "Can we come back another day, Mom?"

Christy smiled. "Of course. Let's stop at the Jamieson ice cream kiosk and have a treat before we go home."

"Yeah!" She lifted her hand for a high five and Christy laughed as she complied. They set off for the ice cream stand, which was at the opposite end of the mall. Noelle skipped ahead, again full of exuberant energy, leaving Christy and Ellen to follow more slowly.

Christy glanced at Ellen. "You looked worried when we came out of the store. Any problems?"

Ellen shook her head. "Not really. I'm more perplexed. The call was from Harvey Wrenn and I didn't expect to hear from him."

Christy furrowed her brow, but she couldn't put a face to the name. "Who's Harvey Wrenn?"

"Clayton Green's assistant. Well, his actual title is vice president of Management Processes, but he's more of a personal assistant."

Clayton Green's name dumped Christy back to the large, elegant bedroom where they'd found the developer's body. She swallowed hard and took a deep breath. No wonder Ellen had seemed dismayed. "Why did he call?"

"That's the odd thing. He wants to convene an emergency meeting of the beautification committee to elect a new chair. He was calling to tell me the day and time of the meeting."

"Why would he do that?"

Ellen said slowly, "When Clayton became the chair, he arranged for Harvey to provide secretarial and organizational services." She laughed shortly. "Jeff Darling loved it. Before that he used to have his secretary sit in on the meetings and do the minutes. Once Harvey was involved the secretary could focus on Jeff's municipal work." Jeff Darling was the municipal representative on the committee.

Talking about the committee and the personalities involved helped Christy regain her balance. "Why the haste? Clayton died only a few days ago."

"Harvey said that decisions need to be made. We can't proceed without a chair, so someone must be approved."

Christy's brow furrowed. "Did he say what these decisions were?"

"No, he was quite mysterious." They were almost at the ice cream parlor now. Ellen drew a deep breath. "Do you know, Christy, I am not comfortable with this undue haste. It's disrespectful. I think I'll contact Jeff and see if he has any further information." She nodded emphatically. "Yes. Perhaps Harvey is being overzealous and acting on his own. Jeff may not even be aware of what he's doing."

They reached the small shop, which had a few chairs and tables in front of a long, refrigerated counter filled with a dozen flavors of Jamieson ice cream. "Good idea," Christy said. "Now, who wants what?"

The cheerful discussion that followed pushed aside Harvey Wrenn's unseemly desire for a new chair.

At least for the moment.

~

Built in 1936, Vancouver City Hall was a combination of the Art Deco and Moderne architectural styles. As Ellen walked through the big double doors into the lobby, she appreciated the black and white terrazzo floors, the marble clad walls, and the soaring vaulted ceiling. Even the elevator she entered to take her to Jeff Darling's office was gorgeously appointed with gleaming dark wood inlaid with marquetry designs.

As was usual with public buildings from that period, the ornate reception areas were designed to impress, but the hallways leading to the offices were drab and practical. Her heels tapped on the hard-wearing flooring and echoed off the bare walls. She reached Jeff Darling's office, accessed by a nondescript door like all the others, and entered.

Inside, sitting behind an L shaped desk constructed of man-made wood products, sat a tidy-looking woman in her mid-thirties. She smiled when Ellen entered. "Miss Jamieson. How nice to see you. Jeff is just on a phone call now, but he'll be with you soon. Do have a seat. Can I get you anything?"

As she shook her head to decline the refreshments, Ellen reflected that the phone call was probably bogus, a ploy to ensure she understood that Jeff Darling was an important man whose time was at a premium. While she knew he was busy and he did juggle a lot of files on any given day, it annoyed her that Jeff thought she could be impressed or intimidated so easily.

She sat, carefully ensuring the skirt of her elegant blue silk suit didn't wrinkle. The comfortable, boxy chair was covered in faux leather and like the hallway was practical rather than impressive. She took out her phone and scrolled through her messages. When Jeff emerged from the inner office a couple of minutes later, she was busily typing an email and didn't look up. Two could play the power game.

When he cleared his throat, she glanced over with a smile. "Jeff! Good morning. Have you been standing there long?" She held up her phone. "These devices are insidious. You can't escape their demands." She dropped it into her purse as she stood so he couldn't see that the email had no address and would never be sent.

Jeff Darling was a small round man with thinning hair he combed over a bald spot that was beginning to show on the top of his head. Muddy brown eyes looked out through brown-framed glasses with thick lenses. His mouth, now pursed with annoyance over being outplayed, was a surprisingly unmasculine rosebud. "Lovely to see you, Ellen. You said you wanted to talk to me about the beautification committee?"

He gestured for her to precede him into his office, which Ellen did without any haste. She knew Jeff liked to move quickly. When he walked down a hallway his strides were hasty almost to the point of a race walk. In smaller spaces he bustled. All that energetic movement gave the impression that he was a man of action who got things done. Ellen didn't buy it, though. She knew he could stall with the best of them and only acted swiftly when it suited him.

She nodded agreement as she sauntered past him and into his office. She hid a smile at the annoyance she could feel emanating from him as he followed her inside. The inner door shut with a click as she made herself comfortable at the small glass-topped table in one corner of the office. She would not take the supplicant's seat in front of his massive steel and glass desk.

There were two tubular steel chairs at the table. Jeff sat down in the other and narrowed his eyes at her. "Is this about the meeting?"

Ellen raised her brows. "You knew Harvey was arranging it?"

Jeff nodded. "It was my suggestion. He came to me after Clayton died and reminded me the committee can't get anything done until it has a new chair. He wanted to know who I was going to appoint in Clayton's place. I said we needed to elect someone to the position." He puffed out his chest a little, inviting Ellen to praise him for his insistence on democratic governance.

Ellen smiled, nodded approvingly, and watched him beam. "Absolutely true, but why the undue haste? We are scheduled to have our regular meeting in two weeks. Surely choosing a new chair can wait until then?"

The bright smile faded from Jeff's wide face, replaced with a somber expression. "Time marches on, Ellen." He shook his head sadly. "Time marches on."

Really? He was trying to snow her with a hoary old cliché like that? Something was going on here he didn't want her, or anyone else on the committee, to know about. So what was it? She allowed herself an expression of confusion. "There's no question that time passes. But why must Clayton be replaced in such haste? His murdered body hasn't even been released by the coroner and certainly hasn't been decently buried."

Jeff winced. "I'd forgotten you found him."

"Yes, I did," Ellen said, and shuddered. There was no theatricality involved. The image of Clayton's lifeless body rose in her mind's eye and swamped her emotions with the same intensity it had when she'd walked into the bedroom and discovered his mangled body. "I had my differences with Clayton, but he worked hard for the committee. I think we need to acknowledge his contribution and respect him and not act in a precipitous way."

Jeff's little rosebud mouth tightened. He leaned forward and looked Ellen right in the eye. "Decisions need to be made," he said in a low voice that implied secrets and important government business.

This was more like it. Someone wanted something done and needed input from the committee. That meant a change of land use somewhere in the city that required rezoning, or perhaps a bylaw change before a project could go forward.

She studied Jeff, whose eager expression belied cool emotionless eyes.

They had several projects they were working on at the moment, but she figured she knew which one he was talking about. "The consortium that's bought up all the old buildings near Stanley Park wants a decision from city council on rezoning to allow them to be replaced by a hotel apartment complex," she said.

Jeff blinked and sat back. "How did you know? Did Harvey tell you? I thought he was just calling the committee members to inform them of the new meeting."

"Please, Jeff! Give me some credit. Nothing else we're looking at has the impact that project will have. It's the only thing that could possibly require such swift and disrespectful action."

At the word disrespectful, Jeff narrowed his eyes. "Clayton wouldn't be upset by the request. Nor would he have any objection to our moving forward quickly. His company is in the running to build the project and—"

"Yes, and we've had that discussion before. Clayton should have recused himself from involvement in that file. He was materially involved and therefore biased."

Jeff tapped his fingers on the glass tabletop. "His company hasn't won the contract as yet."

"Not yet," Ellen said evenly. "But he'd worked with Dunnville Investments before. In fact, the building where he was killed was financed by them and built by his company."

Jeff nodded. "True, true, but that doesn't mean he automatically would have won the contract for the new project."

Jeff was pushing hard to ensure the project moved forward. Why? "Developments of this kind are complex and take years to organize. Why the sudden haste?"

Assuming an expression of weariness, Jeff said, "The mayor is getting flack."

Ellen raised her brows. "From whom and about what?"

Jeff licked his lips uneasily. "The local tenants' association got wind of the project and they're starting to organize a protest. The mayor wants to get a sense of whether the benefits from the project will outweigh the upset that will occur when the change is made."

"In other words, when people who have lived in the area for decades can no longer afford to because their cozy, old-fashioned apartments have been replaced with snazzy and very expensive new ones."

"Well, not quite like that, but, yes, we can expect some resistance if the deal is approved."

Part of the resistance would probably come from Lloyd Webster, social warrior, whose wife was currently the prime suspect in the murder of Clayton Green. Were the two connected?

Jeff drummed his fingers on the tabletop again. "The mayor wants the report from the committee sooner rather than later. That means we need to proceed with our discussions. If Clayton were here, he wouldn't hesitate to schedule an extraordinary meeting of the committee. But he's not, so we must elect a new chair and get on with business."

Ellen sat back. She crossed one leg over the other as she studied Jeff. His expression was unhelpful. He was a very good politician. "Are we window dressing, Jeff?" When he frowned and tilted his head in a curious way, she added, "Has the decision already been made? Are the findings of the committee just glitzy packaging to wrap the deal in glossy paper and a pretty bow?"

Jeff reared back, his expression offended. "Of course not! That is not how we do business on this council. Ellen, the mayor is under the gun. He needs a decision, that's all. One way or the other, it doesn't matter which."

"I see." Ellen prepared to rise. "There's nothing I can say to convince you to move more slowly? To wait until after Clayton's funeral to open this contentious issue?"

Jeff shook his head.

"Very well." She pushed back the chair and stood. "Thank you for your time, Jeff."

He nodded and stood too. "It's been a pleasure, Ellen."

As she left the office, Ellen thought that it probably hadn't been a pleasure and that Jeff would be annoyed when he discovered she was going to do everything she could to stop the special meeting of the beautification committee.

CHAPTER 11

A sense of frustration followed Ellen as she retraced her footsteps back to the opulent lobby. There, she paused, stepping out of the traffic path to dig through her purse for her phone while she considered her next step.

She could let the issue go. Not many people these days were sticklers for correct behavior and what most probably considered old-fashioned manners. She was. She believed that being respectful of what mattered to people—like the rituals for birth, marriage, and death—was important. She grudgingly admitted to herself that she didn't always manage to be polite to everyone, especially overzealous cops and those she considered evildoers. But she had her standards, and she did try to meet them. That was why this business of convening the committee while Clayton Green was not yet in his grave sat poorly with her.

She found her phone and pulled it out. Then she held it in the palm of her hand, her fingers curled around it, the screen black. She stared unseeing at the people hurrying by on their way to some important meeting, or perhaps coming back from their morning coffee break. If she opened the phone and dialed a number, she was setting a process in motion to counter the plans of Jeff Darling, an elected representative, and

Harvey Wrenn, whose position now was ambiguous. Did she want to? There would be consequences. Would it be worth it?

The thoughts drifted away, leaving an empty, blank void filled with nothing. No healthy mental debate about the pros and cons, no enthusiastic acceptance that she must or must not act. Not even panic she couldn't ponder a decision, let alone make one.

After a few seconds, she shook herself out of the unfamiliar place and activated her phone. She scrolled through her contacts and found the one she wanted—Eugene Sawatzky, the owner and CEO of Sawatzky Restoration and Renewal, a company dedicated to restoring and repurposing old buildings. As she pressed the link, she realized her brain had been working behind that peaceful void. Eugene knew the construction business in Vancouver and if she consulted him to ask for his advice on how to proceed, he'd have a much better idea than she how useful her fight would be.

His line was answered on the first ring by Eugene himself. "Ellen! This is a surprise. How can I help you?"

She felt a rush of old warmth in the center of her being and smiled at the sound of his voice. She'd known Eugene for most of her life. They'd been lovers once when they'd been at university together. The romance had lasted less than a year, but they'd parted without recriminations and remained friends. Over the years their paths had crossed often and regularly. "Eugene, could you meet me for lunch today? I need advice."

"Let me check my schedule." There was a slight pause, then, "I have an hour between noon and one. Will that be sufficient?"

Grateful, Ellen said, "Yes, perfect." They briefly discussed where to meet, chose a restaurant near Eugene's office, then she rang off. Relief surged through her and renewed her confidence. Maybe she'd pursue this, maybe not, but at least she would be able to decide.

The restaurant was more local bistro than gourmet cuisine and they knew Eugene. He and Ellen were seated at a corner table with no one nearby so they would be able to talk confidentially. The food was simple, quick but homemade. After they'd ordered, Eugene smiled at her and said, "Tell me what's on your mind and I'll see if I can help."

Ellen smiled back at him. In his fifties, he remained a good-looking man. His hair was still thick, though silver shot through the wheat-colored blond. His face had once been thin, but over the years had filled out. Blue eyes, as warm as a summer sky, still burned bright with intelligence, over a beak of a nose and a wide mouth. As usual, he was dressed in a dark, well-cut suit, dress shirt, and a silk tie. These days, he spent more time in the office liaising with clients, dealing with architects, decorators, and suppliers than he did on his construction sites. She trusted and respected him, which made asking her questions so much easier. "I spoke to Jeff Darling this morning."

"Ah. The special meeting of the committee."

She nodded. "I admit I was shocked when I received Harvey's text. Clayton was his boss and, I thought, his friend." She wrinkled her brow, envisioning the two men's interactions. "I know they worked closely together, and they always appeared to be in harmony. It seems wrong to rush replacing Clayton as the chair. Why can't it wait until after he's been properly laid to rest?"

Eugene nodded, warmth and some amusement in his eyes. The expression made Ellen remember that he was something of a risk-taker while she had always had a strong sense of propriety and tended to do what society deemed right.

"What did Jeff have to say?" Eugene asked.

"He wasn't sympathetic. Apparently, Dunnville Investments, the consortium behind the redevelopment in the West End, wants a decision as to whether the area can be rezoned. So does the mayor, which means Jeff does too." She flattened her mouth in disapproval. "Therefore, Clayton must be replaced, swept aside as if he never existed."

The amusement in Eugene's eyes deepened. "So dramatic, Ellen."

She shot him a sideways look then laughed, rather ruefully, because he was right.

He laughed too, before he sobered. "Dunnville is made up of men who have their fingers in many pies, most of them international. Not surprising since most of the investors are from outside Canada. Prices in our housing market are rising exponentially, so adding to the stock of private homes in desirable areas like the West End is an excellent invest-ment. That the low-rise buildings there now tend to be rental spaces only makes it more enticing for a developer. They're adding retail stock in an area that is in high demand. They can charge premium prices for each unit and be quite certain of receiving them."

She nodded. "That makes sense." She added thoughtfully, "People like Lloyd Webster and his group won't like it."

"Many people, not just Lloyd, won't like it." Eugene raised his brows and fixed her with a pointed stare. "I've heard the link between Clayton and Dunnville was closer than any of us imagined."

"What do you mean?"

Eugene drew a deep breath, then blew it out. "I have no proof."

Curious and curiouser. Eugene didn't usually prevaricate this way. "I'm willing to listen."

He tipped his head in something that was almost a nod. "Clayton's company, FGC Inc., isn't just a favored bidder on Dunnville projects, but the only bidder."

Ellen blinked as she considered the information. "Clayton never disclosed that when we started discussing the potential of rezoning the area."

Smiling thinly, Eugene raised his hands. "If you remember, Clayton was always careful to remind us that as chair, he had no vote in the deci-sion process, unless there was a tie. However, in a slow and subtle way he did push the discussion toward agreeing to the rezoning."

"You think he was acting on behalf of Dunnville Investments?"

Eugene nodded. "While at the same time Dunnville's CEO lobbied the mayor and other city councilors."

"And now the mayor wants a decision from us. But why the unseemly haste? We only review the requests and gather evidence. We recommend, but our suggestions don't have to be accepted. Why try to rush this through? Why not make the decision without our input?"

Eugene stared down at his water glass, watching as he rubbed his thumb up and down its length. "Clayton's company doesn't have a good reputation in the industry. There's speculation that he bribes building inspectors and other city employees to bring his buildings in on time and under budget." He looked up. "It's also said that the consortium uses him because of those contacts and his willingness to bend the rules. So, with Clayton dead, what will happen next? Who is his heir? Will FGC continue as it is? Could it be sold? Or change its style—go legit and build their massive complexes properly and to code? Which would mean, of course, that the square footage costs would go up and profits down."

"I had no idea," Ellen murmured. "I still don't understand why the decision needs to be made so quickly and why we need to be part of it."

"Ah. It all boils down to money and optics. A significant amount of property in the area has changed hands over the past year, which means Dunnville has sunk a considerable amount into the project. The mayor wants the development to go through because he believes the tax revenues from high-end residences, stores, and a hotel will benefit the city. But area residents tend to be middle or lower income and an older demographic. A good chunk of them have lived there for most of their lives. They'll get a lot of sympathy from the press and social media if they're evicted because their homes are being razed."

"He doesn't want to be seen as pushing for the rezoning." Her eyes widened. "He wants us to recommend it." A moment later her jaw had hardened as indignation flared. "He wants us to take the responsibility, so he can avoid any flack that results."

Tapping the side of his nose, Eugene nodded. "Exactly. Now that Clayton is no longer with us and able to guide the committee to the appropriate recommendation, the consortium—and the mayor—want to rush us into a choice we wouldn't necessarily make if we took our time and studied the data."

"Eugene. If I convince five members—a majority—of our committee to vote against a special meeting, would you be willing to be one of them?"

He leaned forward with a broad smile. "Ellen, for you, anything."

She blushed and cast him a quick look from under her lashes.

"And let me say," he added. "I am not disappointed. You, of all the people on that committee, are the most able to lead us in defiance."

There was amusement in his eyes as he added, "Not because you want to break the rules, but because you want to enforce them." He lifted his water glass in lieu of anything stronger. "Bravo!"

She laughed, inordinately pleased by his praise, and clinked her glass against his. "To success!"

CHAPTER 12

W hile Ellen was getting input and reassurance from an old friend, Quinn was interviewing Clayton Green's wife, Roberta.

The Greens lived in an enormous home in the suburb of White Rock. The house was located on a small street not far from popular Crescent Beach. Parking along the street was by permit only, but the wide driveway in front of the house was empty of cars, so Quinn pulled in there. He figured Roberta would be busy with him and if someone else in the household wanted him to move his car, they'd know where to find him.

Built on an irregular lot, with the driveway below the main level, access to the house was up a flight of stairs that led to a small lawn. A short curving path cut through this, leading to a wide covered porch that ran the length of the building. When he reached it, Quinn paused to study his surroundings.

The view from the porch was stunning. He could see the golden sand beach and the deep blue sea before him. A little distance away was White Rock's pier, a popular visitor attraction. In the other direction, he detected the white glimmer of snow-clad Mount Baker south of the city in Washington State.

Impressed despite himself, he turned back to the house. Entrance was through double glass doors. On either side were three quarter length windows, then a set of French doors leading out onto the porch. Another set of three-quarter length windows flanked both sets of French doors, making the front wall of the house one of glass and ocean views.

On the porch itself was a small table and chairs to one side. He could envision Clayton and his wife sitting there, drinking their morning coffee or enjoying a drink before dinner. At the other end was a grouping of comfortable lounge furniture. Clearly the porch was designed to be an outdoor room, meant to be used and enjoyed.

He grinned to himself as he rang the doorbell. He thought Christy would love a spacious porch like this one, where she could sit outside and enjoy the action around her without having to perch on her front steps. The neighborhood and this house told him it would cost a fortune to live here, unlike her compact Burnaby home. But then, she was now the custodian of a quite enormous fortune, so price wouldn't be a problem. Not that he was going to suggest she go house shopping. He liked her living down the street from him and as far as he knew, she liked living there too.

The woman who opened the door was attractive, dressed in a pair of blue slacks and a simple sheath shirt that was a soft green paisley. Her dark hair was styled in a well-cut bob, her even features carefully, but not heavily, made up. Her eyes were a warm brown, but Quinn read caution in them. Roberta Green had agreed to talk to him about her husband's death, but only if he used her as a source, not as a central character in the article he planned to write. He was fine with that. At this point, his goal was to help Jodie's defense by finding out as much about the dead man as he could. He'd write an in-depth article later, but its structure would emerge from the data he collected, not from any preconceived notion of what he thought it should say.

"Quinn Jamieson," he said, holding out his hand. "You're Roberta Green?"

She nodded and shook his hand, scrutinizing him. He'd expected that and dressed carefully in a sports jacket, dress shirt, and chinos. Neat, tidy, respectable clothes that were meant to put her at ease. Apparently, his strategy worked because she stepped back and gestured for him to come inside. "The living room is this way."

The walls of the living room were a cool white, the furniture low and modern. Rectangular sofas and chairs surrounded a coffee table made of golden teak. The same wood provided the gleaming flooring. Bathed in light from the many windows, the simple design echoed traditional beach cottages, but in a considerably upscale way.

Quinn flashed Roberta a smile as she followed him into the room. "Great house. Nice place to live."

At that she relaxed and laughed. "My family has owned this property forever. We had a house in Kerrisdale, where we lived in the winter, but when school was over Mom moved us kids down here and we spent the summer at the beach. I loved it. I still do."

Quinn nodded, staring out the windows to the sea beyond. "I'm not surprised."

"Would you like anything? A coffee? I baked some cookies."

"Sure. Both would be great." He watched her wend her way through the artfully placed pillars, positioned to simulate traditional rooms in an open space layout. Everything about this house evoked traditional values in modern design. It was beautifully done, and he suspected the person behind it was Roberta herself.

When she came back a few minutes later, he was settled on the sofa facing away from the fabulous view. He wanted the light on her face when he talked to her and the shadow on his. She carried a tray with a coffee urn, cream and sugar bowls, two mugs and a plate of cookies. She set it on the coffee table, then sat on the sofa in front of it, opposite Quinn. After pouring a cup, she handed it to him, then nudged the plate of cookies his way. "Chocolate chip, heavy on the chips. Have one."

The cookie was chewy rather than crunchy and melted in his mouth. "Delicious. This is a bakery grade cookie."

She relaxed even more. "I don't have the opportunity to bake much any more. My kids don't live at home, and I don't need the extra pounds. But—" She broke off, took a sip of her own coffee, then carefully put the mug on the table. "I bake when I'm stressed. I find the process soothing. I think it reminds me of my mom making cookies when we were kids and we didn't have to worry about anything more bothersome than if the tide was going to cover the beach all day so we couldn't spend our time lying around on the sand. Have another one."

Quinn did. "I'm sorry for your loss, Mrs. Green. It must have come as a painful shock."

She looked over his shoulder at the blue ocean view. "I was in Toronto visiting friends when the police called to notify me. I'd flown out a couple of days before. Clayton said he had a meeting so he couldn't even drive me to the airport to see me off. My last words to him were polite, distant, and cool." She sighed. "A guilt inducing way to end a marriage, even when the marriage had become little more than a business arrangement."

Saddened, because he thought Roberta Green was a very nice person, he said, "What was your husband like, Mrs. Green?"

"Oh, do call me Roberta," she said. "It seems silly to be so formal." She drank more coffee, her hands wrapped around the mug, her elbows propped on her knees as she leaned forward in her seat. "Clay was a simple man who pretended to be complex. He liked pretty young women, lots of money, and power over his peers. He got the first and the last, but not the middle."

Quinn looked around at the obviously high-end house and said, "Property rich, but cash poor?"

She laughed. "Heaven's no. The company is doing well, thanks to Harvey Wrenn. No, Clay's problem was that the money is all mine. I own Ferguson Construction, not him, even though he renamed it Ferguson Green Construction and called it FGC. He was my manager. I provided him with an excellent salary, but I expected him to pay all his expenses out of it, just as I pay mine from the profits the company brings in."

"An unusual arrangement," Quinn said, raising his brows.

She nodded. "Ferguson Construction was my father's creation. My parents had no sons, only my sister and me. Neither of us was interested in the business, so my father planned to sell it when he retired. Then Clay came along. He joined the company, started dating me, and before we knew it plans had changed. Clay married me and Dad gave him more and more responsibility. When Dad died, he left the company to me and gave my sister the Kerrisdale house and a cash settlement."

"But he didn't leave Clay a share in the ownership?"

She shook her head and the ghost of a smile flickered over her lips. "By that time Clay's tendency to enjoy extramarital affairs was no longer a secret. Dad disapproved. He realized the best way to keep me safe financially was to make sure I held the purse strings."

Quinn studied her. Her expression was serene, and he couldn't detect more than a hint of bitterness in her voice. She was either accomplished at hiding her emotions, or she was truly unconcerned by her husband's behavior. "Did you know about his current affair?"

"Jodie Webster," she said in a thoughtful voice. "A bit older than his usual women, but she had the added benefit of being married to Lloyd Webster." She took a sip of coffee. "He hated Lloyd Webster with a passion. Said he was an interfering toad who was a pain in his ass."

Quinn laughed. "He can be."

"You know him? Then you probably know Jodie too. I met her once or twice at social events. She seemed like a nice enough woman, if a bit over-shadowed by Lloyd."

"Do you have any idea why someone would murder Clayton?" Quinn asked.

"Do you mean, did he have any enemies?"

He nodded.

She shrugged. Picking up a cookie she nibbled it while she thought. "On the surface, Clay was charming. Most people he met casually thought he was lovely. People like Jodie fell into his sexual trap because he knew how to make them feel like they were one of a kind and so special they deserved the best. It wasn't until he was ready to move on that they realized they'd been used, that he didn't have an emotional commitment to them."

Shaking her head, she said, "I expect he had a great many enemies, Quinn, but who they were I couldn't tell you. Once the kids were grown, I didn't bother keeping tabs on him anymore. We went our separate ways. I spend most of my time here in the beach house, while he lives in our downtown condo." She stopped, put the mug carefully on the coffee table with suddenly shaking hands. "Lived. He lived in our downtown condo." She covered her eyes with her hands. "Oh God. Lived, not lives."

"Roberta…"

Drawing a deep breath, she dropped her hands. She shook her head at the concern in his voice. "No, I'm okay. It just hit me. It's been happening ever since I heard. I go along fine for a time, then suddenly I feel the need to weep."

"I'll take off then," Quinn said, rising. "Perhaps we can speak again another time."

She rose too as she nodded gratefully. "Thank you. Yes, I'm fine with that. I know what you write will be balanced and as close to the truth as it's possible to be."

She preceded him to the door, where she smiled valiantly as she bid him good-bye. As the door closed quietly behind him Quinn turned to face the fabulous ocean view. Roberta Green knew her husband well, but he thought she still cared a great deal more for him than she believed she did.

For her sake it was a good thing she had an ironclad alibi for the day of his death. Unfortunately, nothing she'd said helped Jodie or made her look any less guilty.

CHAPTER 13

The next morning, after she and Christy had taken Noelle to school and Ellen had seen Christy off to the Jamieson Trust offices, Ellen pulled out her phone and called Portia Quance to schedule a meeting. Her secretary announced Ms. Quance had a half an hour at eleven o'clock. Relieved, Ellen took it.

The Quance Hotel was a heritage building in Vancouver's West End. Built nearly one hundred years before when wood was the usual construction material in Vancouver, it was red brick. Seven stories high, it sprawled across a city block. The rooms were large and spacious, with an art deco vibe that made the hotel an in-demand location for travelers who looked for a hotel room that was more than just a clean bed to spend the night in.

Ellen's father, the Jamieson who founded Jamieson Ice Cream, had taken his family there to stay while the Jamieson mansion in Shaughnessy was being built. The hotel was located not far from one of the English Bay beaches and she had memories of running free on the hot golden sand, and diving into the chilly north Pacific for the duration of a long, glorious summer.

The hotel had a different name then—Portia had bought it some twenty-five years ago and given it her last name—but the building and the location remained the same. Was that wonderful, long-ago summer why she'd always had warm feelings for Portia? Ellen shrugged off the question because she had no idea what the answer was. What she did know, was that Portia had been a fixture in Vancouver society for those twenty-five years and Ellen trusted her.

Now she stood before the double doors that opened into the hotel lobby, dressed in a very un-beach-like costume of Italian leather heels, a silk, long-sleeved dress in a solid navy with no pattern to relieve it, and no jewelry except a gold chain with a diamond pendant that had been her twenty-first birthday gift from her parents. She looked down at Stormy, who was twining around her feet, absolutely delighted to be included on this outing. "Remember our agreement, Frank."

Yeah, right.

"This hotel is cat friendly. There has been a local cat in residence since before Portia became the owner. You must act as if you are one of the area cats who decided to visit. You cannot seem to have come with me. Portia would never understand me bringing my cat to a meeting. I know her to be a cat lover, but business is business and that's how she will perceive this meeting."

I get it, Aunt Ellen! I'm going in undercover.

"Yes, well, I sincerely hope so. Now, when I go inside you race through the door, as if you're a stray cat taking advantage of an opportunity."

Got it.

They went to the door. Ellen opened it, put her foot on the sill, and raised the other to follow. Stormy took advantage of the moment to bolt through her legs, almost tripping her. Ellen stumbled into the lobby, her hand on the doorknob the only thing keeping her from falling on her face. "That cat!" she said, thoroughly annoyed.

One of the front desk staff hurried over to her. "Ma'am, are you okay?" He looked around for the offending cat, but Stormy had already found a place to hide and was nowhere in sight.

"Yes, I'm fine. I wasn't expecting an animal to rush into the hotel behind me." Not quite true, but it sounded good. "I'm Ellen Jamieson. I have an appointment with Portia."

"I'll let her know you're here," the man said, smiling. "I'm sorry about the cat, but all the local felines come to visit the hotel at one time or another. I'm certain they talk to each other and broadcast that it's a good place to bed down on a cold night."

They do. Not many places as partial to cats as the Quance.

"How interesting," Ellen said. She was responding to Frank's comment, but the front desk agent thought it was his observation she was replying to. He nodded cheerfully and asked her to sit in one of the well-padded chairs in the lobby while he notified Portia she was there.

Ellen's seat had a lovely view of the beach and she thought fondly of that summer long ago. "Your grandparents brought Frank senior and me to this hotel when we were pre-teens. It was a wonderful summer. Your father was a fantastic sandcastle builder." She kept her voice low. She didn't want to sound like a loony old lady when the front desk agent came back to fetch her.

I don't remember much about Dad, or Mom.

"No, I suppose not." Ellen decided she'd better get off the subject of Frank's childhood. After his parents' death she and the former Trustees had raised him, with her as the primary guardian. Single and unprepared, she hadn't been the best mother.

Fortunately, Portia herself arrived a few moments later. Slender, elegant, somewhere in her early or mid fifties, Portia Quance was an intelligent, sophisticated woman who had never married. There were rumors she'd had affairs and that she was currently in a relationship with the high-energy executive chef at her own hotel, but Ellen had no idea if the gossip was true. She wondered if Clayton Green had ever pursued Portia, and if they had been lovers. Perhaps she'd find out today.

They embraced and exchanged air kisses. Portia smiled. The expression lit her attractive features. "You're here about the committee meeting, I expect."

Ellen nodded.

"Good. Let's discuss this in my office." She led the way to the bank of elevators.

"Is your office on the second floor?" Ellen asked. She'd seen Stormy slinking around the edges of the chairs in the seating area. If he wanted to follow them to the office, he couldn't hop into the elevator. He'd have to take the stairs.

Portia nodded. "Yes. Would you prefer to walk up?"

Out of the corner of her eye she saw Stormy charge across the lobby to the grand staircase that led to the second floor. He raced up the steps. At the rate he was going he'd get to the top before the elevator ever arrived at the ground floor to pick up her and Portia. "Oh, no. I always assumed your office was behind the front desk, that's all."

Portia smiled. The elevator arrived. "My front desk manager's office is there. The GM and I have offices on the second floor." The doors slid open and they stepped inside.

The second floor was as beautifully appointed as the lobby. The cream-colored walls rose to crown molding installed by an expert plasterer a century ago, and plaster medallions surrounded chandeliers dripping with crystal. Portia led the way to a polished dark wood door, discreetly labeled with a gold plaque, steps away from the grand staircase. Stormy followed them inside just as the door was closing.

The suite consisted of a small reception area, leading to a hallway, from which several offices opened. Portia's was at the end and down another shorter corridor. She gestured Ellen inside.

Stall her, Aunt Ellen, so I can get in before she shuts the door.

Not quite sure how she could do that but concerned that if Portia closed the door Stormy would be stuck in the hallway and very exposed, Ellen advanced into the room. She hovered near the doorway, smiling brightly and saying, "What a lovely space." Her position, and her idle comment, forced Portia to pause, to answer before she closed the door. Stormy slunk along one wall and disappeared underneath her desk.

"Thank you," Portia said. "I love this room. It's the view, I think. So beautiful and soothing."

The room was a corner office, so windows made up two of the walls. The view was across English Bay to Point Grey in the south, then west to Vancouver Island. In between were vast expanses of ocean and sky, today varying shades of deep blue.

They sat in comfortable chairs facing the windows. Portia got right to the point. "Are you trying to stop Harvey Wrenn from convening the committee?"

Ellen nodded. "Initially I thought pushing up the date of our next meeting was simply disrespectful when Clayton was murdered so horribly. But when I spoke to Jeff Darling, I discovered it was rather more sinister than that."

Sinister? Must you be so dramatic, Aunt Ellen?

"Sinister?" Portia raised her brows and Ellen wondered briefly if she was one of those people who could hear Frank.

"Perhaps I'm being a bit extreme, but Jeff told me the real reason for the meeting was to discuss the redevelopment project of that area just down the beach from you."

"The low-rise apartment buildings and the block of storefronts." Portia sounded thoughtful. Ellen wasn't sure how to read her response.

"Yes, that area. Apparently, Dunnville Investments, the consortium behind the redevelopment, wants the city to sign off on the project and the mayor is keen on it, but there's likely to be a lot of bad press and possibly demonstrations, so he wants backup supporting the decision."

Portia raised her brows. "He doesn't want to be the bad guy."

Ellen nodded. "Exactly."

"I've met some of the investors behind Dunnville and their CEO as well. He's from an old Ontario family, with connections into both the provincial and federal governments. It will be very hard to turn their proposal down. I expect the mayor is under a lot of pressure."

And we will be too. Portia didn't say the words, but the implication was there. Ellen said carefully, "I'm not saying we shouldn't discuss the project, but I don't think we should rush to make a decision."

"Well, I don't need to discuss anything," Portia said. "My decision is made. The project includes two towers, one forty, the other thirty-five stories. The complex will be massive. The towers will dominate the area and impede the views of many of the buildings not directly on the waterfront. It's a typical Dunnville-FGC project, all about money, not what the city or the people who live here need."

Now we know where she stands on your problem, ask her about Green.

Ellen almost said, "I'm getting there," but she bit her tongue before the words popped out. "You sound like you don't have a lot of respect for Clayton."

"Clayton was Dunnville Investments' puppet," she said flatly. "He liked to think he fit right into their crowd, but he didn't have their deep pockets and he lacked their ruthlessness."

"I knew the members of the consortium behind Dunnville were wealthy international investors, but ruthless?" Who were these people, anyway?

"Ruthless," Portia said, nodding. "One made his initial fortune running guns. Another deals in drugs. A third is linked to the black market and organized crime in Eastern Europe. I could go on, but I think you get the picture."

Not a good idea to cross them, Aunt Ellen.

Ellen lifted her chin. She was a Jamieson. She was not about to be intimidated by ones such as these. "I will not be the mayor's patsy."

Portia grinned. There was an element of reckless enjoyment in her smile. "Neither will I. Tell me what you need from me, and I'll do it."

The voice groaned. *This is so not a good idea.*

Ellen wanted to say, "Stuff it, Frank." Instead, she grinned back at Portia. "We'll start with getting the meeting postponed and move on from there."

CHAPTER 14

Christy poked her nose into Isabelle Pascoe's office and said, "I'm heading out, Isabelle. I'll see you tomorrow."

The office manager at the Jamieson Trust, Isabelle looked away from the computer screen she was studying and smiled at Christy. She had dark brown hair, bound into a tight bun, and warm brown eyes. "Oh, that's right. You're visiting that real estate agent, Miss Kippen. The one who was with you when you found the body."

"Actually, Miss Kippen found the body. I've never seen anyone quite as freaked out as she was when she ran from the room. If the police hadn't insisted that we remain in the building I don't think she would've stopped running until she reached Calgary."

Isabelle laughed, but she said, "Poor woman. I don't blame her. I think I'd be terrified if I stumbled on a murder."

Christy nodded. "It wasn't pretty." She hitched her purse higher on her shoulder. "Anyway, I thought I'd look in on her to make sure she's okay. Call me if anything comes up."

"Of course, but I'm sure it won't be necessary. See you tomorrow."

As Christy walked down the thick cream carpet to the reception area, she reflected that Isabelle was correct. She'd taken over the post as the CEO of the Jamieson Trust and the senior Jamieson last fall when the

Trust's embezzled fortune was recovered. Initially there had been a lot to do. She'd appointed new trustees to replace the ones whose actions had led to the disappearance of the money, set up a new charitable foundation, and designed a plan to restore the Jamieson good name in the community. Along the way, she'd helped solve a couple of murders that threatened to derail her program.

But now everything was chugging along smoothly. Harry Endicott, one of the newly appointed trustees, was managing the investment portfolio of the Trust, while Isabelle oversaw day-to-day management. Christy's role had begun to focus more and more on generating ideas, reviewing potential recipients of the foundation's grants, or attending social events. She didn't need to be in the office every day. It was April, almost the end of the school year. She was seriously contemplating taking the summer off to spend it with Noelle.

On her way to Miss Kippen's office, she made a short detour to pick up a box of hand dipped chocolates from her favorite chocolate shop, then she walked briskly to her destination, which was not far away.

She'd made the appointment that morning, expecting to have to wait a day or two, but Miss Kippen's calendar was clear and there'd been no problem arranging a visit today. That seemed rather ominous to Christy. She'd had the impression that Miss Kippen was a successful realtor, even if she'd never been able to sell a unit to Ellen. She was a hard worker who didn't see an unproductive showing as a failure, but rather an opportunity to find an even more special dwelling for her client. Christy liked her and hoped that the shock of finding a body hadn't dimmed her positive spirit.

The Ruby Cronin Agency where she worked was located in a suite as luxuriously appointed as the Jamieson Trust offices. From what Ellen had told her, their clients were high-end and the residences they represented sold for millions. The receptionist was as carefully groomed as the perfectly clear desk she worked at. She smiled and said, "Mrs. Jamieson. Welcome. I'll just buzz Shelley to let her know you're here."

It always disconcerted Christy when people she'd never met called her by name. It was an easy trick, she knew. She had booked an appointment, so it was reasonable to assume it was her when she walked in the door. A quick check on the internet and the receptionist could easily have found a photo of her to confirm. Still, she had to swallow a sudden bout of insecurity, as she nodded.

After a moment on the telephone, the receptionist rose. "If you'll follow me?" She led Christy along a corridor painted a delicate ecru to a good-sized office furnished with a desk, visitor chairs, and a file cabinet. Miss Kippen sat at the desk, which was covered with papers. Her hands rested on top of them, as if she'd suddenly realized it would be a good idea to tidy the desk before her visitor arrived but hadn't had a chance to put thought into action. Her dark hair, usually smooth and carefully styled, stuck out at odd angles, as if she had been running her fingers through it, while she'd paired a bright orange blouse with a teal blue suit. The color combination was jarring.

The receptionist frowned, possibly in disapproval of the chaos on the desk and or perhaps at Kippen's rather wild appearance, but when she turned to Christy, she'd smoothed her features into a smile. "Would you like a beverage, Mrs. Jamieson? Tea? Coffee? Something cold?"

Christy looked at Shelley Kippen, who was biting her lip, as if she was afraid the receptionist would tell on her for having a messy office. She smiled at the receptionist and said, "No, thank you." Then she went into Kippen's office, shutting the woman out by closing the door behind her.

Miss Kippen blinked.

Christy aimed her smile Kippen's way. "Hello, Shelley. I hope you don't mind my dropping in for a visit, but I wanted to see how you were doing after that dreadful experience the other day."

Miss Kippen shuddered.

Christy put the box of chocolates on top of one of the piles of papers. "I stopped by Sinfully Delicious Chocolates on my way here. I thought some chocolate therapy would be a nice way to round out the afternoon. I do love their chocolates, don't you?"

She opened the box. The heavenly scent of freshly made chocolates drifted out, perfuming the room.

Shelley's eyes narrowed as she sniffed the air, catching the aroma and sighing a little as she did. She scrutinized the contents, selected, bit into the irregular ball, then groaned with appreciation. "This is wonderful."

She ate the second half of the chocolate with the same intense enjoyment. When she'd finished chewing, she dusted her hands together, and contemplated the box again. "I've never been to that shop. Where is it?"

They talked about the store, the woman who owned it, and the process of chocolate making while they each consumed several more chocolates. When Kippen finally sat back, she looked a good deal less harried, and more her usual cheerful self. "Thank you for that treat, Mrs. Jamieson."

Christy too sat back. The chocolates were lovely, but she'd had enough for the moment. "Do call me Christy. After what we went through together, I don't think polite formality works anymore, does it?"

Kippen's mouth flipped up in a wry smile. "It's turned my life upside down." Her eyes glazed, as if she was back in the display suite, remembering the moment when she found the body, then she refocused and pulled herself together. "May I ask how Miss Jamieson is doing?"

Christy didn't suggest Shelley adopt a more informal manner with Ellen. They both knew it wouldn't be appreciated. "Ellen is resilient." She laughed. "She's offended that Clayton Green had the bad manners to get himself killed in the apartment she was scheduled to view."

Shelley stared blankly for a moment, then she too laughed.

"I'm afraid Ellen will not even consider buying a unit in that building, though."

Kippen shook her head. "No, of course she wouldn't. In fact, I think it's going to be difficult to sell those units to anyone until the murder is solved and the media turns its interest to something else." Her mouth drooped, then hardened. "I certainly won't be showing any of them. In fact—" She broke off and shrugged.

Christy raised her brows in a question, but didn't ask it.

Waving her hand, Kippen said, "I'm not sure I'll ever show a home again!" Her expression was guilty, the words rushed as if she was making a horrible confession.

"I'm sorry to hear that, because you're an excellent real estate agent, Shelley."

Her eyes widened. "Really? Even though I've never found a property that meets Miss Jamieson's standards?"

"Ellen is picky. It's not your fault."

"She can be quite daunting." Shelley didn't sound dismayed by that, but her expression was gloomy. "Is that why you're here? Is Miss Jamieson anxious to view another residence?"

"Oh, no. I think Ellen wants to wait awhile before she goes house shopping again. No, I wondered if you'd had any side effects from that day."

"I still have my job, though I don't know for how long. Ruby—that's Ruby Cronin, my boss—does a lot of work with Mr. Green. We list all the suites in his buildings. I'm not sure what's going to happen now that he's dead."

"Is the brokerage in danger of closing then?" That seemed extreme to Christy. The Cronin Agency listed the best of the best residences available. Surely there was enough money in the kitty for Ruby to land new clients.

Kippen shook her head emphatically. "No, it's not that. It's..." She sighed. "It's me. Ruby's mad at me because I found the body. Originally Miss Jamieson was scheduled to view the unit the day before, but she wanted you to come along and you weren't available until the next day, so we agreed to meet at the same time that day. I didn't see any problem. No other visits were scheduled on that morning. I had an appointment I had to rush off to just after I talked to Miss Jamieson, and I forgot to change the time of her appointment in our database. In fact, I didn't add it until the next morning. But there was no problem. As I said, no one else had booked for that time."

"But...why would that matter to Ms. Cronin?"

Kippen sighed. "Ruby is a stickler for details. She checks our appointments for the next day every evening. And..." She drew out the word waving her hand back and forth in a so-so gesture and leaned forward. "She's under Mr. Green's thumb. I think she reports every visit and how they went to him. I bet she wanted to be able to tell him that Ellen Jamieson was viewing one of his suites. Maybe she even expected him to be there to add a personal touch."

Christy frowned. "That seems like a very close relationship."

"He employed her before she started the agency and there's a rumor they were lovers when she worked for him."

Christy found herself pursing her lips in disapproval, in an expression that closely mirrored one she'd seen many times on Ellen's face. "That's not right."

Shrugging, Miss Kippen said, "That was Clayton Green. He used sex to control women. Everyone knew it. If Clayton paid attention to you, you were someone special. Ruby must have been important to his organization because he never bothered with women who didn't matter."

"He sounds like a horrible man."

"I thought so, but he was good-looking and he had nice manners. Women were disappointed when he split with them. It wasn't until the relationship ended that his lover felt slighted."

From what she'd learned of Jodie Webster's experience with Green, Christy thought Shelley had the man's M.O. exactly right. "Ruby must be upset about Green's death, then."

Miss Kippen tilted her head thoughtfully. "You know, I don't think she is. As I mentioned, I know she worked closely with him, but I'm not sure she was comfortable about it. In fact, from things she let drop, I'm not sure she liked him much."

"A jilted lover thing?"

Kippen nodded, then she put her elbow on her desk and rested her chin on her palm. "If Ruby fires me, I'm not sure I'll stay in the business. I haven't been able to show a house or condo since it happened. Honestly, I don't know if I'll ever go into a stranger's home again. The thought of finding another body..." She shuddered.

"Pretty awful," Christy agreed. "But it's unlikely it will happen again."

"You think so?"

Christy wanted to say she knew so, but of course she couldn't. Instead, she nodded. "When the cops find the killer, you'll feel a lot better." She laughed and nudged the box of chocolates. "In the meantime, chocolate therapy works."

Kippen laughed too, her expression brightening. "Especially with chocolates as good as these."

~

An hour after Christy finished her conversation with Miss Kippen, Ellen walked into the Cronin Agency and asked for Ruby Cronin. The perfectly put together receptionist checked with Ruby to see if she was available, then announced that Ms. Cronin would see her.

As if Ruby would refuse, Ellen thought as she followed the receptionist down the ecru hallway.

Ruby stood as Ellen entered and gestured to a seat. "You're here about the meeting."

She was nothing if not direct. Ellen raised her eyebrows. "News travels fast."

Ellen sat in the chair Ruby had offered. They were meeting in the agency's conference room. It was a compact space, decorated in soothing cream with almond accents, the oval table a warm maple, the deep padded swivel chairs upholstered in a soothing café au lait. The room was an interior space, so there were no views to distract. It was meant for business, discussing options, closing deals.

Ellen was prepared for that. She was fresh from her conversations with Eugene Sawatzky and Portia Quance. With their support, she was hopeful she would be able to thwart Jeff Darling and his plan to force the beautification committee into action.

Ruby smiled thinly. Like her conference room, she was beautifully turned out in an expensive bronze-colored suit that blended with the decor. The shade looked good on her, with her warm toned skin and dark hair, currently bound up into a knot at the back of her neck. "Jeff was on the phone to me the minute you left his office."

Ellen raised her brows. "Seeking allies?"

"The mayor wants the development to go through, Ellen, so Jeff wants it too."

"I thought the meeting was supposed to be about electing a new chair," Ellen said.

Ruby threw back her head and laughed. "Of course it isn't. It's all about endorsing the West End development. Choosing a chair is a mere formality."

Ellen blinked. She hadn't expected Ruby to be so open. "I have four people who are against the project. That's a majority no matter who is chair. The committee won't endorse the project."

Ruby shook her head. "Your math is off, Ellen. Jeff has invited Harvey Wrenn to replace Clayton on the committee. You can be sure Harvey will support rezoning the area. He wants the project to go through."

Ellen sucked in her breath. "You're telling me that between them Jeff and Harvey will force the committee to recommend the project go forward."

"We don't recommend, Ellen, as you well know. We report. We gather information. We discuss the benefits and the drawbacks. In the end City Council can throw out anything and everything we decide. They can pick our report to pieces and choose the shreds that work best for them."

"You assume this is a done deal."

Ruby shrugged. "It is what it is."

"Why is this development so important? It will destroy a lovely family neighborhood in a desirable part of the city and replace it with a transient population that depersonalizes the area."

Ruby sat for a moment, studying her. Then she nodded. "You're right, but a project like this one will add millions in tax dollars and raise property values all over the West End. That makes people happy and happy people vote for the politician who made them happy."

"All those families who are displaced by the loss of their homes when the apartment buildings are torn down won't be happy," Ellen retorted coolly.

Ruby laughed. "No, but they probably will have moved to the suburbs because they can't afford to buy one of the new suites. They won't be voting for Jeff or the mayor."

"It will take years for the project to reach the point where buildings are torn down and people are evicted," Ellen protested.

"Yes, but the rezoning is just the first step. Do it now, then announce the project later. Dunnville Investments will acquire the land and put the package together. By the time FGC starts tearing down the buildings everyone will have forgotten who was instrumental in getting the zoning changed and putting the process in motion."

"So Dunnville Investments hasn't acquired the full package yet?" Ellen said slowly, thinking as she spoke.

Ruby shook her head. "They've purchased enough properties to make them anxious, though."

Ellen frowned at that. "Why would they be concerned about their investment? Property in the West End does not lose its value."

"True enough," Ruby said coolly. "Investing in West End property will always get you a good return. That's not enough for international financiers like the men behind Dunnville Investments, though. They want spectacular profits from every project they endorse. Quite honestly, Ellen? If the rezoning isn't done now, Dunnville is ready to walk. Their link to this city was Clayton. He knew how to ensure projects were approved and moved smoothly through all the red tape the city throws at new construction. With him dead? The benefits have to be pretty big for them to stay. Toronto's real estate market is as hot as ours is and luxury apartments are what buyers are looking for. The Dunnville CEO is from Toronto. Do you think he hasn't been nattering at them to focus their investments on his own city?"

"Then why bother with this project? Why not move their assets to Toronto?"

"They may yet. None of the investors behind Dunnville want to call attention to their involvement. That's why Clayton was so important to them. He was splashy and photogenic, and he knew how to make the press feel good about every project he did. Harvey Wrenn is now managing FGC and he'll make sure everything runs smoothly. He doesn't have any of Clayton's panache, though. Unless everything is tied up quickly the whole deal will fall through."

"Well," Ellen said, pulling her purse toward her and starting to rise. "From my point of view, that's good to hear."

Ruby shook her head as she rose as well. "You know, this whole mess is all because of Jodie Webster."

Startled, Ellen paused. "How so?"

"The rezoning hearing is next month. If she'd only waited until after it happened to kill Clayton, the project would have been well underway. Dunnville Investments would be happily acquiring the property block they need, and I'd be making a fortune in the process." Her lips twitched into a rather nasty smile. "Lloyd would have been happy too."

Ellen lifted her brows in an imperious way. "I can't imagine why. The people he serves would soon be evicted from their homes."

Ruby nodded and laughed. "Exactly. He would then have been able to mount protests and gain much needed media attention. Donations to his foundation would be pouring in."

"Good heavens," Ellen said.

Ruby laughed again. "You see? A win-win for all involved."

CHAPTER 15

"If you ask me, this is a disaster." Gloomy, emphatic, Roy shook his head.

The disaster in question was Jodie's arrest that afternoon. Christy wasn't particularly surprised. Although they had uncovered a good deal of negativity in Clayton Green's personal and business life, they didn't have a suspect nearly as compelling as Jodie to offer Patterson as an alternative suspect.

The landline rang shrilly in the kitchen. Roy cringed.

Quinn glanced at him. "Are you going to answer it, Dad?"

Roy looked down as he shook his head.

This was the third time the phone had rung since Christy had arrived to spend the evening with Quinn. That was ten minutes ago. They'd been discussing what would happen next and how they might help Jodie, but the ringing phone kept interrupting. It was annoying. "Is there any reason you don't want to answer, Roy?"

He shot her a wary, almost shifty-eyed look. With his long hair escaping from the tie at the back of his neck, well-worn jeans, and a soft, almost threadbare checked cotton shirt, he could have passed for a street person with a somewhat manic secret he was afraid to let slip to those in authority. "It's Evelyn, my sister-in-law—Jodie's mom. She's been calling all afternoon and leaving messages. Since we don't normally talk much, I assume she wants to know what's happening."

Quinn, who was drinking a beer, pointed the bottle in his father's direction. "And what we're going to do about it?"

"Trevor is down at the station with Jodie. What else can we do?" Christy asked. She wasn't sure why either man was so reluctant to speak to this Evelyn person. How scary could one woman be?

"That won't satisfy Evelyn," Roy said pessimistically. "When she delegates work, she expects results."

"We'll take action tomorrow, after Trevor fills us in and we've decided on a plan," Quinn said. "You can tell Aunt Evelyn that when you talk to her."

"If," Roy said.

Quinn shook his head. "When, Dad. Otherwise, she'll be phoning all night and neither one of us will get any sleep."

The doorbell rang. Quinn put his bottle down and stood to answer.

"This place is busier than Grand Central Station," Roy muttered, and Christy laughed as the phone rang again.

Because of the noise of the telephone, it was impossible to hear who was at the door. Christy assumed it was Ellen, who had stayed at their house to look after Noelle. The only reason she'd be coming over now was if there was a problem. That thought had Christy on instant alert.

She needn't have worried. Heavier male footsteps sounded on the stairs and moments later Sledge's shaggy blond head and long rangy body appeared.

The phone cut off and Christy said with a smile, "Hi, Sledge. Good to see you." She thought with some amusement that Frank would be upset he'd missed Sledge's visit, since he was such a big fan. He'd elected to stay with Noelle and was probably curled up on her bed, both of them fast asleep by now.

Sledge sauntered over to the sofa where she sat and bent to give her a peck on the cheek. Like Quinn he was wearing jeans and a sweater. Though the two men were of similar build, Christy thought the style looked better on Quinn, though she knew Sledge's legions of fans wouldn't agree with her.

"Good to see you, too. Quinn tells me there's been a break in the case." He straightened, then chose a chair to sit on, leaving the sofa beside Christy for Quinn.

"Hardly a break," Roy said bleakly. "Jodie's been arrested. That about shuts it down, at least from the cops' point of view."

Quinn came in from the kitchen where he'd been getting a beer for Sledge. "As Trevor's fond of saying, the defense doesn't have to find the killer, they just have to provide reasonable doubt that the accused is guilty. So we'll keep digging and do what we can to undermine the crown's case." He handed Sledge the beer. "What brings you over tonight?"

Sledge took a long drag from the bottle, leaned his head against the back of the chair, closed his eyes, and sighed. "Mitch and Hammer are driving me nuts."

Roy snorted. Quinn said, "Mitch I get, but why Hammer?"

Sledge sighed again and reluctantly straightened. "We've been in talks with these two agencies who want to represent us, you know?"

They all nodded.

He took a pull of beer, then gestured expansively with the bottle. "Mitch and Hammer want this woman who's affiliated with one of the big agencies in the States. Well, more than affiliated. She's a branch plant, actually."

Quinn settled in beside Christy. "And that worries you?"

In Canada, a branch plant was a wholly owned subsidiary of a US corporation. The company might act independently, but more often it would take direction from the US parent company. "Not really. Well, maybe a little. No, it's not that there's anything wrong with her and what she's offering. It's more..." He gestured again, his arms out wide, the beer sloshing in the bottle. "I like the other guy. He's cool, you know? He knows the scene. He gets it."

"He talks the talk," Christy murmured. She held a glass of white wine in her hand, and she lifted it, watching Sledge over the rim as she sipped.

"But does he walk the walk?" Quinn finished, amusement in his eyes.

Sledge flattened his mouth in a rueful expression. "That's the problem. Mitch says he can see right through him and there's no depth. Hammer says his gut is telling him there's something off about the guy."

"Sounds like two good reasons not to go with this Toronto fellow," Roy said.

"The branch plant woman is full of big ideas," Sledge said.

"Nothing wrong with that," Roy said, eying him thoughtfully.

"Nooooo." Sledge drew out the word, doubt in his tone. "But she's also bossy. She didn't say, 'this is what I think the band should do.' She said, 'First you'll do this, then you'll do that.' And 'this is what your assistant will focus on' not 'should be focused on.'"

"Whoa! Is the assistant the problem?" Quinn asked, laughing.

Sledge looked sulky. "Maybe. Hammer loves the idea. I hate it. I don't want someone chasing after me with a tablet which has my every move inscribed on a daily calendar and telling me what I can and can't do."

"You're at an impasse," Quinn said.

"Yeah." Sledge leaned back in the chair again. "Kim came up with a good idea. She suggested we invite the two candidates to lunch or dinner and see how each of them does in a social setting. Maybe I can find a connection with the branch plant woman. Or maybe Hammer will take to the Toronto guy."

"When do you do that?" Christy asked.

"Each one gets their own lunch, starting with the branch plant woman tomorrow." He paused, shook himself like a big dog emerging from a lake. "So, enough about me. Fill me in on what's been happening in the case."

"Apart from Jodie being arrested, not all that much," Roy said gloomily. The phone rang. He slid his gaze toward the kitchen. His expression was guilty.

"You'd better answer it, Dad," Quinn said, amusement in every word.

Roy looked at his watch and sighed. "Yeah. I guess I should." He levered himself to his feet then lumbered across the living room, reluctance in every stride. "I'll be back in a minute."

"Take your time," Quinn said. In a lower voice meant only for Sledge and Christy, he said, "If that is Aunt Evelyn, he'll be on the phone for the next half hour."

～

In the kitchen, Roy's hand hovered over the phone, then he gave himself a little shake, far less emphatic than the one Sledge had just done, and picked up the phone.

"I hope you are going to tell me you've been working on getting my baby out of the clutches of the police, Roy Armstrong."

Trust Evelyn to lead with aggression. "We're doing our best, Evelyn." There was no way Roy was ever going to admit to his sister-in-law that he'd been avoiding her calls. "Jodie's got the top lawyer in Vancouver with her. He's not going to let the cops take advantage of her."

"You're not answering my question, Roy."

Evelyn Crowther had a firm way of talking. She made statements, she ordered, she demanded. There was nothing soft or sinuous about Evelyn. She met you head on and expected to be the one who won the encounter. Vivian, Roy's late wife, had had something of that same energetic self-confidence, but hers had been modified by an enormous curiosity and a willingness to look at a problem from every angle.

Since all he knew was that Jodie had been arrested this afternoon and taken downtown for questioning and presumably, for booking, Roy had no answer for Evelyn. That was why he had been avoiding her calls. Now here she was expecting him to provide her with a wealth of detail he didn't have and the worst of it was he wanted to give her an answer that would make her happy.

He drew a deep breath and plunged into the deep end, aware there was a good chance he was about to drown. "Evelyn, I don't have any information. I haven't heard anything all day."

There was a tense silence, then Evelyn said in crisp, clear tones, "You didn't try, did you?" She spaced the words evenly, adding emphasis, fueling them with guilt.

Roy closed his eyes and rubbed the bridge of his nose. "Evelyn..."

"Now you listen to me, Roy Armstrong. This is how we're going to proceed. You give me the contact information for that high-priced lawyer of yours. Then you tell me the name of the cop who thinks my daughter is a murderer so I can put him straight. After that you get up off your ass and go out and find whoever did this. Understood?"

"I heard you, Evelyn." There was no way Roy was going to throw Trevor under the wheels of Evelyn's earthmover, but he didn't mind sacrificing Patterson. He figured if anyone could handle Evelyn Crowther under a full head of steam, Patterson could.

"Well? My phone is ready. Spit out the data."

Roy snuck a look into the living room. The young people were chatting, relaxed and cheerful. He was envious. Worse, he was jealous. He wished he were there and not here. Anywhere but talking on the phone to an angry in-law who always thought her sister could have done better for herself than a flaky novelist who was also a social activist.

When Roy didn't speak, Evelyn's voice hardened, became insistent. "Well? I'm waiting."

Roy cleared his throat. "Patterson. The cop's name is Patterson."

"First name?"

"First name?" Roy repeated. He sounded vacant even to his own ears.

"I can hardly call the police station and ask to speak to a cop named Patterson. They'll just blow me off. The police respond to chain of command and authority. I need the full name of the cop, so I'll sound like I know what's going on when I talk to his commanding officer."

"You're going to talk to Patterson's boss?" Roy imagined the detective's reaction. She wouldn't be happy.

"I'm going to talk to the chief of police and let him know his boy has botched the investigation. And that's only the start."

Roy would like to be a fly on the wall for that exchange. As he imagined how it would go, he started to feel better about this whole conversation. He said with more enthusiasm than before, "It's Billie Patterson."

There was a little pause as she typed in the name. "William? I suppose Billy is a nickname."

"I have no idea," Roy said truthfully. "You know parents nowadays. Call their kids the most outlandish things."

Evelyn grunted disapproving agreement. "Name and contact info for this lawyer you've found."

Emboldened by his success in mixing up Evelyn over Patterson's name and gender, Roy decided to get creative. "You know me, Evelyn. No head for numbers."

"Look it up on your phone. I'll wait."

There was impatience in her voice. Roy could imagine her tapping her finger on whatever piece of furniture was nearby, as if that would help hurry him along. He grinned as he said, "No can do, I'm afraid. I'm talking to you on the landline and my cell's upstairs on my bureau." He stopped, then added, "I think." Just in case she expected him to run up to his room to hunt for it, like an underperforming middle manager. "Might be in the car. Or in the bathroom."

"Why would you have your phone in the bathroom?"

Evelyn sounded scandalized. That was great. He was getting to her. This was beginning to be fun. "Well, you know."

"No, I don't. And I don't want to know. What's the name of this lawyer? I'll look him up."

"Best to call McCullagh, McCullagh, and Walker. They'll know how to get hold of him."

Evelyn repeated the name, asked if McCullagh was Mac or Mc, then said, "What are his details?"

"He's a partner."

"Getting information out of you, Roy Armstrong, is like trying to find water in the Sahara. What's his name?"

"I wish I could tell you more, Evelyn, but I don't have a lot. I asked McCullagh, McCullagh, and Walker for their best and they sent someone." Well, that was a lie, but he wasn't going to rat on Trevor and sic Evelyn on him. He, Roy, had to deal with her because she was family—of a sort. Trevor didn't.

"That's it?" she said. "You didn't get a name? All the pertinent details?"

"I'm not the one who was arrested, Evelyn. I figured the lawyer would tell Jodie his, or her, name when he or she arrived."

"Why don't you just say they like everyone else," Evelyn said on a sigh. "Honestly, Roy, sometimes you get so precious with this language stuff I could pop you one."

"Good thing you're on the phone, then, and not standing in my kitchen with me. Quinn would get upset if we started beating on each other and breaking the crockery. He's like his mother that way, prefers brain over brawn."

On the other end of the phone line, Evelyn sighed again, more deeply this time. "Okay. I get it. I went overboard. I apologize. I'm so worried about Jodie. Between that louse kicking her out of her own house and this cop targeting her, I feel so helpless."

"I get it," Roy said. And he did. When Quinn had been at the height of his international correspondent career, there had been times when he went off the grid. Then Roy hadn't known where he was, if he was in danger, if he was even alive. It made both him and Vivian crazy, but usually she was better able to handle the crazy than he was.

"Did the cop look into Lloyd as the killer?" Evelyn asked after a moment.

"I don't know," Roy said, rather relieved she was no longer demanding contact details.

"Because that man is a loose cannon. Killing the guy who seduced his wife is exactly the kind of thing he'd do."

"Maybe." That initial sense of relief was rapidly turning into alarm as Evelyn's voice gained strength and indignation.

"No maybes about it. Lloyd Webster acts on impulse, then justifies it with highfalutin words afterwards. He's their man. Why didn't that cop arrest him instead of a good, decent girl like my Jodie?"

She practically bellowed the last bit. Roy decided enough was enough and he was done. "Why don't you ask Patterson or the chief of police?"

"I will. And if I don't get any satisfaction, I'm coming down there to sort this out myself."

"Great. You do that."

"And I'll stay with you until we can get Jodie released. Family solidarity and all that."

Horror enveloped Roy. "What? You can't!"

"Why not?" There was petulance in the tone. Roy could imagine her eyes narrowing and her mouth thinning.

"Because Jodie's using our spare room."

"Jodie's in jail. I'm coming as soon as I can."

Roy's brain screamed no, no, no! His voice said, "Listen, Evelyn, I've got to go. Talk to you later."

He hung up as she started to say something that wasn't good-bye. Then he strode into the living room and said, "We've got to find the real killer fast, or our lives will turn into a living hell."

Christy blinked at this announcement. Sledge smiled, amusement lighting his eyes, and drank beer. Quinn observed him with resignation. "What did Aunt Evelyn say?"

"She's coming down to Vancouver and she's going to stay with us."

That made Quinn sit up. "She can't. Jodie's using our spare room."

Roy's eyes were flashing now, and he was working himself up into a bigger state than he'd been in for his dramatic entrance into the living room. "That's what I said. Would she be polite and promise to stay at a hotel? No! Not only that, but she's going to harass the cops."

Quinn relaxed at that. "No problem there. Patterson can handle it."

Jabbing his forefinger at no one in particular, Roy said, "She doesn't bother with underlings. She's going to start with the chief of police. I wouldn't be surprised if she drags in the mayor as well."

"I don't think the mayor would appreciate that," Christy said. "Ellen told me the mayor is pressuring her committee to vote on whether to recommend the rezoning for a new project in the West End. Clayton Green was involved both with the committee and in the development of the project. I'm sure the mayor would like to see his murder solved quickly."

Frowning, Quinn looked at Christy. "That's hardly arm's length. Green should have resigned from the committee when the project came up."

Christy shrugged. "You'd have to ask Ellen about that. It sounds to me, though, as if this is a politically charged situation. Maybe Jodie's been caught in the middle of a couple of warring parties."

"Maybe. Green's company was a player in the development industry in this city. I think it's worth looking into the company, including past projects and partnerships."

Roy said mournfully, "Evelyn won't care about Green's company, even if the mayor does. Her goal will be to have Jodie released."

"Would he do it?" Sledge asked. He still looked amused. He'd never been one to be overawed by position or authority.

Roy sat back down on the chair he'd been using before the phone call. He nodded glumly. "If he's smart, he would. If he didn't, Evelyn would never stop pestering him unless he resigned his office and moved out of town."

Sledge laughed. Quinn said, "Aunt Evelyn's not that bad, Dad."

Roy waved a finger at him. "Just you wait and see."

Quinn grimaced in a disbelieving way. Roy said, "Evelyn believes Lloyd is the killer. She wants me to prove it."

Surprise had Quinn raising his brows. "Why does she think he did it?"

"Jealousy because of the affair," Roy said.

"Mad passionate love," Christy said lightly. "I'm sorry to say I think she's wrong. From the way Jodie and Lloyd acted the day Ellen and I took Jodie over to her house, I don't think Lloyd cared that Jodie had a lover. He was angry because the lover she chose was Clayton. If the victim had been Jodie herself, I could see him as the murderer, but not Clayton Green."

"Even if he was angry at Green, rather than jealous of him, that still could be motive," Roy said, stubbornly—and perhaps a little desperately—defending his theory.

Christy shook her head. "But that's just it. He wasn't angry at Green either. He was angry at Jodie for putting him in the position of losing face to Green."

"Still..." Roy thought for a moment. "Does he have an alibi for the time of the murder?"

Christy shook her head. "He says he was in his house taking a business call because he didn't have time to go into the office. That conflicts with Jodie's statement that she went back to the house to pick up some clothes at the same time. Neither of them saw the other, though, so one of them is lying."

"Or both," Sledge said.

Christy looked at him sharply, then nodded. "Yeah, or both."

"I'll have to go see him," Roy said, still focused on the danger of a visit from Evelyn. "If I can get something useful out of him, maybe Evelyn will stay up in Whitehorse."

"Take Frank," Christy said, helpfully. "Lloyd can hear him, but like Jodie, refuses to admit it. Frank took great pleasure in needling him when Ellen and I were over there. That rattled him and he said more than either of us expected. Maybe it will work again."

"Good idea." Roy rubbed his chin. The gloom on his face gradually lifted as he thought. Finally, he grinned. "We'll go to his office. Disconcert him. Push him off his game. Lloyd likes to present himself as intense and caring, a defender of the little guy, but dependable, a man of action. He wouldn't like his secretary to see him talking to a cat."

Christy laughed as she imagined the scene Roy was planning. "I like that. I think it would do him good to be shaken off his soapbox."

"This guy sounds thoroughly unlikeable," Sledge said.

"He has his moments," Quinn said. "If you're tackling Lloyd, Dad, I'll dig into the business side of Green's background. His wife Roberta told me Harvey Wrenn was basically running the company even before her husband's death. That sounds like Green himself was into other things."

"Besides women, you mean," Christy said.

Quinn flashed her a smile as he nodded. "Yeah. I'll see what I can find out."

"I still think a woman could be involved. Quinn, you told me Roberta knew about Clayton's affairs and that his liaison with Jodie was nothing new. That means there are probably several women who could be holding a grudge against him because they were dumped. Or maybe just because of the way he broke with them. Ruby Cronin, who owns the real estate agency Miss Kippen works for, may have been one of them. If I can find one or two others, Trevor could make the argument that Jodie wasn't the only woman who was angry at him."

"Worth a try," Quinn said.

"When you have some names, we'll tell Evelyn. She'll dangle them in front of the mayor and the chief of police like carrots in front of a donkey," Roy said. He liked that idea. He hoped it would keep her from showing up in Vancouver, determined to drag him and everyone else into the immediate rescue of her daughter.

"And if they don't bite?" Quinn asked, quirking his brow.

"She'll use them as a goad instead." Roy shook his head. "One way or another, she'll get her point across."

CHAPTER 16

Lloyd Webster's office was in a low-rise red brick building on West Broadway, an easy commute from his Kerrisdale house, though a much longer drive for Roy coming from Burnaby. That annoyed him and got him thinking about Lloyd and his tendency to create a plausible picture rather than to live an authentic life.

The building itself was nothing special. There were several small storefronts on the ground floor, including an upscale diner that boasted its trendy gourmet sandwiches were made with only gluten-free bread, a women's clothing shop advertising new and gently used designer fashion, and a jewelry store that sold hand-crafted items made of repurposed materials. Inside double glass doors a small, well-maintained lobby was tiled in black and white stone. On one wall was a listing of the tenants of the building. Adjacent to it were two small elevators. Beside them was a gray metal fire door labeled *Stairs*.

Roy pushed the elevator button, then scrutinized the tenant list while he waited. The disgruntlement he felt as he drove in had been augmented by a twenty-minute battle to find parking. It had now reached fuming proportions because Lloyd's non-profit wasn't listed on the building's tenant list. Of course, Roy already had the address, so it didn't matter to him, but he was quite sure that the anonymity was a deliberate request on Lloyd's part. He wouldn't want the world to know his for-the-people organization rented space in a nice building in comfy Kitsilano any more than he wanted people to know he lived in well-to-do Kerrisdale.

The elevator arrived and Roy picked up the cat. Stormy didn't like elevators, so it was a good idea to hold him during the ride even though he was wearing the dreaded harness and leash. As usual, Stormy had protested the use of the halter, but Roy had flatly refused to take him on the road trip unless it was on. Frank wanted to go, so after some internal dialogue, he'd managed to persuade the cat to condescend to wear it.

Lloyd's office was on the sixth floor. The elevator door whooshed open into a small foyer. Carpeted in a dark blue hard-wearing broadloom, it led to a hallway that transected the building. The walls were painted a soft cream that managed to minimize the harshness from the fluorescent lights in the ceiling. Roy stepped out of the car and put the cat on the floor. The door slid closed behind them. They stood for a moment in the quiet hush of an empty hallway.

Which way?

"He's in 601," Roy said, peering at the directional signs mounted on the opposite wall. "To the left and all the way to the end."

He let the cat precede him down the corridor. Stormy wasn't the fastest walking companion. He liked to meander from one wall to the other, stopping suddenly if some interesting smell caught his olfactory senses. Roy had nearly tripped over him more than once, so he moved cautiously behind the cat, rather than striding out as he would have if he'd been on his own. As a result, the trip along the corridor took considerably longer than it needed to, adding to Roy's frustration. That he could have picked up Stormy and marched down to the office with due speed, but did not, thus making the slow amble his fault, made everything worse.

As he approached the door to 601, he wondered why he had bothered coming here. Lloyd would tell him he had been at home without an alibi just as he'd told Ellen and Christy. He'd continue to be a suspect. Evelyn would descend from Whitehorse to make his, Roy's, life miserable, and he'd have solved nothing.

Well. Are you going to open the door?

Somehow, they'd reached 601. He must have been standing there for a minute or two gazing at the door unseeing. He shook his head, mentally telling himself to smarten up, pushed open the door, and let the cat precede him inside.

The interior of 601 was many steps up from the hallway. Here the carpet was a plush beige. The receptionist sat at a console made of a dark hardwood that looked like the real thing. It took up most of the width of the room and was as impressive as any Roy had seen in a major conglomerate. Behind the receptionist was a feature wall painted a rich viridian green. The other walls were cream, tinted green to complement it. It didn't look like the entryway to an organization dedicated to helping the destitute and downtrodden. It did look like a nice place to work, though, probably why it was what it was.

The attractive young woman behind the reception console looked puzzled when she saw Roy enter the suite, possibly because they received few visitors, probably because of the cat. People rarely expected to see a cat on a leash. It was a curiosity that either caused interest and delight, or bewildered disapproval. Stormy tugged on the leash indicating he wanted to inspect the room. Roy let go and it dropped to the floor. Now that they were inside the suite the cat was safe enough on his own.

"Hello. How may I help you?" the woman said in a friendly enough way.

Roy smiled at her. "I'm here to see Lloyd."

She frowned at that. "Do you have an appointment?"

"Nope," Roy said, still smiling in a friendly way.

Her frown deepened. "I'm sorry. Lloyd isn't available at the moment—"

Sure he is. Stormy can smell him.

"Tell him his uncle's here," Roy said, cutting ruthlessly into her excuse.

She still looked dubious, so he added, "And his mother-in-law is about to descend from Whitehorse, breathing fire and repossessing his house."

Her eyes widened. "Evelyn?"

Roy thought it odd that Lloyd was sharing details of his personal life with his employee, but issues on that level of intimacy were between Lloyd and Jodie. "Yup, Evelyn. You sound like you've heard about her, so you'll know I'm not kidding when I say Lloyd needs to talk to me."

She nodded and picked up her phone to dial his extension. She relayed Roy's message, then said, "I know you asked not to be disturbed, but it does seem to be urgent."

He's going to tell her he won't see you. Let's just go to his office.

Roy nodded. The receptionist put the phone down. Her expression was troubled. "I'm sorry, sir. Mr. Webster can't be disturbed."

Stormy wandered into the short corridor that led from the reception area to the offices in the back and disappeared.

"That's too bad," Roy said. "I came all the way from Burnaby." He made it sound as if he'd just trekked from one side of the province to the other.

She nibbled her bottom lip, clearly uncomfortable. "Perhaps you can call and set up an appointment next time?"

Roy sighed. "Okay." He looked around. "Now where's my cat got to?"

He knew, of course. Frank and Stormy had gone directly to the source. They were probably in Lloyd's office by now.

That was confirmed by a shout from the inner office. "You again! What the hell are you doing here? Get out!"

The receptionist was visibly startled.

Roy smiled cheerfully. "The little devil. So that's where he got to. I'll just go get him." He didn't wait for her okay before he ambled off after the cat.

He found Stormy sitting on a large, beautifully made double pedestal desk of gleaming walnut. The desk was positioned in front of a window and set so that the user was facing the door, with the light at his back. A filing cabinet in the same wood was against an adjoining wall, which was painted forest green and adorned with framed First Nations prints. The carpet was the same plush beige as in the reception area.

Lloyd dragged his gaze away from the cat as Roy entered the room. He was wearing a dress shirt with no tie. Roy shut the office door behind him. A suit jacket hung from a peg on the back of the door. Roy supposed that his tie was carefully rolled up and stashed in one pocket.

130

"Since I'm here," he said, "we may as well talk." He sat in one of the simple armed chairs in front of the desk and crossed his booted ankle over his jean-clad knee.

"What do we have to talk about?" Lloyd said. His tone was belligerent, but he eyed the cat warily.

"Evelyn has decided you're guilty of the murder and she wants your hide. Unless you've got a rock-solid alibi, she's going to tell the mayor and the chief of police you did it and then she'll make sure you're arrested." He paused for a minute to let that sink in. "You know Evelyn. When she sets her mind to something it happens."

Evelyn sounds like fun. When can I meet her?

"In a few days," Roy said amicably. He watched Lloyd carefully. Sure enough, the man paled.

"She's coming south in a few days? But...how can she? She has a company to run."

Lloyd really could hear Frank. Roy sent a pointed look toward the cat. Stormy yawned in response, then padded across the desk so he could sit down on top of whatever Lloyd had been working on when they arrived.

She has a kid to save. That trumps work any day.

Roy thought so too. Lloyd looked confused.

"She seems to think you haven't been a good husband to Jodie," Roy said.

He hasn't.

"It's not my fault!" Lloyd burst out. "She was the one who had the affair!"

Roy shot him a disapproving look. "And why was that? Something lacking in your relationship?"

Why ask him? I can tell you. He's a jerk and she's fed up with him. Simple.

"I'm not a jerk!" Lloyd's expression was somewhere between guilty and annoyed. "I have no idea why she took up with Green. Maybe she was bored."

Astounded, Roy said, "How can she be bored? She's raising two teenagers and working a full-time job, not to mention running your household. She probably had no time to even think, let alone be bored."

"She made time to be with Green," Lloyd said with a rather smug smile.

There was that. Roy didn't intend to let Lloyd get the upper hand, though. "When did you notice she was acting differently?"

Lloyd looked over Roy's shoulder and shrugged.

"You didn't!" Roy wagged his finger and allowed himself a superior smile.

Lloyd's eyes narrowed. "I did, once I thought back over the last couple of months."

Such a prince of a man. Hindsight is a beautiful thing.

Shaking his head, Roy said, "So Green told you he was sleeping with Jodie, then you realized she'd been acting differently."

Lloyd nodded.

"Did you ever wonder if it was true or not?"

Lloyd frowned. "I'm not sure I get where you're going with this."

He's suggesting Green might have been playing you. Winding you up to watch you squirm.

Lloyd's expression was so astounded it was clear this possibility had never entered his mind. "She didn't deny it when I questioned her."

Roy nodded. "I guess you were really mad when you found out."

"Of course I was! My wife was sleeping with my enemy. What do you expect? That I wouldn't mind?"

Roy tilted his head thoughtfully. "Your enemy. That's a strong description. People hate their enemies. Did you hate Clayton Green?"

"What? No! We never agreed on anything and I thought he was a money-grubbing jerk with no principles, but I didn't hate him."

"Ah." Roy held up his forefinger and waggled it. "He was your adversary then, not your enemy."

Lloyd rolled his eyes and said, "Whatever."

Roy wagged his finger again. "Not so. Using the correct term is important. For instance, murdering an adversary is very different from killing your enemy."

Lloyd blinked as he stared at Roy.

I think you've lost him, old man. Way too complex. You need to bring it down to kindergarten level.

A wash of color rushed up under Lloyd's skin, reddening his cheeks. "Now listen to me—"

"One is coldblooded and planned. The other is decided in an instant and done on a rush of hot passion." Roy nodded as Lloyd narrowed his eyes. "Which one did you do? Premeditated or spur of the moment?"

"You think I killed Clayton Green?"

Roy raised his eyebrows.

Stormy stood, arched in a stretch, then pawed the documents he'd been sitting on, apparently attempting to make a more comfortable bed for himself. Papers went flying.

"Hey!" Lloyd yelled.

The cat is bored. He wants this idiot to confess so he can go home and chase the squirrel.

"I'm not going to confess. I have nothing to confess! You need to leave."

Roy narrowed his eyes. "So, you're saying you didn't meet Clayton Green in the display suite in Seymour View Tower then shoot him dead."

"Of course not!"

"I don't believe you."

Lloyd hesitated.

More papers sailed off the desk as Stormy used strong hind legs to propel them into motion. *Spit it out. If you've got an excuse, now's the time to use it before the cat decides shredding paper is more fun than pushing it around.*

Eying the cat, Lloyd's jaw hardened. "Without Clayton Green my foundation is going to be in a cash crisis. I didn't like Green, but he was useful. Everyone knew him, or knew of him, and lots of people didn't like him. All I had to do was to drop his name, tell potential donors that he had a project close to approval. That was enough to get the bucks pouring in, because he had a lot of enemies out there! People who wanted to cause him problems and were willing to pay for it." He stopped, drew breath, calmed down. "I didn't want Clayton Green dead, even if he was sleeping with my wife. He was too important to my well-being."

That self-serving statement was so Lloyd Roy believed it. Still, he aimed a stern look at him and said, "Do you have an alibi for the time of the murder?"

Lloyd looked relieved and nodded. "I was at home, getting ready for work, then on the phone trying to connect with one of my donors."

We know this. You already told me. There's no way to prove it, remember? The voice was weary, bored. The cat sat on the remaining papers and licked his paw.

Roy cocked a brow. "Landline or cell?"

"Cell. He sent me a text at ten-twenty saying he'd have to reschedule. I replied immediately. You can see my log if you want."

Roy shook his head. "Won't work, man. With a cell you could be anywhere, including in the presentation suite staring at the body of the man you'd just killed—or murdered."

Lloyd blanched. "That's disgusting!"

Roy shrugged. "Possibly. Certainly more blunt than you're used to, but it's true. You have no alibi."

"I didn't kill him! I had no reason to."

There was a sigh and the cat jumped off the desk, managing to scatter the remaining papers as he went. *This is getting us nowhere. Let's go.*

Roy sat for a minute longer, tapping his chin thoughtfully. Frank was right. Lloyd couldn't prove he was at home and he clearly wasn't going to admit that he'd killed Clayton Green. He wouldn't be able to call Evelyn with absolute proof that Lloyd was the killer. This interview had been a waste of time.

He'd put both feet on the floor and his hands on his knees, preparing to stand up, when a thought occurred to him. As he rose, his smile was wicked. "Evelyn planned on staying with me, but you know, when I tell her you claim you're not guilty, but don't have an alibi, she's going to want to keep an eye on you. Best place to do that would be in your house, in your spare bedroom."

Lloyd's mouth fell open.

Roy nodded. "Yup. Your next couple of weeks are going to be busy. Evelyn has a way of organizing people so they work to her schedule. Have fun."

CHAPTER 17

W hile his father was busy trying to find a way to throw Lloyd under Evelyn's bulldozer, Quinn got to work finding out as much as he could about Clayton Green and his company. A quick search online generated a lot of positive, if not gushing, details about how Green had grown the renamed Ferguson Green Construction Company from a medium sized operation that built homes for individual clients, to a player in the mega project business. That fit with what Roberta had told him about her husband's involvement in her family company, but it wasn't what Quinn wanted to learn. This was the official corporate story, meant to draw in customers.

It was the surface. He wanted the depths.

He moved his search to the newspaper morgue he had access to.

Green's growth strategy began with small single-family home developments in the suburbs. If he had his dates right, Quinn thought, this cautious expansion began when Green's father-in-law, the man who founded the company, had still been involved in the business. Gradually, though, the projects grew, and included large townhouse developments, as well as small apartment buildings. Then, about ten years ago, FGC leapt from low-rise apartment buildings and townhouses into mega projects.

The first was a spectacular retail and housing complex in Surrey, a suburb in the Metro Vancouver region. Similar projects in other locations in the greater Vancouver area followed. The Seymour View Hotel and Tower where Green had been killed was the latest and most ambitious to date.

The projects generated a lot of press, as did Green himself. He attended social events in support of local charities. He was a spokesperson for rezoning and redevelopment, championing higher density construction across the region. He was photographed with local politicians, and with provincial ones as well. He appeared to be a man of influence, respected by the people around him.

Quinn didn't buy it, so he dug deeper into FGC Inc.

The company had always offered a turnkey product. If you wanted a house built, FGC would oversee every aspect of the project—acquisition of the land, finding an architect, arranging building permits, the actual construction. Later, when FGC began to build small apartments and townhouse complexes they used the same pattern but added sales or leasing of the units to the list of options. The process continued for their mega projects, changing only in scale.

That information made Quinn pause and consider. A development the size of the Seymour View Hotel and Tower was a massive undertaking. Not only did it require considerable expertise and careful planning, but the cost would be enormous. Financing would need to be in place, and it would have to be secure. If the backers pulled out of an immense project like this one and replacements couldn't be found, construction would stop, and Green could find himself on the edge of bankruptcy.

Green's move from townhouse complexes into mega projects ten years before was a sudden leap. Had he begun to work with Dunnville Investments all those years ago? Was FGC essentially the construction division of that company, appearing to be arm's length, but closely allied to it? Quinn thought that was a strong possibility. If so, what was Dunnville Investments and who were the people behind it? From conversations with Christy and Ellen he knew rumor claimed the money men behind the company were international financiers of dubious reputation, but what was listed in official channels?

Not much, he found. Dunnville Investments was a subsidiary of an anonymous numbered company registered in the Caribbean. The details were buried deep, and though he searched, he couldn't find the names of the investors.

There was a company website, which proudly announced that Dunnville's mission was to provide the finest in luxury residences in the heart of Canadian cities. A list of projects in Toronto, Calgary, Ottawa, and Halifax, as well as those in Metro Vancouver, proved Dunnville was allied with developers other than Clayton Green.

A CEO who seemed to be a combination of general manager and company spokesperson ran the company. According to the website, his name was Ethan Byrne. That made Quinn sit up and take notice.

The Byrne name was well known in Canada. An old establishment family, there had been Byrne members of parliament, Byrne senior civil servants, Byrne members of the judiciary. In private life, the Byrnes had their fingers in a dozen different industries and were well connected and wealthy. Because every family had its share of renegades there had even been a few very un-Canadian robber barons. For the most part, though, the family was viewed benignly by the media and considered hard-working and down-to-earth, even though they were so incredibly rich.

The Byrne who worked for Dunnville Investments was the son of a Regional Chief Justice in the Superior Court of Ontario. That was a prestigious position, and it was held by his mother. His father appeared to enjoy unlimited access to the Byrne fortune and spent most of his time sailing the kind of yachts that competed in the Olympic games.

Quinn found that combination intriguing. With an industrious mother used to wielding power and dealing with an independent and intelligent workforce, and a self-indulgent father content to do only what pleased him, Ethan Byrne could be anything from a self-driven go-getter to one of the Byrne family rogues. He decided it was time he found out which the man was.

Paper records could only go so far. For the real drama behind Ethan Byrne, Dunnville Investments, and Clayton Green's construction company, he needed a source, and one wasn't hard to find. Bernie Oshall, an old friend from high school, was an urban planner. He worked for one of the few suburbs that didn't have an FGC mega project somewhere in its jurisdiction. Quinn wondered why and he figured Bernie could tell him.

They met for lunch at an unpretentious little restaurant. Bernie was delighted to see him, but he was no fool. He knew Quinn was a freelance journalist and he knew about Clayton Green's murder. He put the facts together and was ready for Quinn's questions.

While they ordered and waited for their meal to arrive, they talked about the usual haven't-seen-you-in-a-while things people gab about when they're old friends. Bernie mentioned his wife, Emily, and how fast his kids were growing. Quinn talked about Christy and his father. Bernie asked about Quinn's new book, which had been a runaway bestseller over the previous Christmas season and that led, not surprisingly, to the reason Quinn had sought him out that day.

"So, you're working the Clayton Green murder?" Bernie said casually, as his plate of chicken potpie with salad was placed before him. He inhaled the rich scent of chicken and spicy gravy and smiled as he picked up his knife and fork.

Quinn nodded. When he called and asked to meet, he'd told Bernie he wanted to pick his brain on how urban planning worked. It was an easy step from there to Clayton Green, whose notoriety and sudden death would be of interest to anyone in the construction business. He waited until the server placed his chicken leg lunch before him, then he said, "Green was involved in some big projects in the Metro Vancouver area. I know the surface stuff, but I haven't been able to find a lot of details. I'm hoping you can help me."

"What kind of details?" Bernie asked. He scooped up piecrust and rich sauce and chewed thoughtfully as he waited for Quinn's reply.

Quinn didn't waste any words. "Who are the money men behind Dunnville Investments?"

Bernie's features brightened with amusement. "Ah, that's the big question we'd all like to know. Ethan Byrne keeps that information close." He ate more pie as he considered. "I don't have specific names, but it's rumored that there are six investors and they're international billionaires who made their fortunes through criminal activities."

Quinn's brows went up. He hadn't expected that. "Ethan Byrne, whose mother is a superior court judge, works for international criminals who may be using a numbered company to launder money in Canada?"

Bernie grinned. "Interesting thought, isn't it?" He sobered quickly and added, "All of this is speculation, mind, and I'm only telling you because I know you'll check it out carefully before you use it."

"Okay," Quinn said. Normally he didn't allow the people he interviewed to dictate how the information they provided was used but agreeing to Bernie's request this time wasn't much of a concession. Ensuring the details were correct before he published was the way he worked. "What do you know about Green and his company?"

"FGC built a couple of townhouse complexes here fifteen or so years ago, before I joined the planning department. They were large developments—one was a hundred townhouses and the other was just under two hundred. The houses sold at premium prices for the time and were marketed as luxury homes." Bernie sighed and looked down at his pie, moving his fork uneasily through vegetables and gravy. When he looked up, his expression was grim. "The buildings haven't aged well. There are problems with leaks around the windows and the foundations of some of the structures appear to be unstable. There's rot in the rafters and the roofs leak. I'm told that inside the buildings the finishings started to fall apart within four years of construction."

"So, Clayton Green and his company don't build a quality product," Quinn said.

Bernie shook his head. "When Green first hooked up with Dunnville Investments, a good ten years ago now, he applied to build one of his mega projects out here. The site he and Dunnville proposed was in an old warehousing district and city council was excited at the idea of replacing the empty buildings with a combined housing and shopping complex. By that time, though, we'd already started to hear complaints about the two townhouse complexes so my department scrutinized Green's proposal carefully. In the end, we recommended that the city not agree to the project and they didn't. Green moved it to Surrey instead. I've heard that the complex they built is already experiencing difficulties, even though it only completed construction about seven years ago."

Quinn pondered that while he ate some chicken. "Why do you think that is?"

Bernie fiddled with his pie some more and shook his head. "Poor building design and engineering, perhaps? Choice of building site?" He shrugged and looked away, then back again. His expression said he'd made a decision, one he was finding unpleasant carrying through. "The site chosen was, like our warehouse area, priced to sell, but geologically it wasn't a good fit for a several story shopping complex and three thirty-floor towers. If proper supports are installed, they can provide the necessary stability. If it's not done correctly, or inferior products are used, over time problems can ensue. Using inferior construction materials throughout the build, both on the exterior and in the interior, doesn't help. There are rumors he cut corners at every level. You name it. Green did it."

"What about the provincial building code? Don't contractors and developers have to build according to it?"

Bernie nodded. "They do and every city has building inspectors whose job it is to check to make sure the proper permits have been acquired and that the developers adhere to the code while they build. But not all building inspectors are equal. Some are more diligent than others. Some are more...honest than others."

Keeping his gaze steady on Bernie's, Quinn said, "You're talking about inspectors on the take?"

Bernie grimaced and nodded. "It happens. Less often than you'd think, but it does happen."

"What about Dunnville Investments? What would their role be in this?"

"That's not as easy to define. Ethan Byrne would certainly have input into the selection of the building site. I imagine his organization would be involved in the design and look of the structure, and the choice of interior fittings, you know, like chrome or brushed nickel in the bathroom, hardwood or carpeting on the floor. For the major construction materials, like the concrete and the steel girders, the stuff that no one sees, I expect they'd leave that to Green."

"From what you're saying, both Green and Dunnville would have been involved in the decisions that resulted in the premature decay."

"Yes," Bernie said heavily. He looked desperately unhappy, as if he felt FGC's practices were a major stain on the whole building industry and he, personally, was ashamed, even though he had nothing to do with them.

Clayton Green had been murdered in the show home in his latest project. Could the assailant have been a former purchaser who felt cheated when his or her luxury apartment deteriorated with undue speed? It seemed a long shot, Quinn thought. How about an urban planner, like Bernie, who had endorsed one of his projects, then had to deal with the fallout from angry purchasers? Probably more likely, but still not a solid motive for murder.

"Tell me something, Bernie. If the people who purchased units in one of Green's buildings had problems FGC wouldn't or couldn't resolve, what would they do?"

Bernie shrugged. "Once construction is finished and the unit owners move in, a condo corporation is formed to manage the building. The association would be accountable for any exterior or structural problems, while individual owners would be responsible for the interior of their suite. For the first year after construction, owners can go to the developer and request problems be fixed. Unless it's owner caused, the developer usually sends in a crew and does what's necessary. I've heard complaints that FGC doesn't answer emails or phone calls and makes it difficult for buyers to get satisfaction that way. There's also a new building insurance program that all developers are required to pay into. The condo corporation could have to apply to that. If they couldn't get satisfaction there, they'd have to take legal action and threaten to sue the developer. It could take years to be resolved."

"If ever," Quinn said.

Bernie nodded. "If there's a widespread problem, like the leaky condo scandal in 1998, the government might get involved, but for a specific building, the legal system is a condo corporation's best bet."

And a condo corporation was made up of every owner in the development. Quinn knew because the townhouse complex he lived in had one and he went to the meetings. They'd never had any major problem with their buildings, but he could imagine how annoyed he'd be if the place had started to fall apart and he was faced with special levies to repair what a developer had not properly done. Still, he couldn't see an individual owner being so enraged that he or she would go out and shoot the developer. There were too many levels where annoyance could be vented and frustrations eased before it got to the level of murder.

No, unfortunately, despite Green's shady business practices and his relationship with a company owned by unscrupulous men, he didn't think they were likely to find the murderer amongst irate homeowners. He'd have to keep looking for now.

CHAPTER 18

While Quinn was finding out about building codes from his friend Bernie Oshall, and Roy was doing his best to ensure Evelyn Crowther wasn't going to be hunkering down in his townhouse when she came to Vancouver, Christy was sitting on her front porch watching her daughter host her very best friend Mary Petrofsky and two other little girls from the school.

The afternoon sky was a lovely deep blue. Fluffy white clouds drifted lazily across it, bunching into shapes and images defined by a lazy imagination like Christy's as she idly watched Noelle, Mary, Lindsay, and Erin. The four girls were burning off energy playing hide and seek. Lindsay, a dark-haired girl who'd recently had a growth spurt that had her towering over the others, was the seeker. Mary Petrofsky had just scrambled into the small crawl space underneath Christy's porch. Noelle was crouching behind the large bush on the other side of the road and Erin had taken off. It looked like she was planning to duck into one of the carports further up the street. As Christy watched her race along, she noticed Ellen coming down the road, having parked her new Mercedes in the lot at the top of the hill.

Lindsay finished counting, opened her eyes, and chanted, "Come out, come out, wherever you are." No one came out, of course, although

Christy detected a quiet, almost stifled giggle from Mary. Lindsay put her hands on her hips and looked around, then she started hunting.

Ellen, wearing heels and a very nice dress in a blue pattern, topped with a short jacket, marched firmly down the steep hill. She was almost at the Armstrong house when Lindsay danced over to Christy, a coaxing expression on her face, and said, "Mrs. Jamieson, did you see where Noelle went?" She made play with big trusting eyes, begging for help.

Christy laughed, then ran her finger over her mouth. "My lips are sealed."

Lindsay pouted, but the whole exchange evoked a giggle from beneath Christy. It was swiftly suppressed, but apparently not quickly enough, as Lindsay shouted, "Ah-ha!" and bounded up to Christy where she peered through the openings between the steps and came eye to eye with Mary. She shouted, "Got you!" which resulted in uproarious giggles on Mary's part followed by shrieks of delight on Lindsay's.

Across the street, Noelle's head popped up above the top of the bush as she inspected the action. She narrowly avoided capture when she dove back down as Lindsay turned, looking for her next victim.

Mary Petrofsky crawled out from under the porch. She had a spider web in her hair and a dead leaf attached to her sweater. The ground surface under the porch was made up of large chunks of gravel, but some smaller bits of stone adhered to her palms. She brushed her hands together to dislodge them while Christy removed the spider web and plucked off the dead leaf. Then Mary bounced after Lindsay, who was prowling up the road looking for her next capture. Both girls said hello to Ellen as they passed, but they were intent on the game and didn't pause.

As they headed away from Noelle's bush, her head popped up again. She was frowning. Christy almost laughed. Evidently waiting to be caught was less fun than being caught and joining the search.

Ellen reached the short walk that led to the townhouse. Christy moved over on the steps, opening a place for her to sit. A year and a half ago Ellen would never have considered sitting on porch steps in front of her home, but the past months had mellowed her. She was still Ellen Jamieson of the Vancouver Jamiesons, but now she was also Noelle's great aunt and an important part of a complicated family that rarely did anything the normal way. She'd learned to be flexible—or at least more flexible than she'd been before she'd moved in with Christy and Noelle.

She sat down on the steps and put her purse down beside her. Then she placed her elbows on her knees and rested her chin on hands. "What's the game?"

"Hide and seek."

There was a shout from up the street, followed by loud giggles. Mary Petrofsky appeared from the inside of a neighbor's carport and skipped onto the roadway. Erin, still tiny and waiting for a growth spurt, her black hair in a pixie cut, raced after her. Lindsay loped behind them both, easily catching up with her longer strides. Behind her bush Noelle's head had disappeared again at the first shout. Now that there were three of them searching for her, she was determined to cling to her hiding place if she could.

"How did the meeting go?" Christy asked. While Quinn and Roy were working on the murder, Ellen had been at a meeting of the Vancouver Beautification Committee.

Ellen grimaced. "As you might expect." She'd tried hard to keep it from happening, citing her three supporters who made up a majority on the small committee, but without success. Harvey Wrenn, who organized it, was adamant it was necessary. Jeff Darling supported him. As a city councilor, Jeff's voice carried weight so Ellen's motion had been quashed.

She stared glumly at the three searching girls, dancing about, darting here and there as they searched beneath porches and inside carports for Noelle. "I suggested Jeff be chair, but he refused, oh so charmingly. His excuse was that he was the city representative on the committee, so it wasn't his place to assume the chair position. Really," she said, straightening and shaking her head, "what he wanted was to have one of the people against the development be made chair so he couldn't vote against recommending it."

"Who got the job?" Christy watched Mary Petrofsky peek around the edge of Noelle's bush then dart away without revealing Noelle's location. She smiled. Mary looked very pleased with herself.

"Eugene Sawatzky. Jeff said that as chair his name would be the one on the report and his reputation as a respected member of the construction and development industry in Vancouver would add weight to our findings."

"Surely, Eugene would not want to be associated with a recommendation that he didn't approve of," Christy said.

Ellen sighed. "He protested. In fact, he refused the position." She put her chin back down on her hands. "Jeff ignored his protests and appointed him anyway."

After sighing again, she straightened as Lindsay galloped into Christy's carport, apparently still searching for Noelle.

"She's not there!" Lindsay bellowed as she danced out. Mary Petrofsky giggled, and Erin tilted her head in a questioning way.

"Manners," Ellen muttered, but not too loudly. She shook her head as the girls raced off in another direction. "Once Eugene was made chair, Harvey told us we had two guest speakers. One was a member of the planning department who had come to talk to us about the vital importance of the project to the city. The other was a building inspector. Of course, we couldn't refuse to listen to them since they had made time out of their busy days to talk to us. Imagine! The cheek of the man, arranging something like this to force our hand!"

Lindsay, who had run past Noelle's bush to peer around the side of the last house on the block, turned back to the street. There she paused, her hands once more on her hips as she surveyed the area. Watching her idly, Christy said, "This development must be very important to some people."

"Oh, yes," Ellen said. "The city planner was clearly a believer and very motivated." She shrugged and added grudgingly, "I must admit his enthusiasm was infectious. If I didn't know the area and know that it's an attractive, quiet neighborhood with mature trees and friendly, involved residents, I might have been persuaded. As it was…"

"You were not."

"No, I wasn't."

The hide-and-seek game was nearing its close. Lindsay shouted, "I see you!" and pointed, then raced to the bush. Noelle popped up, laughing so hard she bent double, holding her side. Erin and Mary Petrofsky converged on the bush about the same time Lindsay reached it. The four girls collided and went down in a tangle of limbs and laughter.

Stormy bolted from beneath the bush, spooked by the noise and action. The cat bounded up the stairs. *Who knew little girls could play so rough!* He disappeared inside the house.

Christy laughed.

Ellen said, "That cat!"

The girls stood and dusted bits of dirt and bark mulch off their jeans. Then they skipped over to a grassy area and sat cross-legged, settling into deep conversation.

They were deciding what was up next on the agenda, Christy thought with affectionate amusement.

Ellen said, "I didn't mind listening to the urban planner. The other man, the building inspector..." She shuddered. "I didn't like him at all."

Christy glanced sharply at her. Ellen had sounded concerned, hesitant, almost frightened, a very un-Ellen tone of voice. "Why?"

"There was nothing I could put my finger on," she said slowly. "He was a pleasant-looking man. No horrible facial tics or scars to make him seem scary. He had a reasonably trim body and he dressed well. But there was something—Oh, I don't know. Something in his eyes, I guess. In the way he looked at people. At women."

Christy raised her brows and waited as Ellen searched for words. Finally, she said, "He leered at us. At each one of us in turn. Portia Quance gave him a cold stare that only made him sneer at her, but Ruby Cronin looked at him once, then pursed her lips and wouldn't look at him again. And Amie Foran! Well, she couldn't meet his eyes and she fidgeted with her pen throughout his talk as if she hated being in the same room with him."

"He sounds like a creep," Christy said.

Ellen nodded.

Christy wrinkled her nose. "You said he sneered at Portia when she glared at him. How did he react to the other two?"

Ellen thought about that. "He smiled, coldly, I'd say, at Ruby, but he positively ogled Amie. No wonder the poor girl didn't want to look at him."

"Nasty," Christy said.

Ellen nodded.

Over on the grass the conflab was breaking up. The girls would be heading their way in a moment. "How did he react when you glared at him?" Christy asked.

Ellen looked at her and smiled faintly. "I didn't. I didn't acknowledge him at all. I treated him as if he didn't exist. When Jeff introduced him, I turned to Portia and made a quiet comment he couldn't hear. She looked right at him and laughed. She's very quick, Portia is. We annoyed him, I think."

Christy laughed. "Yeah, I guess you would."

There was no time for more. The girls had come to a decision. They bounded across the road. Noelle shouted, "Mom! We're hungry! Can we have a snack?"

Christy stood. "Come inside and wash up. I've got some brownies in honor of today."

There was a general chorus of "Brownies! Yay!" as the girls stampeded up the stairs.

As she and Ellen stood to follow, Christy said, "Let's talk about this later, when it's quieter."

The worried frown disappeared from Ellen's brow as she laughed. "Good idea."

CHAPTER 19

*T*revor *is at the Armstrongs' house. The news isn't good. I told them to come over here because you couldn't leave Noelle. They'll be over later, after Noelle is asleep.*

The cat rubbed against Christy's shins. She reached down and patted him. He meowed in response and rubbed his cheek against her hand before he trotted out of the kitchen.

Christy wiped the counter, took a quick look around to make sure everything had been put away after dinner, then nodded to herself in satisfaction.

In the living room Noelle was watching a show Christy had recorded that afternoon. It was a pre-bedtime treat, so she waited until it was over before she said, "Okay, kiddo. Time to get ready for bed."

Noelle, predictably, said "Awe, Mom!"

Ellen, who was also watching the kids show with a rather glazed expression, said, "Mind your mother, Noelle."

Noelle shot her an innocent look neither adult bought into as she said, "Yes, Aunt Ellen."

Ellen's raised brows said she knew exactly what Noelle was up to. It made Noelle giggle as she switched off the television and jumped to her feet with a remarkable amount of energy for just before bed. "Come on, Stormy. Race you up the stairs!"

She got a head start, of course, since she'd called the race, but despite her pounding feet, Stormy beat her to the top.

The end-of-day energy dissipated with remarkable speed. A half an hour later, Noelle was in bed, reading a book and yawning. Fifteen minutes after that, Christy went up to tuck her in and turn out her light. She was already drowsy as she murmured good night and rolled on her side. Curling up behind her knees, Stormy yawned. Frank sighed. *We'll be down in a few minutes. The cat wants a little nap.*

Christy left them to it and went back downstairs. She was in the kitchen making coffee and setting cookies onto a plate when the doorbell rang a few minutes later.

"I'll get it. You stay and finish up."

Christy looked up. Ellen was standing in the kitchen doorway. Christy noticed she'd changed her clothes and was now wearing a long-sleeved dress that emphasized her trim waist and slim hips. She'd also freshened her makeup and tidied her hair. For Trevor, Christy assumed. Suppressing a smile, she nodded. "Thanks." Then she wondered if she should run upstairs and replace her jeans and sweater with a nice dress as Ellen had. Too late, she decided with an internal sigh. She probably wouldn't even make it to the stairs before their guests were in the living room. She ran her fingers through her hair, straightened her sweater, which was her favorite teal blue, and decided she looked fine.

There was a murmur of voices from below, then, as she predicted, Christy heard male footsteps on the stairs. A few minutes later Quinn and Roy appeared. Roy had a bottle of Drambuie in his hand, which he plunked onto the counter. "Figured we might need this."

Christy raised her brows. Behind his father, Quinn sent her a warm, appreciative glance, and smiled. Then he sobered. "Things do not look good for Jodie."

Ellen came in with Trevor. He was dressed in a dark gray suit, white shirt, and blue silk tie, probably the clothes he'd worn to the police station when he'd been with Jodie while she was interrogated. The tie was loosened, the top button of his shirt undone, and his features were set in troubled lines. The combination reinforced Quinn's worried comment.

Ellen ushered the men to the kitchen table where she'd already laid out her pens and the leather folder that held her special paper. Christy followed with the plate of cookies and mugs of coffee. When everyone was settled, she said, "Stormy wants a nap, so Frank will join us later."

They all nodded. Trevor said heavily, "Jodie admitted under questioning that she was at the display suite the morning of Clayton Green's murder."

Ellen, holding a fountain pen aloft, ready to take notes, froze. "Good heavens. She confessed to killing Clayton?"

Trevor shook his head. "No. She says he was alive when she left him, but she was there in the display suite with him and it's only her word that he was alive when she left."

Christy took a cookie. They were chocolate chip, Noelle's favorite, and Ellen had made them with the girls that afternoon, after their hide and seek game was over and all the brownies had been consumed. It was a miracle that any remained for this evening's visit. "Is Patterson still looking for the perpetrator?"

Trevor shook his head. His jaw tightened before he said, "The case is officially closed. The police believe they have the culprit. It's up to us to prove someone else is guilty."

"We'd best get on with it, then," Roy said.

"Patterson must have solid evidence for her to arrest Jodie. Has she disclosed what it is?" Quinn asked.

"Video footage from security cameras in the lobby show Jodie arriving at ten a.m., then taking the elevator that goes up to the floor the display suite is on. She looks angry, determined. When the cameras catch her again, it's about fifteen minutes later and she's visibly upset. One of the construction crew, whose job is to make sure guests coming to view the display suite are signed in and have hard hats, has testified that Jodie was crying when she left the building." Trevor shook his head. "The CCTV camera footage is bad enough, but it's corroborated by a witness. It's not surprising Patterson is sure she's got her killer."

"How can that be?" Ellen was frowning. "What about the gun? What about fingerprints? Don't they need more evidence? Can they expect to convict someone on video footage alone?"

Trevor sighed. "The gun is still missing. I suspect it will never be found. The caliber of the bullets suggests it was a small handgun, easy to conceal when the killer exited the building. Jodie says she's never handled a gun and wouldn't know how to fire one. Unfortunately, this plays into Patterson's theory that the killer was inexperienced and fired erratically. As for fingerprints, Jodie's fingerprints are there in the bedroom. Crown counsel accepted Patterson's evidence when the warrant for Jodie's arrest was issued."

Crown counsel was what prosecutors in British Columbia were called, Christy had learned. Their involvement meant that the authorities believed they had their perpetrator. Trevor was right. For the police, the case was closed.

Quinn tapped the table with his fingers. "Do the police know the exact time of death?"

Trevor shook his head. "They have a window. Green was seen entering the building just before ten o'clock. He spoke to the greeter and said he had a visitor coming up to the display suite. Ellen and Christy, along with their real estate agent, entered the display suite about eleven, and found his body during their tour of the apartment. There was only them in the suite, so the killer had been and gone by eleven."

"An hour is a pretty big window," Roy said. He was pouring Drambuie into small liqueur glasses and looking grim. "Who else did those cameras catch going up in the elevator?"

Trevor shot him a small smile. "Good point. One I tried to make to Detective Patterson, though she wasn't really interested." He pulled out his phone and opened a notation app. "Let's see. Ruby Cronin, the real estate broker whose firm is handling the listings for the suites in the building, arrived at nine forty-five and went up in the elevator. Her purpose, apparently, was to unlock the display suite and give it a quick run through to make sure it was clean and everything was in place. She returned to the lobby shortly after ten. By that time both Clayton and Jodie had been seen entering the elevator. According to the greeter, Ruby comes in everyday to inspect, then open, the suite, so nothing unusual there."

"Is there any proof that's what she did?" Roy asked.

Trevor shook his head. "There are no cameras on the display suite level, or in the suite itself."

Excited now, Roy's hands rose in silent emphasis. "So, she could have shot Green herself!"

"No," Ellen said. "Remember—Jodie was with Clayton in the display suite from ten to ten fifteen. Ruby had already returned to the lobby by that time."

Trevor nodded. "Correct. I think we can eliminate Ruby from our suspect pool. Two other people are seen in the video footage, both arriving around the same time Ruby does." He scrolled down his page. "Amie Foran is an architect. She told the greeter that she was working on a project for Green and that he'd given her permission to look around the building. The greeter wasn't surprised. Apparently, Ms. Foran is a protégée of Green's and she often drops in to check out the construction process so the greeter nodded her through. The elevator camera shows her entering the car about nine forty-five. She exits a half an hour later, then leaves the building without speaking to anyone."

"I wonder what she was up to," Ellen murmured.

"When exactly did she leave?" Quinn asked.

Trevor consulted his notes. "At ten eighteen, three minutes after Jodie was seen exiting."

"Interesting," Quinn said.

"Yes, it is, but Jodie claims she left Green alive and she departed only a short time before Foran. That makes it difficult to see how Foran could have been the killer. Still, we can keep her on the suspect list and look deeper into what she was doing."

They all nodded. "You mentioned there were two people. Who's the other one, Trevor?" Christy asked.

Trevor scrolled through his notes. "A city building inspector by the name of Howard Stoke. He arrived about nine forty-five, shortly after Foran. He can be seen on the tape peering at areas in the lobby and writing notes on a form of some kind that was attached to a clipboard. He went up in the elevator about nine fifty. He returned to the lobby at ten thirty."

Roy, who had been looking gloomy, brightened. "So, his whereabouts during a crucial period haven't been verified."

"No," Trevor said, agreeing. "We need to keep an eye on Stoke to find out exactly what he was up to."

Ellen frowned. "Howard Stoke came to the meeting of the beautification committee this afternoon. He was there to convince us that new construction would benefit the West End." She moved her pen, this one filled with a pleasing peacock blue color, through her fingers. "Amie Foran wouldn't meet his eyes. Nor, for that matter, would Ruby Cronin."

Trevor shot her a keen look. "Do you think there's something there?"

"Stoke could be a bully, one of those hide-bound types who doesn't think women have any place on a construction site." Ellen shrugged. "Then again, he leered at every woman in the room when he came in. Amie is the youngest and least experienced of us. Perhaps she just found him unpleasant."

Trevor's mouth hardened at this, but he nodded. "Could be. He's certainly worth digging deeper into."

"Agreed," Quinn said. "Anyone else?"

"The construction crew took their mid-morning break at ten thirty. They stream out the door, some of them pulling out cigarette packages, others already on their phones. They return at ten forty-five and disperse throughout the building. The only individual who wasn't crew who entered the building around that time was Shelley Kippen, the agent who showed Ellen and Christy around. She arrived at ten forty-five, went up in the elevator, then re-emerged five minutes later. She spoke to the greeter, gathered two hard hats, and waited for Christy and Ellen."

"She must have been up to the display suite, making sure it was open," Christy said.

Nodding Trevor said, "That's her claim. She says she exited the elevator, made sure there was no construction going on in the area, or material cluttering up the foyer, then returned to the lobby. She asserts she didn't go into the suite until she was with you two."

LISTEN TO THE CAT!

"And there was no one else?" Christy asked.

Trevor shook his head. "That's it."

"That narrows our field considerably," Roy said. He sounded gleeful. "It's got to be the building inspector or the architect."

"Why would either of them want Green dead?" Quinn asked.

"They wouldn't," Ellen said slowly. She'd been furiously taking notes, but now she was tapping her lip with the pen. "Amie is still at the beginning of her career. She is keen to work on big projects like the ones Clayton specialized in. In fact, I'm sure she's hoping to get a contract to design or be part of the design team for the West End hotel apartment complex if it goes through. I've seen her chatting with Clayton numerous times, networking and making a connection. With him dead, that puts her career move in jeopardy."

There were nods around the table. She continued, "Howard Stoke works for the city. What would make him feel so strongly that he'd want to kill Clayton?"

"A good point. Is there no one else?" Christy asked, feeling rather desperate.

Trevor shook his head. "That's why the evidence is so devastating against Jodie. Patterson has a rock-solid case."

"All we can do is keep digging," Quinn said quietly. "I think the answer lies with Clayton Green. Who he was, who he did business with, how he treated people, the promises he made—"

"And maybe didn't keep," Christy murmured.

Quinn flashed her a smile and nodded. "Exactly."

"If you're looking deeper into Clayton," Ellen said, "I'll see what I can find out from Amie Foran."

"I'll help you, Ellen," Christy said.

"What will happen to Jodie? Will she be allowed out on bail?" Roy asked.

"She's been granted bail," Trevor said, "but the judge set it high, since it looks like premeditated murder. The only way she can pull together the cash is to use her house as collateral. Lloyd's name is on the deed along with hers, making them co-owners, and he refuses to allow her to use it. Until she can provide the funds to the court, she must remain in jail."

"Good thing Evelyn is coming to town," Roy said. "She'll sort out Lloyd and get the cash."

"Can't be too soon," Trevor said gloomily.

CHAPTER 20

Ethan Byrne wore his dark blue, pure wool suit well. Quinn priced it at upwards of five thousand dollars and from the tailoring guessed it was Italian and handmade, a huge contrast to Quinn's more casual garb. The white shirt beneath was fine cotton, the tie burgundy silk. His dark blond hair was styled and sleek. As Quinn was ushered into his chic, modern office he smiled, showing white even teeth, and held out his hand in greeting. As far as Quinn could tell, the smile was easy and unforced. It made Byrne's rather nondescript features light up and appear handsome.

"Mr. Armstrong, I read your book. Fascinating case," he said as he indicated they should sit in one of the tubular steel chairs positioned so the occupants could take advantage of the floor to ceiling windows that overlooked the Burrard Inlet and the North Shore Mountains beyond.

"Yes, it was," Quinn said. He chose a chair that put his back to the view and forced Byrne to sit so the light from the window was on his face.

"I didn't know Frank Jamieson personally, although we were both alumni of the same university. He was three years behind me, and our paths never crossed. His death was a tragedy."

Quinn thought calling Frank's murder a tragedy was a bit much, but he was interested in where Byrne was taking this, so he simply nodded agreement.

"I gather you're close friends with Frank's widow," Byrne said.

His expression, grave when he spoke of Frank's death, was thoughtful now, interested more than judgmental. Once again, Quinn wondered where this was going. His research had told him that Ethan Byrne wasn't married, or currently in any committed relationship, but he had been known to date the sisters and daughters of establishment families. It wasn't too big a jump to suspect that he might consider Christy fair game.

If he did, he wasn't going to get an introduction from Quinn. He raised his brows and said flatly, "Very close friends."

Amusement leapt into Byrne's eyes. Mentally, Quinn cursed. The man had been testing him to see how he'd react, and he'd taken the bait. Okay, score one for Byrne. The round wasn't over yet.

"I'm surprised you didn't meet Frank or Christy at some point in the past. I'm sure there are social events all of you would have attended," Quinn said, watching him.

Byrne shrugged. "Dunnville Investments has properties all over Canada. Initially, we managed them from offices in Toronto, but we're committed to being green and that includes minimizing travel. Vancouver has become an important city for us, so we opened this office two years ago. I divide my time between the two cities."

"When you say divide what do you mean? Two weeks here, two in Toronto?" Quinn asked

Byrne shook his head. "No. When we have a project either beginning or ready for market, I spend most of my time in that city." He held his hands out in front of him, turning the palms up. The gesture was both dismissive and an invitation to join him. "I'm sure you know the building where Clayton Green was killed is one of ours. We've just begun ramping up our marketing for the apartments and I'm negotiating with a hotel to flag the property. In addition, we're working on a new project that hasn't yet received planning approval. Between them, I expect to be here for several months."

"How does Green's murder in your display suite affect your marketing plans?" Quinn asked. Byrne was giving him more information than he'd expected. He wondered if the man simply liked to talk, or if he was deliberately laying a trail.

Byrne's hands dropped and his rather thin lips tightened. "Clayton's murder could not have come at a worse time. Many of the suites were pre-sold, but the buyers have a back-out clause if the project runs behind or if the property fails to conform to the prospectus. We've had several purchasers cite failure to conform as a reason for refusing to complete their deal."

That sounded like a convenient excuse to Quinn. "How does Green's death constitute a failure to meet expectations?"

"Lack of security," Byrne said, annoyance clear in his voice.

"I guess they have a point," Quinn said with considerable enjoyment. He liked the idea of giving Byrne a little dig of his own.

"The purchasers who backed out will regret it later. The building is in the news now, but in a couple of months people will have forgotten anything negative ever happened there. Or if they haven't, the notoriety will drive the prices up instead of down."

There was a bite to Byrne's words, an edge of malice Quinn noted with interest. "The loss of revenue must be concerning to the shareholders behind Dunnville Investments."

"My directors realize this is a short-term issue." The words were clipped.

So, Byrne was taking heat from his investors. "Rumor has it that the major shareholders in Dunnville Investments are men with ties to organized crime. Not really the kind of people you want to cross."

The expression on Byrne's face smoothed out, so it was impossible to guess what he was thinking. "As is usually the case, the rumors are wrong. The investors are all wealthy, but they have acquired their wealth in the normal way."

Quinn didn't know what "the normal way" of amassing wealth was. Winning the lottery? Picking the right horse at the racetrack? Commodities trading? Inheriting a pile from a workaholic ancestor? Inventing the next big thing? Working hard at growing a business one painful step at a time? He knew an evasion when he heard it, though. He wondered if any of the men behind Dunnville Investments might have been so annoyed with Clayton Green that they would kill him.

He kept his expression interested as if he accepted Byrne's statement about his bosses and figured it was time to move on. "What did Clayton Green do on one of your projects?"

Byrne relaxed in his arty, modern—and in Quinn's opinion, uncomfortable—chair. "Clayton developed the projects from the beginning. He would present a proposal to us that included the location and cost of land acquisition, projected use of the building, proposed architect or architectural firm, and estimated construction costs. Clayton was a thorough man, so he also included projected revenues from rental or sales. My shareholders and I would then discuss the details and decide if we were interested." He shrugged. "If we were, we'd take a closer look at the project. Was the building right for the audience we market to? Was the market potential realistic? What were the profit margins? That sort of thing. If we thought the project worthwhile, we would ask Clayton to create a detailed estimate along with a construction schedule. We'd review that as well. If everything was according to our standards, we'd sign off on the project. At that point, Clayton took over completely."

"A project like the building in which Green was killed must have a huge price tag," Quinn said.

Byrne nodded. He stared at Quinn with watchful eyes and a carefully controlled expression. "The construction process is not inexpensive."

"And yet you left the project in Green's hands without oversight?" Quinn said. He let surprise and doubt seep into his voice.

Byrne's expression lightened and he laughed. "Of course not. Clayton sent me weekly updates, including a detailed breakdown of expenses and a review of costs and potential cost overruns." He leaned forward. "Clayton Green was an excellent manager, Quinn. He brought his projects in under budget and on time. I'll miss working with him."

Quinn nodded as if this sounded perfectly reasonable to him. "I suppose Green liked to show off his achievements. Did he ever take you on site tours?"

Perfectly at ease now, Byrne laughed again. "Of course. Clayton Green was a proud papa. When I was in town, we'd schedule many visits to the site. He'd itemize every addition since my last visit. We'd talk over what was working out and what needed to be reviewed and changed. As I said, we worked closely together."

Smiling, Quinn said, "So the crew knew you."

Stiffening, Byrne said, "I wouldn't say that. I doubt any of Clayton's workmen knew me as an individual. Rather they saw me as a guest, someone Clayton brought to the site to impress." He shrugged. "I doubt any of them would remember me."

That, thought Quinn, was probably untrue. With his expensive clothes and confident manner, Ethan Byrne stood out. Whether the crew members liked him or not was another matter, but they would notice him and remember him. "When a project nears completion, there must be lots of changes every day."

Byrne nodded, again with that careful, watchful look on his face.

"And Clayton Green, being, as you say, a proud papa, must have wanted you to view those changes pretty regularly."

Byrne nodded again. "And I wanted to see them. That's why I establish myself in Vancouver toward the end of each project. Finishing touches are important and I want to make sure that every aspect of design and construction are perfect."

"So, you visit the site more frequently."

"Yes. Look, what has this to do with Clayton's murder?"

"I'm trying to understand how Green worked. What was normal, what wasn't. I get a sense he interacted more closely with some people than with others, you being one of the people he was close to. Am I correct?"

Slowly, Byrne nodded. "Clayton and I had a good working relationship."

"And you were familiar with the building."

"Yes." Anger sparked in Byrne's eyes. "But let me be clear, Armstrong. I didn't kill Clayton Green. I had no reason to. Nor is his death to my benefit. In fact, it causes me a great many problems."

"Such as?"

"My directors are keen on the proposed hotel, apartment, and shopping complex in the West End. Clayton was the guiding force behind that development. On his advice, we've purchased some of the land, though there are other important properties needed to create the parcel. Without him to ensure zoning permission is granted, the project may not go forward. If that happens, we'll have to sell off the original land purchase. My investors wouldn't be happy about that."

"Why? In this market you'll probably make a profit."

"But we will not make the kind of return they expect," Byrne said.

"Your bosses will hold you responsible for a zoning change not being granted?"

"When my directors go forward with a project, they expect to see it completed. They don't like failure."

Quinn raised his brows. "You sound worried about your job."

Byrne studied him for a few moments. Finally, he said, "Property development is big business all around the world. My investors are in Canada because we have a stable government and a healthy economy. Our cities are desirable places to live. Building mega projects is profitable and provides a good return on investment. But there are many places that have the same criteria. There's nothing keeping the shareholders of Dunnville Investments in Canada. And if they no longer wish to do business here and move their assets to another country, I will indeed be out of a job."

Quinn scrutinized him with raised brows. "I expect you have a tidy sum tucked away for rainy days like that."

Byrne laughed. There was a bitter edge to the sound. "You'd be surprised." He stood. "I must return to convincing those who bought suites in the Seymour View not to back out. It's been a pleasure talking to you."

"And you," Quinn said. They shook hands. As he left the expensive, minimalist office, Quinn thought about their conversation. He wondered if Clayton Green was as important to Byrne and Dunnville Investments as he'd said. Green's company was large and multifaceted, not a one-man operation. Surely the people who worked there would be able to successfully complete the work Green had brought in.

The more he thought about that, the more unlikely Byrne's concerns seemed. The only way to find out what was true was to go to the source. Time to talk to Harvey Wrenn.

CHAPTER 21

"Ellen and Christy Jamieson to see Amie Foran." Clad in a silk dress, handmade Italian heels, a chic spring coat whose beige color complimented the soft rose of her dress, Ellen was very much a Jamieson. She raised a brow as she spoke, her tone neither demanding nor intimidating, but it was quite clear she wasn't prepared to be kept waiting.

The receptionist, young and well dressed, responded with a smile and action. She stood and gestured toward a hallway. "Of course! We're pleased to have you visit us, Ms. Jamieson, Mrs. Jamieson. We're all set up in the conference room. Please come with me."

Christy let Ellen precede her as they followed the receptionist down the hallway into a medium-sized space with clerestory windows and pale blue walls. A long refractory table made of reclaimed hardwood took up the center of the room. On it was a tray with cups, saucers, a coffee beaker, and a teapot. Unlike the table, which looked like it might have once done service in a monastery's dining hall, the chairs around it were a modern swivel style that would allow participants at the table to turn toward each other. They looked comfortable, along with being practical for a modern business setting.

The receptionist stood just inside the doorway gesturing for Christy and Ellen to enter. Ellen chose the chair at the end of the long table, leaving the head for Amie, while Christy sat beside Ellen. Once they were settled, the receptionist smiled and asked for their preference, then poured and distributed the cups. "Ms. Foran is with a client—a previous appointment running late, I'm afraid—so Mr. Wright, our senior partner, will be here in a moment."

"I came to see Ms. Foran," Ellen said. She was frowning, her expression disapproving.

"Of course," the receptionist said quickly. "Mr. Wright simply wishes to make sure you aren't inconvenienced by an unavoidable delay." She smiled again. "If you'll excuse me, I'll just let him know you're here." She nodded, then moved soundlessly on the thick pile carpet, exiting the room, and gently shutting the door behind her.

"Well, I did not expect this." Ellen glanced at her watch. "Amie is not usually tardy."

"She probably won't be long," Christy said. "If the receptionist doesn't let her know she has to wrap up her earlier meeting, I'm sure Mr. Wright will as soon as he leaves us."

"I think Wright wants to know why we're here and what we want Amie for. He's probably envisioning a big contract for a new Jamieson mansion and wants to make sure his firm receives the commission."

Christy didn't have a chance to respond to Ellen's rather cynical comment. The door opened admitting a large man Christy estimated was in his mid forties. His hair was somewhere between red and brown, and he had a beard that was more than a scruff and neatly trimmed. He was dressed not in a suit and tie, but in dark blue chinos and a long-sleeved black sweater. The pants were good quality and the sweater appeared to be the finest cashmere. Christy put his appearance together with the decorating in the conference room and decided that Wright was branding both himself and his firm with an expensive arty look. She supposed if they were here to have a building designed, Wright would be pushing for a stark, geometric appearance.

His hand outstretched, he came over to the table. "Ms. Jamieson. Mrs. Jamieson. I'm so very glad to meet you both."

They each murmured a polite response

Wright sat at the head of the table and clasped his hands before him. "I understand you are here to meet with Amie Foran."

He paused, clearly expecting a reply, or more likely hoping for an explanation. Ellen simply said, "Yes."

Wright smiled, showing white, crooked teeth. If he were one of your favorite people, Christy supposed the smile would be considered charming. As it was, she thought it calculating and rather predatory.

"Amie is one of our newest associates. Her designs are innovative, but she can be influenced by classic architectural styles as well. We believe she has a bright future ahead of her."

"I never doubted it," Ellen said. Christy noted that she had assumed her most regal manner, cool and in control. Wright's eyes narrowed at her uninformative answer.

Apparently unwilling to be diverted from his purpose, he pressed on. "Do you have a piece of land picked out yet? Or would you like to have Wright and Associates assist you in finding the property location as well?"

"No," Ellen said.

Wright frowned. Christy almost laughed. He was clearly trying to figure out which of his two questions had resulted in Ellen's negative answer and he wasn't having much success.

"No?" he said, the smile firmly in place, but rather fixed now.

Ellen raised her brows. Her expression said he'd been crass to expect an explanation. "I came to speak with Amie about an issue being debated by the Vancouver Beautification Committee, which we both sit on. I'm sure you're aware of her participation. I won't take too much of her time, but there are some points I need clarification on before we write our report for the mayor."

Wright stood. "Ah, the committee. Yes, of course. I'll leave you to it, then. I'm sure Amie won't be long." With a polite nod he was gone.

As the door closed behind him, Christy did laugh. "He couldn't get away fast enough."

"Time is money," Ellen said lightly. Her mouth was pursed in a disapproving way. "I'm sure he has other potential clients to harass."

Christy toyed with her cup as she said, "Do you know much about Wright and Associates?"

"They design houses for the upper one percent who can afford large properties and big, sprawling residences. Wright himself likes angular styles and lots of light, so his houses feature floor to ceiling windows as well as endless jagged edges." She paused, then added thoughtfully, "I quite like his designs. They are very in-the-moment, but I'm not sure how well the style will age."

"Does the firm do any multi-unit projects, like the Seymour View Hotel and Tower where Clayton was killed?" Christy asked.

"That's Amie's focus. She told the committee her passion is to build homes for families in the downtown area that are comfortable and stylish, but high density and affordable at the same time. That's why she joined the committee, I think."

Christy nodded thoughtfully. "So that's the link to Clayton Green. And why she might see him as a mentor."

Ellen tapped her chin with two fingers. "I never thought of Clayton as the mentoring type, but yes, it does explain why she was in the building the morning he was killed."

"Researching and learning," Christy murmured.

Ellen nodded, toying with her cup, then sipping her coffee. She was about to say something when the door opened and Amie Foran hurried in.

Tall and thin with pale skin, big brown eyes, and thick, curling sable hair, she was an attractive young woman. "I'm so sorry to be late. Hi, Ellen. How are you?"

"I'm fine. Amie, this is my niece, Christy Jamieson."

Christy smiled. "Hi, Amie. Nice to meet you."

Amie responded with the usual platitudes and sat down in the chair at the head of the table. "How can I help you?"

"I'm here about Clayton Green's new project."

"Oh. The West End apartment-hotel complex. Yes, it will mean a big change for the area, won't it?"

"It will," Ellen said. She studied Amie's features.

Christy watched her too. Amie's expression was animated, full of enthusiasm, with no apparent reservation that the project would impact the area in a negative way. Christy didn't think Ellen had a supporter to stop the rezoning here.

Amie's features scrunched up in a smile that reminded Christy of Noelle's expression when she had been caught out in a prank she knew she shouldn't have done, but did anyway because it was fun and she wanted to. "Clayton encouraged me to study the construction and design of the Seymour View. He promised me I could submit a design on behalf of the firm when the West End project was sent out to tender. I'm so excited. Mr. Wright has told me that if I win this proposal, he'll make me permanent."

"You're part-time now?" Christy asked.

Amie made a little moue. "Worse than that. I'm a contractor. I have an office in the building, and I'm on the website as one of the firm's architects, but I have to find my own clients. Occasionally, Mr. Wright will send me a referral, but he charges me a larger finders fee if he does. If I bring in my own clients, my operating expenses are less."

"You don't work for this firm?" Ellen's expression was surprised. Christy thought she was also shocked and probably disapproving. She knew she was.

"No, not yet," Amie said. She smiled and shrugged as she said the words. Either she had supreme faith she would be hired on as a full employee, or she assumed she had no other option but to accept Wright's business practice and hope. Christy wondered if she knew that Wright had just done his best to undercut her with a potentially lucrative client.

"A project like the one Clayton was proposing would be a massive undertaking, Amie. Are you sure you'd be up to it?" Ellen asked.

Amie smiled brightly. "Oh, Wright and Associates would be the official architects on the project and Mr. Wright himself would take point. I'd make the original designs, then he and some of the other architects in the firm would weigh in on the details."

Christy guessed that by the time they were finished not much of Amie's vision would remain. "Clayton was taking a big risk empowering a new young architect. He must have had a lot of faith in you."

Amie blushed. "He promised me the opportunity some time ago. I've been helping him out a little and I think he saw something special in me."

Ellen's eyebrows crawled up toward her hairline. "Amie, don't tell me he caught you in his web like poor Jodie Webster."

For a moment Amie's expression blanked, then her eyes widened, and her mouth opened in an oh of surprise. "You mean Lloyd Webster's wife? The one they've arrested for his murder?"

Ellen nodded.

"I read she had had an affair with Clayton. Is that what you meant? You wondered if I'd had a relationship with him?"

Ellen nodded again.

Amie bit her lip and for a moment her gaze slid away from Ellen's. With a sigh, she said, "No, it was nothing like that." Her expression eased into a little smile. "In fact, I wouldn't have minded sleeping with him, but he never asked. I guess he was busy with Jodie Webster."

Ellen's expression turned thoughtful. Christy wondered if she was trying to figure out what it was that Amie had been doing that encouraged Clayton Green, a self-centered man who used people to suit his needs, to mentor her in her career aspirations. If Ellen wasn't considering that question, Christy certainly was.

Rather tentatively, Ellen said, "At our last meeting you seemed to be rather uncomfortable with that building inspector—what was his name? Oh yes, Howard Stoke."

Amie stiffened noticeably. "Howard, yes. He's not my favorite person."

Ellen tilted her head. "Have you met him before? I suppose you must have come across him from time to time."

Amie swallowed. "Yes. Howard works on most of the projects Clayton builds." She cleared her throat. "In fact, I saw him at the Seymour View the day Clayton was killed. I was there reviewing the design differences between the apartment and hotel floors. We bumped into each other there. I think Howard was inspecting some of the structural details."

"Of course. That would be it." Ellen smiled. Amie visibly relaxed. "I'm sure it must have been terribly upsetting for you when you discovered you'd been in the Seymour View when Clayton was killed."

"Absolutely." Amie's brown eyes were wide. "When the police questioned me, I realized I left the building only minutes after Jodie Webster did. How scary is that? I might have been in the elevator with a killer!"

"Being interrogated by the police must have been upsetting," Christy said sympathetically.

Amie's gaze shifted again, as it had earlier when one of Ellen's questions had struck a nerve. "I didn't have anything to worry about because I didn't kill Clayton. I couldn't." She swallowed, emotion suddenly clouding her eyes. "He was my best chance for my future and my career."

So, she did know Wright was using her, Christy thought. At that moment, she felt sorry for Amie Foran.

Ellen sighed. "Well, I guess I have my answer, but I will ask my question anyway. How do you intend to vote on the West End rezoning? I believe we have a real opportunity to stop it now that Clayton is no longer involved."

Amie's expression immediately became chastened. "Oh, I'm sorry, Ellen. I know you think the zoning shouldn't be changed, but I believe the area should feature more high-density housing. Plus, the city will benefit from the revenues that the hotel and the shopping mall will bring in. A win-win all round, as it were. So, yes, I think it should be changed to allow the project to go forward."

Ellen lifted her hands in a well-I-tried kind of gesture and pushed back her chair. "Thank you for your candor, Amie. It's been nice talking to you. If the project does go ahead, I wish you luck with your design bid."

Amie's smile was sweet and at the same time relieved. "Thanks, Ellen."

CHAPTER 22

The afternoon after his appointment with Ethan Byrne, Quinn secured a meeting with Harvey Wrenn at the FGC offices in suburban Delta. The site was a low-rise building of concrete and glass set back from the road behind a parking lot. Fringes of grass softened the edge of the lot and a flower border, newly planted with hardy annuals, added a jolt of color to the foundations.

Quinn found a spot and parked. The building's entrance was in the center of the structure. He pulled one of the double glass doors open and went inside. A middle-aged receptionist dressed in a practical polyester pantsuit greeted him, then directed him to Harvey Wrenn's office, which was on the third floor. "By the elevator," she said with a sniff. "Though that will probably change soon enough." On that intriguing note, Quinn set off.

Wrenn's office, Quinn discovered, was near the elevator, but it wasn't beside it, as the receptionist had implied. His secretary's office was the one by the elevator. Wrenn's office was tucked away behind, protected by the outer office.

Wrenn's secretary, like the no-nonsense receptionist downstairs, was middle-aged and efficient. When Quinn identified himself, the secretary alerted Wrenn that he'd arrived, then led him through to the inner sanctum. She took orders for coffee and disappeared, promising she'd be back in a few minutes.

Quinn studied Wrenn while they settled at a round table on one side of the large room and made impersonal small talk. He was younger than Quinn expected, probably in his early forties, with broad shoulders and a narrow waist emphasized by the stylish dark blue suit he wore. His features were angular, his eyes deep set behind square dark-rimmed glasses. Those eyes, brown and inscrutable, gave nothing away, telling Quinn he'd have to work to get information out of this man.

The secretary returned with a tray holding two mugs of coffee, creamer and sugar packets, and a plate of shortbread cookies that looked homemade. Wrenn thanked her, she nodded, then quietly closed the door as she left.

Smiling, Wrenn indicated the cookies. "From a bakery near the restaurant where most of the staff go for lunch. Please have one. They're delicious." He took one and bit into it with a little hum of pleasure.

He sounded open and friendly, but Quinn wasn't buying it. The man was setting a scene. Why, Quinn wasn't sure yet, but it was what his instincts were telling him, so he'd keep it in mind and see if he could figure out the answer.

He picked up a cookie and bit into it. Wrenn was right, it was delicious. He grinned and said, "What's the address of that bakery? I know someone who would love a box of these."

Wrenn laughed and told him. Quinn wrote it down with a nod of thanks.

"What can I do for you, Mr. Armstrong?" Wrenn said as Quinn finished making his note.

"I'd like to ask you about Clayton Green and how his death affects the company."

Wrenn nodded. "Roberta told me you'd been to see her." He toyed with the cookie he held between his finger and thumb. "She doesn't see any reason why we shouldn't be forthcoming, and she is now the owner of FGC."

From what Roberta Green had told him, she'd always been the owner, but Quinn let that pass. "Clayton Green worked closely with Dunnville

Investments on development projects in the Vancouver area." Quinn made it a statement, but Wrenn nodded anyway. "I spoke to Ethan Byrne. According to him, there's a new project being proposed for the West End, but because of Green's death Dunnville may pull out. I imagine that would mean a considerable loss for FGC."

Wrenn's mouth hardened, and he shook his head, but he said mildly enough, "Ethan is protective of his investors. Until the fundamental components of a project are in place, he makes no promises. It's true the West End development is still in the planning stages, but I'm confident it will go forward. Clayton laid out a road map, which I'm following. I expect to get notice that the necessary rezoning has been completed in the next couple of weeks. After that, we'll finalize the land package and move into the design and development stage. At that point, Ethan will be fully on board."

Quinn raised his brows. "You are quite certain the rezoning will go through? Even though the local community is against it and Lloyd Webster plans to protest it?"

"Lloyd is an intelligent man. He can be made to see reason. Clayton understood that. We've been proceeding with the expectation that there will be hiccups, but we can surmount them."

"So the rezoning application is in the bag, so to speak?"

Wrenn opened his mouth, drew a breath as if he'd been about to reply, then closed it again. After a short pause he said, "The rezoning application has been made and it is being studied. We believe it will be granted."

Ellen would love that. Quinn circled round, back to Clayton Green and the way he ran his business. "When you say that Lloyd Webster could be made to see reason, were you referring to the affair Green had with Webster's wife?"

"Why would you think Clayton's personal affairs were part of his business strategy?" Wrenn's gaze didn't waver, but his eyes were watchful.

Quinn shrugged. "The timing of the affair seems suspicious. Lloyd was against the West End project and was likely to use his organization to protest the rezoning. The news that his wife was in a relationship with the developer would undercut his position."

"Clayton had a...flexible...personal code." Wrenn was choosing his words carefully, keeping his voice bland, without a hint of disapproval.

"Did he get involved with Jodie Webster so he could blackmail her husband?" Quinn asked bluntly.

Wrenn winced. "I can't tell you that. Clayton dropped some hints that indicated it might have been part of his thought processes, but he never admitted anything to me directly."

"You've been running the company since Green's death?" Wrenn nodded. Quinn thought he looked relieved they were no longer on the subject of Clayton Green's flexible morals.

"Roberta asked me to step in while she figures out how to move forward," Wrenn said. "I'm happy to do so."

"I imagine your first job will be ensuring the West End project goes forward."

"While it is certainly an important focus, it's not my first priority." Wrenn leaned forward, his expression earnest. "I want to change the way the company does business. Clayton's primary motivation was to ensure maximum profits, particularly when those profits lined his own pocket. He believed that once a project was finished and the building delivered to the owners, our role was done. It didn't matter if, in five or ten years, there were problems with the building envelope. Or if the foundations were starting to crumble, because enough care wasn't taken at the beginning of construction. That was the problem of the owners, not the company that built the property. I don't agree. I believe that if we're constructing luxury dwellings, we need to make sure we're providing a luxury product. That's how I intend to go forward."

The remark about the foundations and the building envelope fit with what Bernie Oshall had told Quinn about the company's reputation. "Lining his own pocket is a very suggestive statement. Are you saying that Clayton Green used fraudulent practices to run his business?"

"I am saying that Clayton's...flexible...moral code allowed him to feel comfortable with behaviors I wouldn't accept."

"What kind of behaviors?"

Wrenn waved a hand in an airy, dismissive way at odds with his statement. "Unethical ones."

Worse than substandard construction? Intrigued, Quinn wasn't about to let this go. "Like?"

Wrenn pursed his lips and behind the heavy glasses, his dark eyes flashed. "I think I've said enough."

Quinn studied him. During their conversation today Harvey Wrenn had given him the impression that he was a careful man who measured his words and wasn't inclined to blurt out impetuous statements he'd later regret. Stopping now, saying he wasn't going any further, wasn't an ending; it was an excuse. An opportunity for Quinn, perhaps, if he could figure out what the unethical action had been.

What would be unethical in the construction business? Wrenn had already implied Green used substandard materials, so it must be something even more problematic. What went along with using second-rate materials? An incompetent crew that cut corners? Could be. Or maybe it was an incompetent crew *and* crappy materials. Both added up to shoddy workmanship and poor quality, but Quinn didn't think either would have Wrenn refusing to describe them.

What else was there?

How about bribery? Green needed public officials to sign off on the mega projects he built. He probably donated to city councilors' election funds. Did he also bribe them?

And how about other officials who could make or break a project? Planning department officials like Bernie, building inspectors...

Building inspectors. "Did Green have a building inspector on his payroll?"

Wrenn sucked in his breath, looked down, then raised his eyes to meet Quinn's. "How did you guess?"

The hiss of breath and shifting gaze came across as theatrical to Quinn, but he was willing to play his part in the scene Wrenn was directing. "Was it several people? Or just one?"

"One man. Howard Stoke. He's worked for the city for years. He and Clayton went to high school together."

"Old pals," Quinn said lightly.

Wrenn nodded. "Yes. Clayton knew what Howard liked."

Quinn felt the shiver of excitement that told him he was on to something. "And what did Howard Stoke like?"

The answer wasn't what he expected.

"Women," Wrenn said. His expression was somber, his tone heavy with disapproval. "Young, attractive, and the more reluctant, the better."

∾

"Did he give you any names?" That was Trevor. His tone was demanding, his features tight with disgust and anger.

It was ten the next morning. Quinn had arranged the meeting the night before but had refused to talk about what he'd discovered while Noelle might conceivably overhear. Now she was safely in school, and the adults could talk freely. Trevor, Quinn, Ellen, Christy, and Roy had assembled in the Armstrong's kitchen. They were drinking coffee, but not eating melt-in-your mouth shortbread cookies. Quinn never did stop by the bakery Wrenn had recommended.

Now he shook his head in answer to Trevor's question. "I pushed him. I told him the accusation was explosive and he'd better be able to back it up, but he refused to identify any of the victims. He said the women Green had forced to have sex with Howard Stoke had been punished enough. He wasn't going to drag their names through the mud."

"How extraordinarily gentlemanly of him," Ellen said tartly. "He evidently knew all about Green's procurement scheme while it was in action, but did nothing to stop it. I should think that makes him an accomplice if nothing worse."

"It depends when he found out about it," Trevor said. "There's a possibility he only discovered it after Green died."

Ellen raised her eyebrows. "Do you believe that?"

"It's unlikely," Trevor said, "but Wrenn deserves the benefit of the doubt until we can find proof of his involvement."

"Then we'll have to look," Christy said. She shuddered. "Honestly, I'm less and less surprised someone murdered Clayton Green. I'm amazed this Howard Stoke guy wasn't gunned down too."

Roy rubbed his chin. He'd been listening to the conversation with a frown, pondering the implications, Christy supposed. Now he spoke up. "That's a good observation, Christy. If a woman wanted retribution for what she was being forced to do, wouldn't she go after the actual perpetrator?"

"Perhaps Stoke was next on the list. I certainly wouldn't weep if one of his victims eliminated him." From her fierce expression, Ellen would probably be applauding the killer and urging her on.

Trevor shook his head, though there was the hint of a smile on his mouth. "Fortunately, we only have to deal with one murder at the moment. When Harvey Wrenn told Quinn about Stoke and the women, he gave him some clues. Young, attractive, reluctant. Reluctant implies women who wouldn't ordinarily prostitute themselves for gain. Young could mean women who are at the beginning of their careers, who need—or needed—Green's help to get ahead. Wrenn wouldn't name names. Could it be that was because the women were already suspects in the murder?"

Ellen stiffened. "The women on my committee?"

"Shelley Kippen?" Christy said at the same time.

They looked at each other. Ellen shook her head. "I don't think it could possibly be Miss Kippen."

"She's attractive and young. She may not be at the beginning of her career, but she's still working to get ahead," Christy said.

"But she was so distraught when she found Clayton's body."

"If she killed Green, she had time to rehearse how to react when she discovered him."

Ellen grimaced at Trevor's observation. "I suppose."

"From what Wrenn told me, this had been going on for some time. I don't think we can rule Kippen out because she's not just starting her career. She could have been one of the earlier victims."

Ellen lowered her gaze and rubbed her forehead. "I'd forgotten about that. How awful. I suppose we must keep Miss Kippen on our list."

"That leaves us with the women on Ellen's committee," Roy said. "Who do we start with?"

"I cannot believe Portia Quance has been victimized this way," Ellen said. "She is secure, well established and has been so for many, many, years. Also, when Howard Stoke came to our last meeting Portia showed no fear of him."

"She might be one of those people who are defiant when they're frightened of someone," Roy suggested.

Christy shook her head. "Being forced to have sex with a man would be a horrible trauma. I don't think it would be that easy to stand up to him, particularly in a public setting, when reputation counts. This is a huge secret. The woman would be on edge, worried he'd make some reference that would have the other people on the committee speculating there was something between them."

Ellen was nodding as Christy spoke. "Yes, I agree. Portia showed no fear of him and throughout the meeting she acted as if they were equals. It was more like he was one of her employees."

"So, we can write Portia Quance off for the moment," Quinn said. "What about the other two? Ruby Cronin and Amie Foran?"

"They were both uneasy, Amie more so than Ruby." Ellen sighed heavily. "Amie fits the description perfectly. She's at the beginning of her career and needs to land the contract for the design of the West End project so she can win a permanent position with her architectural firm."

"Shelley Kippen told me Ruby was able to start her real estate agency through working with Clayton Green. It could be she was one of Stoke's earlier victims," Christy said.

"All three women were in the building the day Green was killed," Trevor said.

Roy nodded. "So, they're all suspects."

Quinn moved uneasily. "Jodie was in the building too. Could she be one of the women Green victimized?"

Roy sucked in a breath. His expression was horrified. "No! Why would she do it? She's not looking for a career in the construction business. She's an accountant with a reputable firm! She didn't need Green's help to push her career forward. She was doing fine on her own."

"Dad, she was having an affair with Clayton Green. Maybe he told her she'd have to do it or he'd use their liaison to harm Lloyd's work."

Roy shook his head.

Quinn continued, his expression grim. "Maybe that's what they were arguing about on the day Green was shot. Maybe he told her what she had to do, and she refused."

Roy pointed a finger at Quinn. "Ha! That's where you're wrong. Lloyd already knew she was sleeping with Green. They had a fight about it. He'd kicked her out of the house. The affair was out in the open. Green had nothing to blackmail her with."

"Maybe, maybe not," Trevor said. "If we can prove what Green was up to, Patterson might be willing to reopen the case, but she also might follow Quinn's line of thinking, and figure Jodie was one of the blackmail victims."

"The case against her could be strengthened by what we find?" Roy's expression was grim.

Trevor shrugged. "It's possible."

Roy slapped his palm onto the table. "That's not okay. We need to sort this mess out. Who does what?"

Ellen frowned. "I think it's up to me. I know the women involved. I must be the one to talk to them."

"I should come with you," Christy said. "Unless Trevor thinks it's better if he speaks to Patterson, I'll be the one taking the information to her. I'd rather be able to speak directly about what was said, than to provide her with a third-party description."

"Yes," Ellen said slowly. Then nodding, she continued briskly, "Yes, I can see that. I'll make the arrangements for the meetings. Can you be available this afternoon?"

"I'll pick up Noelle from school," Roy offered.

"Thank you, Roy. Yes, this afternoon works fine."

"While you're interviewing Cronin and Foran, I'll see what I can find out about Howard Stoke," Quinn said. "He might be cautious, but somewhere there's got to be evidence of what he's been up to."

"I'll help you," Roy said.

Trevor nodded. "I'll talk to Jodie. If Green did try to force her into his scheme, we need to know."

Ellen drew a deep breath. "All right, everyone. Let's get started."

CHAPTER 23

Two women's voices floated through the corridor in the Jamieson Trust, alerting Christy that some of their guests had arrived. She glanced at Ellen who had her head cocked, listening to what was being said.

"What a lovely office. Beautifully decorated." That was Shelley Kippen and she sounded approving, but unsurprised.

"It should be with the kind of money the Jamiesons' have."

That must be Ruby Cronin speaking, Christy thought. So, she and Miss Kippen had come together. When Ellen issued her invitation to gather the three female suspects together here in the Jamieson conference room, she'd provided different reasons for each of them. Kippen had assumed the meeting was to talk about Ellen's future house hunting expeditions and Ellen hadn't contradicted her. Ruby was more cautious, but she too had expectations. She knew Ellen was looking for new luxury accommodations, but she also knew Ellen was dead set against the West End project. For Ruby, it had to be one or the other. Ellen let her believe what she wanted to believe. The important thing was to get her into the conference room with the other women.

Amie Foran had proved more difficult to corral than the other two. Was that because she was the guilty party? She'd been in the building at the time of the murder. It wouldn't have been hard to move from one floor to another, slip into the display suite, kill Green, then disappear onto another floor until it was safe to emerge. Her alibi was thin, only that she was checking features of the building's construction. That meant she was roaming freely through the Seymour View and was unlikely to have someone to corroborate her story.

When Amie made an excuse not to attend, Ellen spoke to Daryl Wright, Amie's boss at Wright and Associates, and asked him to send her over. She wasn't quite so blunt in her phrasing, but she achieved her goal. Amie had confirmed she'd be at the meeting today.

The architect is late.

The cat was curled up on one of the chairs, annoyed and bored. Frank said Stormy liked the spring and he liked being outside at this time of year. The air was scented with fresh green growth, warming earth, baby birds, and active squirrels. The weather was perfect, not damp and cold like the winter months, or hot and dry as in the summer. There was always something to watch or chase, activity was constant. When he grew tired, the grass was soft and plump with new moisture, and it smelled delicious.

Frank wanted to be part of this meeting, though, and he'd always been a sweet-talker. Evidently, he'd convinced the cat to give up his sunny afternoon rambles for an indoor meeting. That was probably because they'd missed the discussion when the meeting was arranged. Stormy had been outside chasing his archenemy the squirrel, leaving Frank completely out of the loop. Now it was payback time.

Ellen said, "She'll be here. She may not want to come, but she will."

"Your guests, Mrs. Jamieson." Bonnie King, the Jamieson Trust's receptionist and all-round clerical help, stepped to one side to allow Ruby Cronin and Shelley Kippen to enter the room. Her eyebrows were raised, and her mouth pursed. Evidently, she didn't approve of visitors discussing the Jamieson financial situation in her hearing.

Christy stood. "Welcome. Thank you for coming. While we wait for Amie Foran to arrive, would either of you like tea or coffee?"

They both opted for coffee, so Christy nodded to Bonnie, who slipped away to organize the refreshments. She'd brought coffee and fresh cookies—baked the evening before by Ellen—and returned to her desk before Amie finally arrived. Bonnie brought her to the conference room, introduced her, then disappeared to fetch her a coffee. As she sat down, Amie's expression was both wary and upset, evidence she wasn't looking forward to the meeting.

Ellen waited until Bonnie had delivered Amie's beverage and departed, closing the door behind her, before she began. "We've asked all three of you here today to discuss the murder of Clayton Green."

"Not house hunting?" The dismay in Shelley Kippen's voice and expression was almost comical. Ruby was frowning. Amie clutched her mug and swallowed hard.

Well, duh. Aunt Ellen lives with us. She doesn't need swank new digs.

Ellen shot a quelling look at the cat. None of the three women reacted.

"Why would you be investigating Clay's murder?" Ruby said. "That's a job for the cops."

"The police have fixed on Jodie Webster as their prime suspect. For them, the case is closed," Ellen replied.

Kippen wrinkled her forehead. "You don't think Jodie's the one who killed him?"

Ellen shook her head. "No."

Ruby shrugged. "What makes you think the cops have it wrong? They're the ones who have all the evidence."

Ellen took a moment to select a cookie from the plate in the center of the table. "Jodie says she's innocent, but her alibi is weak. However, new information has come to our attention that supports her claim."

When Christy and Ellen had discussed how to handle the meeting, they'd agreed that Ellen would do the talking, while Christy focused on the reactions of the women. Now Christy studied their faces as Ellen dropped her bombshell. Shelley looked intrigued. Ruby was disdainful, almost bored. Amie's eyes were wide and frightened.

Ruby shrugged again. "Don't mess around playing private detective and wasting my time. Take it to the cops."

Kippen nodded. Amie bit her bottom lip.

Ellen placed her cookie on the small plate in front of her, then she carefully dusted her fingers with a starched linen napkin. "The information is sensitive. It concerns Howard Stoke." She glanced up as she finished, adding emphasis to the name.

The reaction was immediate. Ruby stiffened, though her expression didn't change, Shelley's eyebrows rose toward her hairline, and Amie's shoulders hunched as she bowed her head to look fixedly at the table.

"Howard Stoke, the building inspector? You think he killed Clayton Green?" Shelley asked. She sounded amazed and her expression as she reached for a cookie, was intrigued.

"No." Ellen deliberately paused to take a sip of coffee before she said, "The evidence we have suggests that Clayton was forcing women to have sex with Stoke. The sexual favors were a bribe to ensure Stoke okayed each phase of construction on FGC projects in a quick and expeditious manner."

There was a little gasp of dismay from Amie. Ruby's mouth hardened into a grim line. Kippen's eyes widened and she dropped her cookie.

When Ellen glanced her way, Christy nodded. They'd hit pay dirt.

Looking back at the women, Ellen drew a deep breath. When she spoke, her tone was gentle, but her words were relentless. "We believe one of the suites in the Seymour View was used by Howard Stoke for his liaisons. He was in the building at the time Clayton was killed." She paused to give this time to sink in. Then she said firmly, "Each one of you was in the building as well. Which one of you was with Stoke?"

There was a choked off sob from Amie that drew all eyes. She was now hunched inward on herself, her hands crossed defensively over her chest. Her head was down, her hair falling forward to shield her face.

Poor kid. What scum this guy Green must have been. And don't get me started on this Howard Stoke. We need to take him down. The cat jumped lightly from his chair onto the conference table, prowling over to Amie. He nudged her hands with his head and rubbed his cheek against her. When she cautiously lifted one hand to stroke him, he started to purr.

"Amie?" Ruby said. She was frowning, her expression horrified.

Shelley blinked with surprise at the sudden appearance of the cat, but she turned to Ruby and said, "Did you have something to do with this? Is that why you always check the appointments to view the display suites the night before? Were you making the arrangements for Clayton?"

Ruby paled. Her gaze skittered away from Kippen's. "He insisted."

"That's why you were so angry with me the day he died. I didn't pre-book Ms. Jamieson's visit for that morning. Were you afraid we'd catch Stoke in the act?"

"Stoke was in one of the smaller suites on another floor." Ruby had turned away, avoiding Shelley's indignant expression, and looking anywhere but at Amie, whose shoulders were now shaking with silent sobs.

Shelley demanded, "Did you kill him?"

"No!" Ruby closed her eyes as she drew a deep breath. When she opened them again, she said more calmly, "No."

"Then why were you in the building?" Ellen asked. Christy could hear a tart disapproval in her tone. She wondered if the others could hear it too.

Ruby's jaw hardened. "I went to make sure the suite was unlocked and ready for Howard's use. That was it."

"Did you see or speak to Clayton?" Ellen asked.

Ruby shook her head. She looked both aghast and unrepentant at the same time. Expediency battling with ethics, perhaps. "I texted him to let him know there'd be a viewing at eleven, but we didn't meet."

That fit with the evidence from the security camera and the staff greeter on duty at the doors. Ruby had entered the building at nine forty-five and exited at ten o'clock.

"I feel so betrayed!" Kippen moaned.

"Oh, for heaven's sake," Ruby muttered.

"You were once one of Stoke's women." Ellen said to Ruby. She made it a statement. "That's how you got your business going."

Ruby set her jaw, and something flashed in her eyes. For a moment it looked as if she wouldn't reply, then she said, "As Clay's company expanded and the number of projects he developed grew, I could see the potential. I knew he'd continue to be successful, and I wanted his account badly. He promised to give me exclusive sales rights for a little favor." She paused, made a disgusted sound in her throat. "A little favor. Yeah, right.

He made it sound so innocuous. How was I to know what I'd have to do and that it would bind me to him forever?"

"Did he..." There was a quaver in Amie's voice, and she sniffled, but her head was up as she spoke. One hand wiped away tears, the other stroked the cat, whose purr was a loud rumble. He'd flopped over onto his side to provide her with access to his belly, and to show his approval of her continued petting.

Amie cleared her throat and tried again. "Did you have to...submit to Howard too?"

Ruby's eyes locked with hers. There was regret in their depths. Slowly, she nodded. "Yes. For almost a year. Then he got bored and wanted someone new. I thought that was the end of it, but Clayton had other ideas." She stopped. Sighed. "Clayton recruited the new woman, but he told me to make the arrangements for the meetings. Because, he said, Howard knew and trusted me."

"Oh, my," Shelley whispered. "Did you...Did you always use display suites?"

Another sigh from Ruby, then a nod. "If they were available."

"They didn't have to be in Clayton's buildings, did they, Ruby?" Ellen's tone was gentle.

Ruby lowered her head. She rubbed her forehead with her fingertips before she looked up. "No. Once I started my own agency, I had other clients as well as Clayton. I specialized in luxury accommodations and most of them were new builds. I could provide anonymous spaces for the meetings. My involvement gave Clayton deniability. It was a brilliant scheme."

It was sick. Stormy rolled on to his back, all four legs sticking up in the air, still purring madly. Amie managed a watery chuckle.

Ruby said urgently, "Amie, though I organized meeting places, I never knew the women Clayton had recruited. I never suspected you were involved. I am so very sorry."

"What would you have done if you'd known?" Amie sounded more curious than condemning. She stared at Ruby, absently continuing to pat the blissfully purring cat.

Ruby tightened her mouth, looked down, then slid a glance at Miss

Kippen, before returning her gaze to Amie. "I would have told him to back off, the way I did for Shelley."

Ellen's eyes widened. Christy felt her mouth open then form into a silent, "Wow."

Miss Kippen's jaw dropped, then she squeaked, "What? Me?"

Ruby pursed her lips. "Yeah. Howard requested you. It was just after you started. I said no. Clayton pushed and I told him that if he ever approached you for Howard, or if he even tried to get you to sleep with him, I'd expose the whole awful scheme. It would be the end of me, but it would also be the end of him. He saw sense and left you alone."

"Oh, dear." Kippen sounded absolutely devastated. "Oh, my; oh, my; oh, my."

Stormy lazily rolled onto his feet. He sauntered over to Ruby and nudged her hand, which was resting on the table, clenched into a fist.

Ruby looked at Ellen. "Your cat thinks I need comforting."

Ellen raised her eyebrows and said gently, "Perhaps he's right."

Ruby shook her head. "I made my peace long ago. Go help Shelley, cat. She needs you more than I do."

Stormy stared at her for a moment, green eyes unblinking, then he licked the knuckles of Ruby's clenched fist. She uttered a choked laugh. After a final lick, he strutted over to Shelley. When he rubbed against her, she stopped her upset murmurs, sighed, and began to stroke him.

"Amie, the security camera shows you arriving around the same time Ruby did, then leaving at ten eighteen. Were you with Stoke all that time? Did you see or speak to Clayton?" Ellen kept her tone gentle, her gaze level as she spoke. Amie had recovered some of her composure, but her emotions were still raw and on the surface.

She bit her lip as she shook her head. "I didn't even know Clayton was in the building. I was there to be with Howard. I went up in the elevator to the suite. I reached it before he did. He came in. We...well, we did it. When I left, he was lying on the bed, smoking a cigarette."

Ug. What a jerk.

Ellen nodded. "The security camera shows him leaving at ten thirty."

Christy and Ellen exchanged glances. Ellen nodded. Christy said,

"Ruby, Amie, I'm sorry. I need to take this information to Detective Patterson."

Amie stifled another sob. "Do you have to?"

Christy sighed. "I'm afraid so. Not only should Howard Stoke be punished for what he's done, but it gives the case a whole new direction. Clayton has been doing this for many years. That means in addition to you and Ruby, he's forced a half a dozen women or more into this horrible situation. Any one of them could be angry enough to want revenge. Patterson has to be told."

Ruby's eyes flashed. "Do what you must. I won't admit to anything."

At nine o'clock on an overcast spring morning, Christy drove her van into the virtually empty parking lot at Burnaby Mountain Park. Fifteen minutes earlier she'd dropped Noelle at school and when she'd finished her meeting with Patterson here in the park, she'd be on her way downtown to the Jamieson Trust office.

Located on the top of Burnaby Mountain, the park provided spectacular views of the city of Vancouver, but its chief claim to fame was the long slope that rose from the entry road past the parking area. During the winter, when the occasional snowfall turned the Lower Mainland into a white fluffy playground, the park's hillside was perfect for sledding. Neighborhood kids loved it. Neighborhood parents loved it too, and the place was packed with screaming, laughing people.

At this hour on a spring morning the slope was just an attractive hillside greening up with new grass. Christy parked beside the only other car in the lot and climbed out of her van. There was still a chill in the air, making her glad she was wearing a cream-colored overcoat designed to both repel rain and provide warmth over the skirt suit she'd dressed in for work.

Patterson emerged from her vehicle and came round so that they were facing each other. "You said on the phone you have some information for me."

Christy nodded. "It was Quinn who discovered the first clue. Ellen and I followed up. I'll start with his information."

Patterson nodded. Leaning back against the car, she crossed her arms over her chest. Her expression was impassive.

Despite her unenthusiastic reaction, Christy pressed on. She told her about Quinn's interview with Harvey Wrenn and his unexpected disclosure of Clayton Green's bribery scheme.

At that Patterson raised her brows, but she didn't comment. Christy plowed on, describing the meeting she and Ellen had had with the three women in much more detail. She finished up, saying, "After Ruby said she wouldn't talk to you, Amie had a good cry, then she decided she didn't want to talk about it either."

Patterson mulled over the information for a minute, then she sighed. "If what you're saying is true, and I believe it is, I'd love to nail this Stoke guy, but.... Mrs. Jamieson, everything you've brought me is hearsay. All of it, from Harvey Wrenn claiming he didn't know anything about it until after Green was dead, to your disclosure of the details, because the victims themselves are not willing to press charges."

"But doesn't this widen the suspect pool in Green's death? He'd been forcing women into this odious situation for years. There must be many more than just Ruby and Amie. Maybe one of them killed Green."

Patterson shook her head. "There's no evidence from the security camera of unknown females entering the building around the time of death."

"Are there no women working on the construction crew, then?" Christy asked. She could feel momentum slipping away and there was a hint of desperation in her voice.

Patterson looked thoughtful. "Good point. We'll take a closer look at the crew."

Relieved, Christy pressed her point. "And what about husbands or fathers or brothers? If one of them found out that a woman he loved was being victimized this way, don't you think he'd want revenge?"

Patterson swore softly. She glared at Christy. "You know, Mrs. Jamieson, you're a pain in the ass."

Christy laughed. Then she sobered. "I want Howard Stoke to pay for his part in Green's nasty scheme, but I also don't believe Jodie is Green's killer. Maybe one can prove the other."

Patterson shook her head. "Don't get your hopes up. All the evidence indicates this was a woman's crime. A male family member is probably not the killer. I'll go back to the beginning, though, and investigate everyone who was in the building, from the crew to the visitors. I'll speak to Amie Foran and Ruby Cronin. It's possible one of them will open up. If they do, I'll have more chance of getting Stoke to own up."

"We're not going to give up on Jodie, Detective. We'll keep digging into Clayton Green and the people around him. I'm sure the answer is there somewhere."

Patterson's lips twitched into something that was almost a smile, then she shrugged, somber once more. "Knock yourself out, Mrs. Jamieson. I'm quite aware there's nothing I can do to stop you. But be careful." She hesitated. "Let Armstrong take the lead. He's a reporter. He knows how to handle himself. These people are...." She shrugged again.

"Nasty," Christy said. "I understand. We're all being careful."

Patterson sighed, shook her head.

Christy had the sense that she didn't really believe that anything Christy's little group did would be described as careful by the average person. She grinned.

Patterson raised her eyebrows and that tiny smile crept into life again. "Good luck."

CHAPTER 24

T he sun was a vivid orange ball, slowly setting behind the misty blue shadows that were the mountainous spine of Vancouver Island. The day's clear cerulean blue sky was slowly graying into darkness, and a few wispy cirrus clouds were softening the setting sun's salmon tints into pinks and paler yellows.

On the Strait of Georgia, between Vancouver Island and the city of Vancouver, the ocean sparkled in the last vestige of a beautiful West Coast spring day.

Quinn stood on Sledge's massive deck, staring across the ocean to the land beyond. There were times—like now—when he envied Sledge his architecturally brilliant home and it's gorgeous location, but for the most part he was content with his lot. If he and his father lived in this huge house, Roy would rattle around in one part of it, while he was in another entirely. They'd probably never see each other. While there were days when he had to grit his teeth not to snap when his father went on one of his off-the-wall tangents, for the most part they got on well together. He'd spent years as a foreign correspondent, living out of a suitcase or a backpack, sometimes with a crew, but mostly on his own. He found that now he appreciated companionship.

The truth was, he was ready to be part of a family. The desire to rove the world looking for stories had died a bitter death not long before he'd met Christy. Since she'd come into his life, he'd discovered that staying put wasn't the hardship he'd once imagined it would be.

Sledge wandered out onto his deck. Like Quinn he was dressed in jeans and a sweatshirt. In his hands were two bottles of beer. He passed one to Quinn, then took a deep swallow from the other.

"Thanks," Quinn said, raising the bottle in a toast.

Sledge nodded, then leaned his hip against the railing and, like Quinn, stared out over the ocean to the sunset.

When Quinn had arrived a couple of hours earlier in response to an urgent request for company, Sledge had been wound up tight, tension vibrating around him. Gradually he'd admitted the cause—work. What else, Quinn thought, consuming another slug of beer. For Sledge, work included the overwrought emotions of the finalists in the music competition show, as well as the pressures and difficulties around interviewing, then choosing, new management for SledgeHammer.

So, they'd ordered in more food than they could possibly eat from Sledge's favorite Thai restaurant and slowly, as they ate and drank, Sledge had decompressed.

Now, as he stood staring at the incomparable view, he said with a sigh, "My life is going to change one hundred percent."

"Really? I'd expect your career to be more focused with a new agent, but one hundred percent? I don't see it."

"I'm going to become a corporation. No more musician." The gloom in Sledge's voice was evident. It sounded as if he'd just lost a cherished family member.

Still holding his bottle, Quinn rested it on the top of the rail, then half turned his body so he could look at his friend square on. "Become a corporation? I thought you and Hammer registered SledgeHammer as a business a long time ago. What are you talking about?"

Sledge sighed. Sipped some beer. Stared out at the dying sun. "I told you earlier that we chose the US company with the new Canadian branch to rep us, right?"

Quinn nodded.

"Well, we had our first full-on strategy session today. God, what a pile-on. The head guy flew in from New York. The CEO of the Canadian branch, a woman named Justina Strong, who will also be our agent, came in from Toronto. Her SledgeHammer assistant came with her. He's relocating to Vancouver, since Hammer and I don't intend to move to Toronto—despite their none-too-gently made suggestions that we do so. The band's new PR assistant who will travel with us, was invited. The SledgeHammer dogsbody—"

Sledge stopped. His mouth twisted. After a moment he laughed, without much humor. "Her official title is 'band assistant.' I call her the dogsbody because, apparently, she does whatever needs to be done to move obstacles out of our way. Got a parking ticket? She'll organize payment. Need your laundry cleaned? Just tell her and she'll sort it."

Quinn raised his brows. "The kind of stuff you need done while you're on tour."

Sledge drank more beer. "Sort of, except it's permanent. A telephone call away, twenty-four seven. She too will be relocating to Vancouver."

Quinn was beginning to see where Sledge's stress was coming from. He was surrendering his privacy in a way that was different from the loss that came from his stardom. His life was being pushed, step-by-step, from one he controlled to one that controlled him. Sledge was an independent guy. The transformation wouldn't be easy.

There was a moment of quiet while Sledge drank more beer. Finally, his voice heavy, he said, "And I got to meet my very own manager whose job is to guide my personal career beyond SledgeHammer, beyond the TV show, into...God knows what. I sure don't. She seems to have a lot of ideas, though. Endorsements, commercials, maybe a TV series, perhaps movies." Contempt, perhaps even suppressed panic, laced his voice. "Me. On a TV show. Can you believe it?"

Quinn laughed. "You already are."

Caught at the onset of what promised to be a spiraling rant, Sledge cast Quinn a quick look, then drew a deep breath. He shook his head. "Yeah, you're right. I'm overreacting."

"One step at a time. Who knows? Maybe you'll like being a movie star." Quinn lifted his hand, moving it as if he was outlining a theater marquee. "I can see it now, your name in lights. Sledge of SledgeHammer, starring in *Super Singer, Savior of Guitarland*, an action flick for music nerds."

He laughed as Sledge punched him in the shoulder and said, "Jerk."

They contemplated the thought of Sledge as a matinee idol for a minute, then Sledge said wistfully, "I wouldn't mind being an action hero. Maybe I'll mention it to my busy little bee."

"Decide which one you want to be first. Then tell her. Let her figure out how to manage it. Or even if it can be done."

"Take control," Sledge murmured, brightening. "I like that. Good plan."

They tossed around ideas for action roles for a time, until the discussion dissolved into silliness. By then, the worst of Sledge's tension was gone and he was back to his relaxed, rather swashbuckling self.

"Kim is giving a party to introduce our new management to the world. Mitch and the CEO had a guest list a mile long." He laughed. "Kim shook her head when she saw it and said she'd have to find some leavening for all this dough. Expect an invitation."

Quinn nodded. Kim was Kim Crosier, the wife of the music exec who had masterminded SledgeHammer's new management. Beautiful and eccentric, she had latched on to his flaky father and a talking cat after their first meeting at a SledgeHammer concert. Quinn wasn't surprised Kim would see the Armstrongs and the Jamiesons as a fun addition to a serious event.

Fluffy clouds had drifted close to the setting sun, now half hidden behind the shadowed mountains. The vivid pinks and moody mauves intensified. There was something about the beauty of the waning day that Quinn found incredibly peaceful. It grounded him, he thought. Along with the lazy back and forth with Sledge, it allowed his mind to work on the big problem facing him—the murder and his cousin Jodie's arrest. Sledge had heard the bare bones of the case a couple of weeks ago. Now that his search for new management had concluded, perhaps he'd like to get more involved. He might not have time to do any sleuthing, but he was an out-of-the-box thinker, a good person to bounce ideas off.

Quinn laid out what they knew so far, concluding with, "So that's it. Patterson told Christy that she couldn't do much against Stoke unless one or both women provided the information to her directly. She's going to question him as part of the murder investigation, but she's not optimistic about the results. Jodie remains her chief suspect."

"What a slime ball," Sledge said, then he grinned. "Maybe we should find a way to put him and the cat together. I bet Frank could get him to talk."

Quinn laughed. "From what Christy said, Frank would be delighted." He paused, took a swig of beer, then said, "I'm not sure, though, that Stoke and his perversion isn't a rabbit hole."

Sledge raised his brows. "How so?"

"It provides a motive for Ruby Cronin and Amie Foran. The thing is, between what they told Christy and Ellen, and the timing provided by the security camera, I don't think they're any more guilty than Jodie is. I think the killer is a man."

"Didn't you say Patterson is convinced this is a woman's crime?"

Quinn nodded. "Green was shot twice, once through the heart, the other time an angled shot that tore off half his face. They also found bullets embedded in the walls, and one broke a mirror. According to Patterson, the pattern is that of someone not used to handling a gun, who is frightened, upset, and in the throes of a passionate anger."

Sledge rubbed the lip of his bottle down his cheek as he considered this. "Someone who shot off every bullet in the clip and got lucky twice."

Quinn nodded. "Yeah. A woman who came armed to a confrontation with a man who has abused her. A woman who wants closure, but who hasn't thought all the details through."

"Like what a gun feels like when you fire it, how to aim, that kind of stuff."

"Exactly."

"Have they found the weapon?"

Quinn shook his head. "No. From the caliber of the bullets, they assume it's a small, light handgun, the kind of weapon a woman might use."

"Added fuel for Patterson's theory," Sledge said thoughtfully.

"Yes, but a man who wanted to implicate a woman could use the same kind of gun a woman would. It might not be his weapon of choice if he was target shooting, but there's no gender lock on guns. Anyone can use them, no matter what the shape or size. And who's to say that only a woman would be rattled once she started firing? A man who's never used a gun might be just as shook up and end up shooting erratically until he achieved his purpose."

Sledge rubbed his chin thoughtfully. "Okay. So, wash out the crime scene details and look at motive. What do you know about this guy Wrenn, the one who sent you down the rabbit hole?"

"On the surface he's clean." Quinn had checked everyone involved. "His title is vp Management Processes, which seems to be a junk drawer position for anything Green wanted him to do. Mainly, he was Green's personal advisor and ran interference between him and the rest of the company, and the world, as well."

"He would have known about the arrangement with Stoke, then." Sledge raised his brows when Quinn sent him a frowning glance.

"He claims he didn't, until recently," Quinn said, remembering the interview. "Okay. Let's say you're right and he found out about it years ago—or he knew about it from the beginning. Do you think Wrenn is the murderer?"

Sledge contemplated that, then shook his head. His expression was disappointed. "Probably not. Unless it's the heat of the moment, it takes a lot to make a person kill. There doesn't seem to be a lot of intensity in Wrenn's feelings about the bribery scheme. Why murder Green now?"

Quinn nodded gloomily. "And Wrenn wasn't in the building. We know because the camera doesn't record him entering or leaving for that matter."

Sledge laughed. "Forget the camera evidence. Isn't there a large construction crew coming and going?"

Quinn nodded.

"I've been dodging cameras for years. There are ways you can walk into a building and not leave evidence you've been there." Sledge said. "Put Wrenn in jeans and a rough shirt and you've already started the process, because he's expected to be wearing a suit. Add a hard hat pulled low over his forehead to make parts of his face hard to see. If he looked down at his phone as he passed the camera or walked beside and behind someone so he was in shadow, it gets even harder. Trust me, the guy could've entered the building before the security guard arrived and you'd never know unless you checked carefully."

Thinking furiously, Quinn said, "Wrenn isn't the only one who could have done that."

"Nope," Sledge said. He finished his beer and put the bottle on the deck, then leaned against the railing. "So, who are the other guys on the suspect list?"

"Lloyd Webster, maybe Jeff Darling, Eugene Sawatzky in a pinch."

"What about this guy who works for Dunnville Investments and who is so anxious to get the new project up and running?"

"Ethan Byrne?" Quinn rubbed his chin thoughtfully. "I suppose he should be on the list, but his involvement is minor. I don't see why he'd want to kill Green."

"You have to dig deeper into Byrne—into all of them." Sledge grinned at him. "Looks like you've got your work cut out for you."

Quinn nodded slowly. "Yeah, I guess I do."

CHAPTER 25

Quinn had been late coming home the previous evening. He'd gone out in the afternoon, muttering something about Sledge and his new management and hadn't returned until after midnight. By that time Roy had been in bed. It wasn't often that he retired so early, but that afternoon he'd finished a rough draft of his current work in progress, and he was at loose ends.

He'd had dinner, then researched Howard Stoke, Clayton Green, Ruby Cronin, and Amie Foran. He hadn't discovered much and had decided their little detection group knew far more about each of the individuals than the Internet did. Frustrated, he went to bed and had nightmares about Jodie being hung for the murder of Clayton Green.

He woke up at eight o'clock, sweating, the dream still vivid in his mind. Why he'd dreamed she paid the ultimate price for a crime he didn't believe she committed, he didn't know. The death penalty had been abolished in Canada years ago. Jodie might serve a long prison term, but she wouldn't be executed.

He got dressed and went down to the kitchen, grumpy. He needed his morning coffee.

Quinn was already there, holding a mug, and looking way too wide-awake for eight-thirty in the morning.

"Morning, Dad. I've invited Trevor, Ellen, and Christy over for nine-thirty. I think we need to do another information sharing."

Quinn had made a pot of coffee. That was good because Roy needed a cup to jump-start his brain. "I have nothing to add to the information pool," he said, feeling gloomy. "I researched all the main players last night and got nowhere." Maybe that was why his subconscious had sent him to a dark, frightening place he didn't want to visit.

"Interesting," Quinn said. "What sources did you use?"

They talked about what sites Roy had gone to and what he'd found on them while he finished his coffee and poured himself another. When the doorbell rang he went down to greet their guests while Quinn made another pot of coffee.

It was Christy, Ellen, and the cat at the door, and Christy was holding a white box stamped with the name of a bakery in a nearby mall. She handed him the box with a smile, he thanked her, and they all trooped up to the kitchen. When Trevor arrived a few minutes later, the pastries were on a plate on the table and Quinn was pouring coffee for each of them.

He handed a cup to Ellen, who thanked him as she accepted it, then she carefully put the cup on to the table and patted her leather binder. "Shall we begin?"

They all nodded.

"Who wants to start?" Ellen asked, looking around at each of them.

The telephone rang.

Roy, who was closest, reached over to grab the handset. That was his first mistake. His second was to say, "Hello?"

"Do you hear that?" the voice on the other end shouted without taking the time to identify himself.

He didn't have to, of course. Roy knew exactly who he was talking to. He held the phone away from his ear, then pressed the speaker button so the rest could hear.

"She's here! On my front porch. She's rung the bell a dozen times! Now she's pounding on the door and shouting. You have to do something. She's your sister-in-law!"

The almost hysterical speaker was Lloyd Webster. "She" must be

197

Evelyn Crowther, Jodie's mother, recently arrived from Whitehorse. The group listened with varying degrees of surprise, amusement, or disapproval while Roy negotiated with Lloyd.

"She's your mother-in-law," he said. "You deal with her."

"She hates me! She's outraged I won't let Jodie use the house as collateral. God. She just shouted that she knows I'm in here and she won't stop until I let her in. What will the neighbors think?"

"That your mother-in-law is standing on your front porch, and you won't invite her into your house. Lloyd, you're going to have to open your door sometime. Do it now before one of your neighbors gets tired of listening to a domestic dispute and calls the cops to break it up."

Lloyd groaned. "Oh God. If the police come, so will the press. I'll be all over the evening news. The kids will be embarrassed. I'll be labeled a cuckold again. I'll lose more donors."

"Enough," Roy snapped. He was tired of Lloyd's whining. He wanted to get back to the much more interesting activity of dissecting data and building scenarios. "You may not like Evelyn, and you may be mad at Jodie, but the kids love them both. Let Evelyn in, then act like a civilized adult about her visit. When she gets Jodie out of jail—and she will, because she's Evelyn and she always gets what she sets her mind to— accept Jodie back home and treat her like she's your wife and she's important to your family."

There was a long fulminating pause. "Fine." The call was disconnected. In the old days, Lloyd could have slammed the receiver into its holder, resulting in a satisfying crash at his end and an earful of sound at Roy's. Now, to show his displeasure he was reduced to an abrupt departure and poking the disconnect button on his cell phone with more energy than was necessary. As he too disconnected, Roy thought there were some benefits to modern technology.

I'd like to meet Evelyn. She sounds like fun. The cat was sitting on Christy's lap, his head just poking over the top of the table.

"You probably will." Roy eyed the cat. "I wonder if she'll be able to hear you?"

"Is the cat talking about Aunt Evelyn?" Quinn pulled a cinnamon bun apart into bite-sized pieces.

"Frank thinks Evelyn would be fun to know," Christy said.

Quinn grinned. "She is. She likes honesty and straight shooters, she says whatever comes to mind in the bluntest possible way, and she pursues her goals with a single-mindedness that's scary. She's got a great sense of humor, though, and she's willing to try anything."

Quinn was right about Evelyn—and not, Roy thought as he inspected the plate trying to decide which of the breakfast pastries to choose. She liked him, so she showed him her best side. Roy knew she was also possessive and that drive to succeed could leave damaged people in her wake. Lloyd was probably going to be one of them. He mulled that over and found he didn't mind. The man deserved what he was going to get.

"Good to know," Trevor said. "I believe the office gave her my cell number, so I expect her to contact me about how we can ensure Jodie is released."

"Maybe, maybe not," Roy said. "Evelyn works in mysterious ways."

Trevor sent him a long look which Roy ignored as he discovered a blueberry Danish in the collection.

"She should contact me before she does anything," Trevor said firmly. "I'm Jodie's lawyer. We need to work together as a team."

Roy placed the Danish on his plate, then narrowed his eyes at his old friend. "Sounds like you're expecting me to intervene."

Trevor gave him back a bland expression. "If needs must."

No need! Go to Lloyd's house to talk to her. I'll come with you. I can control Lloyd. And maybe Evelyn will hear me too! The cat put his front paws up on the table. His green eyes were bright. *Let's do it now!*

Trevor, who'd never been on an excursion with Frank and the cat, opened his eyes wide. His expression was startled. "That would hardly be professional. And the woman just arrived in Vancouver. Give her a chance to settle in. I'll meet her downtown at the police station tomorrow."

Privately, Roy thought that by tomorrow Evelyn would have annoyed the mayor, sweet-talked the chief of police, and secured a meeting with the provincial premier. Lloyd would have acquiesced in using the house as collateral and Jodie would be out on bail. He decided he'd let Trevor find this out on his own.

"To that end," Trevor said, bringing Roy's attention back to the meeting. "I need to know where we are with the case so we can figure out our next steps. Who would like to start?"

Ellen opened her leather portfolio and drew out a fresh piece of letterhead. She uncapped a pen, smiled at Trevor, and said, "Ready."

He smiled back in a rather goofy way. Roy mentally shook his head.

"I will," Christy said. She ran down what she and Ellen had learned, and Patterson's reaction to their information. "Patterson is convinced the killer is a woman, but if we eliminate Ruby and Amie, as well as Jodie, that leaves Portia Quance, Shelley Kippen, or someone unknown."

"Miss Kippen?" Ellen sounded surprised. "But Ruby protected her. She didn't even know about the bribery scheme."

"The security data shows her arriving in the building at ten forty-five. She entered the elevator, supposedly to make sure the suite was unlocked and ready to view, but what if she found Green there and shot him."

"That sounds highly unlikely. Why would she do that? What would her motive be?" Ellen was frowning. Roy thought she liked the realtor more than she let on.

"That's where the theory falls apart. Perhaps even though Ruby called him off, Green recruited her anyway? Perhaps she lied to us, and she knew about the scheme all along." Christy shrugged. "Because of her presence in the building she's more likely than Portia Quance. But if we eliminate those two, that puts Jodie back at the top of the suspect list."

"What if it wasn't a woman but a man?" Quinn looked around the table. Ellen raised her brows and Christy frowned. Trevor looked interested.

Roy liked the idea too. It was counterintuitive, the kind of outside of the box thinking that appealed to him. It led to some of his best plotting.

He'd raised his boy well.

He wiggled his fingers in a 'give' motion. Quinn grinned.

Christy said, "Patterson agreed to consider the male crew members when she reviewed the security tapes, but Quinn, they believe the crime scene evidence indicates it was a woman who did the shooting."

Quinn nodded. "They don't have the gun, though, so they don't have fingerprints to support that theory or to provide evidence against any one suspect."

"The caliber of the bullets is that of a small pocket pistol. The fire pattern was erratic. They'll argue the pistol is a woman's weapon and an inconsistent trajectory is a woman's emotional reaction to a threat," Trevor said. He was watching Quinn with great intensity. He'd put the opposition's argument on the table. He waited for Quinn to demolish it.

Quinn did. "Guns are not sex specific. Sure, a man might prefer a bigger weapon with more firepower, but what if a man wants to cover his actions and figures the cops will never look at him if he uses a small handgun? And who's to say women are the only ones subject to nerves and fright when they're trying to kill someone?"

Trevor smiled, a faint, almost predatory expression that included narrowed eyes. "Who's the man, or men, you're thinking of?"

"If it wasn't a crew member whose motives we're unaware of, then I'd look at Howard Stoke, Harvey Wrenn, or Ethan Byrne."

Trevor's expression turned thoughtful. "Not Jeff Darling or Eugene Sawatzky?"

Quinn shook his head. "Eugene disliked Green but had no motive. Jeff Darling seemed to be one of his supporters. Again, no motive."

Ellen paused in her note taking. "Neither of those men was in the building. For that matter, neither was Harvey or Ethan Byrne."

Quinn nodded. His lips were curved in a half-smile that was a duplicate of Trevor's. "None of them walked into the building wearing their normal clothing, talked to security, or looked up at the camera, identifying themselves. But what if they entered wearing a disguise?" He outlined Sledge's experience of avoiding surveillance cameras and security guards. "At seven-thirty, the start of the work day, the killer walks onto the job site with the rest of the crew, then leaves with them at the mid-morning break at ten-thirty. The gun is small and light, easy to hide in a pocket. He walks out of the building, but instead of visiting the local coffee shop, he heads off on his own. Maybe he goes down to the waterfront, which isn't far away from the Seymour View, tosses the gun into the harbor, then turns around and disappears. Or perhaps he walks away from the job site to a Skytrain station and disappears. He then disposes of the gun in a dumpster far away from the crime scene."

Roy liked both ideas. He could work with them. "Skytrain stations have surveillance cameras."

Quinn nodded. "But if no one is looking, he'll never be found. If we uncover the culprit, Patterson might be able to track him, but will she look if we don't?"

Trevor shook his head. "No. When we gave her Stoke and the bribery scheme, she had to investigate it. For a long shot possibility like this, when their forensics point in an entirely different direction? The cops have made their arrest. The case is closed. The brass will never approve the money or manpower a quest like this would take."

Sounds like a task for Evelyn.

Roy laughed and the others smiled. Quinn raised his brows, then shook his head as Roy explained.

"It would keep her busy, at least," Trevor said. He focused on Quinn. "Do you have motives for any of these men?"

Quinn shook his head. "No. That's the weakness in my theory. There's also the problem of what the killer did from seven-thirty to ten-fifteen. That's nearly three hours and there are a lot of people working in that building. He could wander around, pretending to look busy for a while, but for three hours? He must have had a bolt-hole. Which means he knew the building."

"That's why you don't suspect Jeff Darling or Eugene Sawatzky," Christy said.

He nodded. "Byrne and Wrenn have visited the site many times. Either one of them could have snuck in, hidden away until Jodie was in the elevator on her way out, then intercepted Green before he left the suite. Howard Stoke was already in the building. Amie left him at ten-fifteen so he had time to do it as well."

"Why would Harvey want to kill Clayton?" Ellen shook her head. "They worked well together. I never once saw a sign of conflict between them."

Suspicious.

"I have to agree with Frank," Roy said, after he'd relayed the cat's comment to Quinn. "No one who works closely with someone else is always in harmony. Maybe there's a reason there was no conflict."

"What are you thinking, Dad?"

Roy shrugged. "Green liked to manipulate people. He didn't mind who he hurt. Maybe Wrenn had a secret. Maybe Green knew it and used it."

"Are you suggesting he was bribing Wrenn the same way he bribed Howard Stoke?" Ellen sounded shocked. "Neither Ruby nor Amie gave any indication Harvey was involved."

Roy shook his head. "Nope. People have lots of different kinds of secrets. Wrenn might have cheated on his taxes. Or could be he has a record and changed his name to hide it. What if he did something stupid when he was in university and blabbed about it on social media, then covered it up and thought it over and done with? Who knows? All that would matter was that he was ashamed of something, and Green took advantage of it."

"The same would go for Ethan Byrne," Trevor said. He raised his brows and dipped his head. "All right. Let's find out what Harvey Wrenn and Ethan Byrne are hiding."

CHAPTER 26

Quinn decided he'd investigate Harvey Wrenn first.

On the surface, Green's VP of Management Processes had lived—and currently lived—a boring life. He graduated from high school with a solid B plus average, which got him into a regional university in the BC interior, rather than one of the province's more prestigious institutions. He'd enrolled in business, graduated with another solid B plus, and got a job at a local property development company as a junior manager.

Two years later, he married his long-time girlfriend who he'd met at university. She was a local girl who was a teacher at an elementary school in the town where she'd grown up, perhaps the reason he'd looked for work in the area. Three years later, for no apparent reason, the marriage broke down and they divorced. With no kids involved and both individuals gainfully employed, they simply split their joint assets and moved on.

Literally, in Wrenn's case. He left the Interior and turned up in Vancouver working for FGC. He began as Clayton Green's executive assistant. Several years later he achieved his current position as VP of Management Processes. As far as Quinn could see, the two jobs amounted to the same thing. Just the title was different.

Two years into working for Green, he bought an angular BC modern bungalow that featured lots of glass and natural wood siding in Delta, not far from the FGC offices.

Since relocating to Vancouver, he'd had several medium length relationships that never progressed to marriage. Each had fizzled out, rather than ending with an emotional bang. He wasn't currently dating anyone, but, interestingly, one of those pleasant, work-a-day relationships that withered away had been with Ruby Cronin.

That had Quinn sitting back and wondering. Thanks to Christy and Ellen, they knew that Ruby was one of Green's victims. Could Wrenn have been involved in Green's insidious bribery schemes? Quinn shook his head as he stared at the computer screen. Why would Green feel the need to bribe his executive assistant?

From what he'd found, Wrenn's relationship with Ruby had been up front. There were even pictures of the two of them on the man's Facebook page. For contrast, everything about the Howard Stoke-Amie Foran affair had been clandestine. Stoke was married, with a family. He needed to keep the relationship a secret. Wrenn didn't. He was single, Ruby was single. They probably met at a business seminar or someone's party and hit it off. There was no reason for Green to be involved.

Still, there was something there that nagged at Quinn. He continued to dig, but nothing he found exposed anything improper in Wrenn's relationship with Ruby—or with Clayton Green, for that matter.

Frustrated, Quinn had decided to call it a day when an email from Kim Crosier popped into his in-box. He assumed it would be the invitation Sledge had told him to expect, to the party introducing SledgeHammer's new management to the world. Though this email was an invitation, it was to a different event. Kim had organized an intimate family barbeque on Saturday afternoon at the Crosier mansion in Southlands. The purpose was to introduce those closest to SledgeHammer to the band's new management. Quinn raised his brows at that. Kim never ceased to surprise him. His brows rose further when he noticed the email was also addressed to his father, Trevor, Ellen, and Christy.

The final recipient, noted in the body of the email, was The Cat, because, Kim said, she didn't think he had his own email address.

Quinn groaned out loud and shut down his computer for the night.

The next morning, he rose early so he could walk Christy and Noelle to school.

The day was overcast in preparation—according to the weather station—for a day of spring showers. With the heavy marine cloud layer, the temperature had cooled. Quinn shrugged his leather jacket on over a sweater and jeans, then he walked the short distance from his house to Christy's. He breathed deep, enjoying the scent of rain in the air. Some people found the Lower Mainland's gray, gloomy days hard to deal with, but to thrive in Vancouver you had to enjoy the rainy days as much as the dry sunny ones. Quinn did and as he sat on Christy's porch steps waiting for her and Noelle to emerge, he experienced a sense of well-being that had him smiling.

When the door opened Noelle was pulling her backpack over her shoulders. Like Christy she was wearing jeans and a sweater under a spring jacket. She shot Quinn a cheeky grin as she bounded down the porch stairs, giving him time for a more intimate hello to Christy before they headed out.

Noelle was her usual exuberant self as they walked over to the school. She chattered, she skipped, and generally radiated unending energy. Clearly, the kid must be a morning person. Apparently, part of the exuberance was due to a scheduled afternoon play date with best friend ever Mary Petrofsky, plus new friends Lindsay and Erin. With that to look forward to, the school day became nothing more than a prelude before the main event.

Having delivered Noelle to her classroom, he and Christy took the long way home, going for a walk along the wooded path that wended its way through the greenbelt between the school and the surrounding housing developments. With the kids in classes, it was quiet, a perfect chance for some intimate conversation, including a passionate kiss or two, which they both enjoyed very much. They were almost home when his cell rang.

He looked at the number and frowned. "It's Roberta Green, Clayton Green's wife. I wonder why she's calling." He'd given her his card the day he interviewed her, but he'd expected to be the one contacting her to ask for further information.

"Go ahead," Christy said, nodding at his phone.

He answered.

"I'm glad I caught you, Quinn," Roberta said. "I've been reviewing Clayton's records so I can figure out what I want to do with the company. As I mentioned when we talked, my father began Ferguson Construction, but I was never really involved. He handed it off to Clayton, who made it into a much grander enterprise than my dad ever imagined. I've been considering keeping the firm and taking a more active role, perhaps for sentimental reasons, but only if I think I can be of some value."

She paused and Quinn said, "Sounds sensible." He raised his brows and shook his head at Christy. He had no idea where this was going.

"Yes, well, I've come up with an oddity."

She hesitated again. Quinn prodded gently. "An oddity?"

She sighed. "Clayton was a bit of a Luddite where computers were concerned. Most of the firm's records are computerized, but when Clayton thought something was important, he'd print out a copy and keep that in his personal files. I've found all sorts of documents from contracts to e-mail correspondence that was the equivalent to an old-fashioned handshake deal."

More hesitation. Quinn said, "Oh, yes?" They were at Christy's front porch now and they both sat down on the steps. Christy was on his side that wasn't holding the phone. She leaned against him and put her head on his shoulder. He wrapped his free arm around her waist. While Roberta mulled over what she wanted to tell him next, he thought about how very right Christy felt snuggled against him.

"You see, I found a printed document that didn't have an email to match it. That's what's odd. Clayton would never delete an email, even if he'd printed it out. But there was no evidence of this email in his in-box or in any relevant folders. I even did a search of his whole computer. It isn't there."

Quinn straightened. He thought Roberta might be on to something. "What was the email about?"

Christy sat up, her eyes wide, her gaze watchful as she listened to his side of the conversation.

Roberta drew a deep breath. "Harvey Wrenn. You must understand, Quinn. Harvey is running the company right now. I had been thinking seriously of appointing him the President and CEO. This...this anomaly has made me question that decision."

"I see," Quinn said patiently. "What exactly did the printout say?"

"It was a resignation letter from Harvey, dated five years ago. The wording was quite abrupt, almost angry."

"Can you read it to me?" Quinn angled the phone so Christy could hear.

"Sure. Just let me get my glasses." There was a moment's pause, the rustling of what sounded like papers, then Roberta said, "Okay. Here goes. *Further to our conversation this morning, I will have to resign. The recent situation has made it impossible for me to continue to work in my current capacity. Our conversation has done nothing to smooth over the vast differences in our personal and professional outlooks. I will be leaving the company at the end of business today.*"

"Is there any indication what the situation was that he referred to? Did Clayton make a note on the hard copy by any chance?"

"No, but he did respond to it and that's also been printed out. He said, *You can't resign, Harvey, and you know why. Take a couple of days. Cool down. Be back on Monday with a smile and your best work ethic.* So hostile, don't you think?" Roberta said, interrupting her reading and sounding upset. "He finishes by saying, *You do a good job, Harvey. The company needs you. Don't disappoint me.*"

"Interesting," Quinn said.

"Yes, it is!" The eagerness in Roberta's voice could have come from relief at hearing someone else have the same reaction she did. "Clayton made Harvey a vice president a couple of months after this. I remember particularly because we had a party for him down here at the beach house. An all-day affair, and when Harvey complimented us on the house and its location, Clayton clapped him on the back and said one day Harvey could afford something like this too. I always thought he was referring to the raise in salary a VP position would bring, but Harvey didn't get a raise, just a fancy title."

"Have you spoken to Harvey about this, Roberta?"

"I did, and he made light of it. He told me a headhunter had approached him about a position in Toronto. He said he didn't really want the job—he wasn't interested in relocating and the company was smaller, working on less interesting projects than our company does. He did the interview though and was offered the job. He claimed he went through the process as part of a negotiation strategy. He thought he could use the job offer as leverage to better his position with FGC."

"But his negotiation with your husband turned hostile."

"Yes. The way he tells it, since he had the new job in hand, he decided to move on and wrote the resignation letter."

"It's plausible. Did he explain why Clayton said he couldn't resign? Or what he had to cool off about?"

"He said that was Clayton's way of reminding him how valuable he was to FGC. He said, too, that at the end of a long week, Clayton would always say, *The week's over. Take the weekend to cool off and climb down. Come back Monday focused and ready to do your best.*"

"So, it wasn't out of the ordinary."

"It was to me." Roberta sounded indignant, perhaps annoyed. "It makes Clayton sound cheerful, almost jolly. As if he's a stalwart leader of men, encouraging his troops to continue despite the obstacles put in front of them. But he wasn't that sort of person. He could be charming, yes, but when he was annoyed—and to me he sounds really annoyed, both men do—he snarled and dug in the knife."

"What reads as off to you?"

"That comment about 'come back Monday with a smile'. There's an edge to it that's so typically Clayton. As if he knew Harvey hated the idea of returning but would be coming back because for some reason he had to. A little reminder that Clayton was in charge and Harvey better remember it and behave."

"That's a lot to pack into one sentence," Quinn said, skepticism in his voice.

"Believe me, Clayton could do it. He oozed charm, but there was always a subtext beneath it. Everyone who knew him well, or worked closely with him, was wary of him."

"Yet, Harvey expected you to believe the disagreement was solved by a simple order to cool off and come back to work." Quinn shook his head though Roberta couldn't see it. "Sounds implausible. Did you press him about it? Ask him what the original disagreement was about?"

"Yes, but he didn't give me much more. He said he and Clayton had argued over a project they were working on at the time and it became heated. When he'd calmed down, he realized nothing was gained by fighting over it and they moved on. Then he laughed and said the rift had been mended ages ago."

"It is possible," Quinn said.

She sighed. "I suppose. Still...Clayton kept that printout, even if, for some reason, he deleted the computer record. I don't know why, but until I figure this out, I'm not confirming Harvey as CEO."

Probably a good plan, Quinn thought. "Thanks for bringing this to me, Roberta."

"Of course. Quinn...You'll let me know if anything...odd...turns up about Harvey, won't you?"

"Sure."

"Thank you." She rang off.

Quinn slowly lowered his cell. "That was interesting."

"Do you think Harvey Wrenn deleted the emails after Clayton's death?" Christy asked

"Yeah, I do. But why?"

"Because Clayton had something on Harvey?" Christy suggested.

"Yeah, but what?"

"I don't think Harvey was being bribed with the women, like Howard Stoke was. Neither Ruby nor Amie mentioned him, and I think they would have if Harvey had also been involved."

"What then? Some transgression from his past he was ashamed of? A stint in prison?"

"Could be lots of things," Christy said. She kissed him on the cheek, then stood up. "I have to change before I head off. Talk about it later?"

Quinn nodded and stood too. "Sure." He drew her close and kissed her. This time it wasn't a friendly peck on the cheek good-bye.

CHAPTER 27

S ledge stood in the quiet of what appeared to be Kim Crosier's sewing room. There was a high-tech sewing machine, light years away from the one he remembered his mother having when he was young; swatches of material, fashion magazines featuring dress designs, pins, needles, and other stuff he didn't recognize.

He'd wandered into this room to get out of the way of the caterers Kim had hired for the family barbeque to introduce SledgeHammer's new management to SledgeHammer's extended family.

She'd arranged the party, Sledge knew, because of him. Because she understood he wasn't completely certain they'd made the right decision. That he needed to be sure that Justina Strong, the Canadian CEO of Causton Entertainment and the woman who would be SledgeHammer's new manager, would work alongside SledgeHammer as a partner, not as a boss. Justina was energetic, intelligent, creative, and enthusiastic, but she was also demanding, not to mention forceful. Sledge was self-aware well enough to know that if she pushed too hard, he'd react and not in a positive way.

The purpose of the party was to let him get to know Justina better in a non-business setting. So far, she'd seemed perfectly reasonable. He'd discovered, much to his surprise, that she came from old Toronto money, that she'd attended a private school, and that she was ruthless enough to make use of the contacts she had in that world if it helped her clients' success. She wasn't married and wasn't in a relationship, so no significant other was at the party for him to scrutinize and perhaps discover another side to her. That was too bad, but he'd work with what he had.

He picked his way to the French doors that opened onto the Crosiers' patio, planning to rejoin the party, which was in full swing out in the expansive backyard of the Crosier mansion. It was almost six and the party had begun mid-afternoon. The weather was cooperating with sunshine and a temperature that was warm enough, but not too warm. Servers garbed in black and white mingled among the guests carrying trays of delectable finger foods, while others took drink orders. Guests were happily munching and imbibing as they mingled and got to know each other. Center stage, at the massive barbeque that dominated the Crosier patio, Mitch was cooking hot dogs and hamburgers, which the caterers were turning into gourmet sandwiches.

It was the kind of bizarre twist on a normal everyday barbeque that would appeal to Kim, Sledge thought, as he opened one of the French doors preparing to slip back outside. It was that quirkiness that ensured a Kim Crosier party was never boring. There was an energy, or perhaps it was her innate positivity, that infused every little detail.

He was, he decided, having a good time even though the party was business. And yet it wasn't.

All of Hammer's family were here: his parents, his brother and sister-in-law, his girlfriend Jahlina Vuong—and Jahlina's parents, which was a surprise. When the Vuongs first arrived, they were rather shy and over-whelmed by the big personalities at the party, but Kim took them under her wing and introduced them around, staying with them until they were comfortable. Until they knew they were part of the extended Sledge-Hammer family. Slowly, they'd opened up and blossomed. Now they were chatting with Christy Jamieson underneath a big flowering cherry tree that was in glorious bloom, loaded with pink flowers, and they were all smiling. Jahlina had looked worried when they first arrived, but as her parents began to enjoy themselves, she gradually relaxed. Now she was standing beside Hammer talking to Justina Strong. His arm was around her waist, and she was laughing.

On his side, his father, Trevor, was here, of course. He was standing with Ellen Jamieson, smiling at her in a way that made Sledge drink deep from his bottle of beer. He still wasn't sure how he felt about his father and Ellen Jamieson, but he supposed the old man deserved a chance at happiness after his cancer scare and his abrupt decision to step away from an active involvement in his law firm.

A few minutes ago, Morgan Causton, the owner of Causton Entertainment, had buttonholed Roy Armstrong. Causton, who liked to hear himself talk, was waving his hands around in energetic accompaniment to whatever he was saying. Roy was watching the wine glass in the man's hand go up and down. Sledge grinned. He wondered if Causton was trying to sell Roy some scheme, or if he was talking about himself, trying to impress Roy, the well-known writer, of his importance. Either way, it didn't matter. Roy had probably tuned out of whatever Morgan was saying and was now focused on keeping himself from being drenched in red wine.

A flash of movement near a little glade of trees caught his Sledge's eye. He saw Stormy the Cat headed his way. The cat's movements were slow and deliberate. In his mouth, caught by the scruff of its neck, was a small gray squirrel. The animal hung limply, apparently dead. The cat was headed directly for the French doors where Sledge stood, intent on finding a quiet spot to enjoy his capture.

Sledge stepped out of the house, closing the door behind him. The cat stopped. He stared fixedly at Sledge.

The Cat wants to go inside.

"Not going to happen."

That's not very sociable.

"I'm not going to let you bring a dead squirrel into Kim's house."

I'm not bringing the squirrel in, the cat is. And the squirrel's not dead. They go limp when the cat catches them.

"Good to know. Why don't you tell the cat to put the squirrel down, then?"

Because he likes to take them inside and play with them.

213

"Play with them," Sledge muttered. "Torture them before he kills them, you mean."

Once he drops it, the squirrel will take off. That's why he wants to go in the house. There are lots of tiny places for the squirrel to hide. He can chase it again. It's more interesting than outside.

"Does Christy let him bring squirrels into her house?"

No. He brought her a mouse once. She made him take it away.

"Then why would he think it's okay to take the squirrel into Kim's house?"

Kim's a softer touch than Christy is.

"And I'm tougher than Christy. Drop the squirrel. If it runs, chase it out here. No going into the house."

"Are you talking to the cat?" Justina Strong, tall and elegant, sauntered up. Her mouth was quirked in an expression perilously close to a smirk. She raised a glass filled with what looked like three fingers of scotch and took a sip as she watched him.

Sledge raised his brows, keeping his expression cool and his voice even. "Yup. The cat and I are pals." He was annoyed by Justina's amusement and sensed that they could be on the edge of their first power struggle.

The cat looked at Justina with wide, interested eyes. He spat out the squirrel, who lay huddled on the grass for ten seconds before it bolted. The cat crouched but didn't give chase. His tail lashed back and forth.

Justina squatted down to pat Stormy's head. "He's a big fellow, isn't he?" She scratched behind his ears. Stormy lost interest in the squirrel and purred.

She straightened as Christy and Quinn wandered over, hand in hand. Christy said, "Did I see that Stormy actually captured a squirrel? There's one that lives in the greenbelt behind my house he's been hunting since we moved in. I don't think he's ever caught it."

This squirrel wasn't as smart as the other guy.

Her glass halfway to her mouth, Justina froze. Slowly, she finished the action and drank. Not the careful, social sip of moments before, Sledge noticed. Instead, she took a big gulp. More, he suspected, than she'd planned.

Christy looked at Sledge, her brows raised. Sledge grinned. Quinn groaned.

Justina glanced from one to the other, her expression puzzled. Then she smiled a social smile and said, "You're Christy Jamieson, aren't you? Kim pointed you out, but she didn't get a chance to introduce us."

Christy nodded and returned the polite smile. "I am. And this is Quinn Armstrong."

Justina nodded. "We met earlier. I think Kim said you were one of the Jamieson Ice Cream Jamiesons."

Christy nodded.

So am I.

Justina froze again. This time she whitened. She swallowed hard and said gamely, "I believe my father was at university with your father—"

My father! Not hers. Hers is a professor.

Christy shot the cat a chastening look, before she smiled at Justina. "I expect you're talking about Frank Jamieson senior. I was married to his son, Frank Junior."

That's me.

Justina choked on the last of her Scotch.

Sledge drank some of his beer. He was enjoying this hugely. Justina could clearly hear the cat, but didn't want to admit she did, and the cat was becoming annoyed at her refusal to acknowledge him. He wasn't sure what was going to happen next, but with the cat involved, it was bound to be interesting.

A typical Kim Crosier party.

Quinn decided to be a killjoy and shift the conversation away from the Jamiesons. "I understand you're from Toronto, Justina."

Justina turned to him with a smile, clearly relieved. "Yes, I am. Born and bred."

Quinn smiled at her in that disarming way he had and said, "Your family has a long history in the city."

Her smile stiffened, turning from friendly to carefully controlled. "We've lived there for several generations."

Quinn already knew that because he'd researched Justina earlier this week after his conversation with Sledge. He'd discovered quite a lot about her, and about her family. His work had a satisfying conclusion. Knowing the history of the Strong family had provided Sledge with the edge he needed to deal with the strong-willed Justina.

Quinn said, "Your dad's a corporate lawyer whose clients include several major companies. He's also influential within the legal community."

Wary now, Justina said, "Is there a specific reason you're asking?"

Quinn nodded. "Ethan Byrne is figuring in a story I'm working on. I'm looking for background information on him, and on his family, anything that might prove interesting."

When Sledge introduced Quinn to Justina earlier in the afternoon, he'd identified him as his high school buddy. Justina had figured out that they were close and had done an impressive job of interviewing Quinn. So she knew he was a journalist. Then she had accepted him as Sledge's friend. Now she was studying him with a cool assessing gaze, treating him like a reporter and preparing to manage what she said and the information she gave him.

Sledge was impressed. The band needed someone who knew how to handle the press. He watched her curiously as she sparred with Quinn.

"The Byrnes are an old Toronto family," she said, speaking easily, sounding as if she was feeding Quinn confidential information. "They've lived in the city since the Family Compact days in the early eighteen hundreds."

Sledge dredged his memory for long ago high school history. If he remembered right, the Family Compact was a group of early settlers who dominated the Toronto social and political scene for years, long after new immigration had expanded the population of the city and the province of Ontario. It was interesting information for a historian, but not all that exciting for a reporter working on a twenty-first century murder case.

Quinn, however, looked interested. "Families tend to die out or move on to other places. But the Byrnes stayed in Toronto and kept their influence, then?"

"Ethan is the current generation," Justina said with a smile, neither confirming nor denying Quinn's reference to the family's influence. "He works for a group of international property investors. His mother, like my father, is a lawyer. She was elevated to the Queen's Bench several years ago."

Quinn smiled. Sledge had a feeling he already knew this. Well, he probably would. Judges were public figures. Quinn wouldn't have any difficulty finding out the basics on Ethan Byrne's family.

"There's money in the family, though, isn't there? Ethan's grandfather started Byrne Furniture and Appliances. That's one of the biggest chains in Canada and its financials indicate it's a profitable enterprise."

Justina stared at Quinn. Sledge could see her assessing him, wondering where his line of questioning was going. "The Byrne family began as general merchants. In the twentieth century they specialized, as you said, in home decor. Ethan's great grandfather invested in prefab furniture manufacturing and they made a fortune."

All of this was available on the Internet. It was on the Byrne Manufacturing webpage, in fact. Sledge waited to see what Quinn would do.

He listened to Justina's carefully composed data with that calm, interested expression that got people to open up to him. Now it didn't change as he said, "Then Ethan Byrne doesn't have to work?"

Justina shrugged. "I suppose not."

"Why does he, then?" Quinn sounded fascinated, as if this load of non-information had exposed the man's deepest, darkest secrets.

Justina raised her brows and smiled. "How would I know?"

She was doing a great job of stonewalling Quinn, which in a normal way he'd applaud. But this was Quinn, and he was not just researching a story, he was trying to get his cousin out of trouble. If Justina had information that could be useful, she needed to provide it.

What would she do if he added his voice to Quinn's? Would she follow his lead? How she responded would tell him a lot and perhaps soothe the concerns he had about their working relationship. Or maybe he'd end up in a battle with her for respect and value.

Either way, he'd know a lot more about his band's new manager.

So, he said cheerfully, "Your father is a high-priced corporate lawyer, and Byrne's mother was a lawyer too, before she became a judge. I'll bet they ran in the same circles and knew the same people and their spouses schmoozed at parties." He raised his beer bottle and drank, then added quite deliberately, "Their kids probably went to the same private schools."

"Ethan went to Upper Canada College, which is an all-boys school," Justina said, some heat in her voice. "I couldn't attend. Besides, he's a few years older than I am. My brother knew him."

"Now we're getting somewhere," Sledge murmured, his gaze locked with hers. She narrowed her eyes.

He'd turned this into a power struggle, and it was one he didn't intend to lose. He knew Justina would be a great manager for SledgeHammer, but he sensed she and the assistants who'd been assigned to the band could become tyrants if allowed to. He didn't intend to be the junior partner in this relationship. It was a partnership with himself and Hammer as the senior members. This was as good a time as any to make that clear.

She added a frown to the narrowed eyes and a silence that stretched and tightened. Sledge smiled. Slowly, lazily. Confidently. That added annoyance to Justina's narrowed gaze, and he widened his smile into a grin.

Her jaw set, she said, "Ethan Byrne is good looking, charming, and a screw-up. He doesn't have boundaries and he indulges himself."

Quinn said thoughtfully, "People without boundaries get into trouble."

"His mother always made sure he stayed out of the system when he was a kid." She said it reluctantly, as if the words had to be dragged out of her.

Quinn caught the implication immediately. "And as an adult?"

She shook her head. "He's grown out of his waywardness. As I said, he now works for a powerful group of international financiers."

Quinn raised his brows.

She said heatedly, "Look. They pay him a huge salary. He doesn't have to go to his grandfather and pretend to be broke. And yeah, he used to borrow money from his friends, then never pay it back, but he hasn't done that in a long time."

"As far as you know," Sledge said. She looked at him sharply. He raised his brows in response. Her lips tightened.

Quinn said, "You like him."

She drew a deep breath, regaining control. "I do. He's fun to be around. If you're looking for a party, he's your guy."

Something that sounded like a snort echoed in Sledge's mind. He looked at Christy, who was staring at the cat. Quinn didn't hear, but he was now adept at reading the signs that indicated Frank was talking. He looked from Christy to Sledge with his brows raised, ready for a rundown on whatever was being said. Justina stared into her glass, the expression on her face making it clear she wished she hadn't already finished the Scotch it once contained.

The snort was followed by a comment uttered in what could only be called a world-weary tone of voice. *I was all about party time too, and I was a drug addict and a wastrel. Makes you wonder about this guy, doesn't it?*

"Oh, Frank," Christy said, deep compassion in her voice.

"Frank?" Justina said, looking from one to the other. "Frank Jamieson? What's he got to do with this?"

"Everything," Christy said with a small smile. "And nothing at all."

CHAPTER 28

After a few more stiff, uncomfortable exchanges, Justina excused herself saying she must speak to Mitch. Sledge watched her go with a wary gaze and grim expression. Christy thought that he was wondering if he'd made a mistake committing SledgeHammer to work with Justina and her organization.

She's trouble.

Christy resisted the urge to reply in kind. Bickering with Frank at a party wasn't something she was prepared to do. She also had to admit to herself that she'd done her share to add tension to the situation when she called Frank by name. It was clear Justina could hear him, but it was also obvious that she, like Lloyd and Jodie, wasn't prepared to admit to having a voice speaking in her mind.

The party began to wind down. Hammer's brother, Kyle, came over with his wife to say goodbye before they gathered up his parents and departed. They were followed not long after by Hammer and Jahlina, and her parents. Justina and Sledge's new personal assistant, a no-nonsense woman called Alice Griffiths, lingered for a while after, but when Morgan Causton and Mitch retreated to the quiet of Mitch's study to discuss potential ways to dominate the entertainment world, Justina departed, taking Alice with her.

Kim sat down on one of the plush patio chairs that could have been used in a living room and sighed. "Good. We're alone. Everyone, sit down. Relax. I do love the quiet after a party breaks up, don't you?"

She smiled a dazzling Kim smile and gestured to the seats around her. Quinn looked at Christy and shrugged. Christy laughed and said, "Why not?" They sat together on a loveseat.

Kim beamed in approval and patted her lap. "Kitty, you can sit here."

My pleasure. Stormy leapt into her lap, did three tidy circles, kneaded her thigh for a moment, then settled down in a tight ball, his head on his paws. Kim stroked him from head to tail. The cat began to purr.

Roy sank into one of the well-padded chairs while Sledge slouched at the end of a sofa, leaving Trevor to join him there and Ellen to take a chair.

"I think that went well," Kim said, staring straight at Sledge.

He stared back. "We got to know Justina better."

She can hear me, but she won't listen! She pretends I don't exist. What is it with people in this case refusing to admit they can hear me?

"Poor kitty," Kim said, stroking the cat soothingly. She looked around at the humans. "You're working on another mystery?"

"The Clayton Green murder," Quinn said.

"Oh, I read about that. They say he was killed by his mistress."

"He wasn't!" Roy said shortly.

"The police suspect Jodie Webster, Roy's niece," Christy said. "She swears she didn't do it, but the police have a lot of evidence that points to a woman and Jodie was on the scene. They're not looking at other suspects, so we're investigating to help Jodie."

"I see." Kim cocked her head. Then she smiled. Impishly. "How can I help?"

The Cat says he doesn't want you to stop petting him.

Christy laughed.

Uncharacteristically tense, Roy's eyebrows met in a fierce stare. Christy returned his look with raised eyebrows. She figured he was stressed over Jodie's fate, but she wasn't backing down.

Roy grunted, then he said to Kim, "Do you know any of the players? We could use some insight."

221

His grim expression didn't faze Kim either. She beamed at him and said, "Since I don't know who the suspects are, I can't say. Why don't you fill me in?"

So, they did. Eventually Quinn said, "We've narrowed the suspect list to five people: Harvey Wrenn, Ethan Byrne, Lloyd Webster, Howard Stoke, and Amie Foran."

"Let's look at each of them in detail," Kim said enthusiastically. "Who wants to start?"

"I will," Ellen said. "Amie Foran told Christy and me that when she left Howard Stoke at ten twenty, she went straight out of the building. That fits with the security and camera timing. Yes, she left after Jodie, so she could have had time to detour to the display suite and kill Clayton, but timing would be tight. I think that precludes her from being a viable suspect."

"And yet, when we were talking to Amie and Ruby Cronin, I got the feeling that they were holding something back," Christy said.

Ellen thought about that. "More Ruby than Amie. Ruby was implicated in Clayton's bribery of Howard Stoke. I think she knows a lot more about that than she'll admit to. Her involvement in that crime may be that you sensed, rather than knowledge about Clayton's death."

"Perhaps." Christy wasn't convinced, but Ellen's explanation fit. She decided to let it ride for the moment.

Quinn took the next suspect. "Like Amie, Howard Stoke claims he left the building after their liaison, though he says he lingered in the bed and had a smoke before he got up and dressed. By his admission, he left the suite about ten minutes after Amie left. He's seen leaving the building after ten-thirty." He paused. "There's no proof Stoke did actually stay in bed, smoking. He could have got up, dressed quickly, then hustled to the display suite, killed Clayton, and still made it down to the ground floor for ten-thirty."

Trevor made a note on his phone. "Stoke doesn't strike me as the neat and tidy sort. If he had a smoke, he'll have left the butt behind. I'll check with Patterson to see if they found anything like that in the apartment he and Amie used. Do we know the suite number?"

Christy nodded and told him. Trevor typed it in.

"What about the other three men?" Ellen asked. "Lloyd Webster, Harvey Wrenn, and Ethan Byrne? None of them have alibis for the time of the murder. All of them say they have no motive to kill Clayton." She looked around the group. "Thoughts?"

Roy sighed. "I'd like it to be Lloyd. He claims he was in his house, on his cell phone trying to connect with a donor when Green was killed."

"Patterson has confirmed that," Trevor said.

Roy nodded. "I expected that, but he never talked to the donor, only received a text from him. A cell call can be made from anywhere. Lloyd could have been in the building, hiding somewhere when the text came in."

"Except, he had to drop his kids at school," Christy said. "That means he couldn't have entered the building until after eight-thirty or nine o'clock. Wouldn't he be noticed?"

"Yeah, that's a problem. And then there's his claim he liked having Clayton as an adversary because he brought in donations," Roy said.

Christy thought he sounded disappointed. He certainly looked frustrated.

Her interpretation was confirmed when Roy added, "Lloyd is dumping Jodie, treating her like she's stinky waste he needs to dispose of. She doesn't deserve that, and I'd like to see him get some payback." His mouth turned down in a glum frown. "Unfortunately, I think he's the weakest of our suspects."

They all nodded. Quinn said, "Our last two, Harvey Wrenn and Ethan Byrne, are better prospects. Wrenn has a fancy title, but at the core, his job was to be Clayton Green's assistant. He's done that for ten years. That's a long time to be in one job. On the surface that implies loyalty to Green and the company, but..."

Ellen tapped her chin. "Yes, but. He admits he's played with the idea of changing jobs, but says he was only doing it to wring benefits out of Green. That suggests a personality that's self-centered and perhaps lazy, rather than loyal."

"Agreed," Quinn said. "Perhaps cautious too. Changing jobs takes effort and it's a risk. Wrenn had made his nest at Green's company. He knew his boss, knew what he needed to do to get by, and didn't want to test himself in a new job."

"That profile doesn't make him sound like a good candidate to murder the man who was paying his salary," Roy observed.

Quinn sighed. "Unfortunately, you're right, Dad. Still, Harvey Wrenn doesn't have an alibi for the time of the murder, so we should leave him on the list."

Trevor said, "What about Ethan Byrne?"

"When Quinn and I were talking to Sledge and Justina Strong, Ethan Byrne's name came up. Justina knew him—quite well from what she said—and he sounds like the kind of person who would plot and carry out a murder if it benefited him," Christy said.

Quinn nodded. "She was trying to be circumspect, but her comments fit with what I found out when I did some research on him."

Trevor's eyes lit up at Quinn's rather grim tone of voice. "Tell me you found some good dirt."

Sledge rolled his eyes at his father's enthusiasm. Quinn laughed. "Ethan Byrne lives in a condo in a high-end building in Yorkville, which is a fashionable neighborhood in Toronto. He drives a Porsche 911. His suits are bespoke and expensive. He's not married, but he's had a series of casual relationships—six months with a top model, a year with a social media fashion influencer, a little longer with an actress who was part of a popular TV series. He and his women are seen at all the trendy places. I found lots of pictures of him with each of them and there were the kind of references that made me think he and his ladies were each using the other to promote themselves."

Christy wrinkled her nose. "I know the type. I've met people like that."

"Yes," Ellen said. "So have I."

Quinn said carefully, "On the surface there's nothing particularly worrisome about Byrne. But..."

"Here he goes again," Sledge said, shaking his head. His eyes were twinkling. "So, what's the big BUT on Ethan Byrne?"

"His condo is rented, not owned. His car is leased. All his credit cards are maxed out. He's a heavy cocaine user. He gambles. And..." Here Quinn paused to look around the circle of fascinated faces. "He's in debt to several casinos here in Vancouver."

"Loses more than he wins, does he?" Roy remarked.

Quinn nodded. "He likes to bet big. Unfortunately, that's not always the best strategy."

"The question is, does he owe more than he can afford to pay back?" Trevor asked.

"I'd say so, yes," Quinn said.

"He sounds like a perfect scoundrel, but how would killing Clayton have helped him if he were in debt?" Kim asked, putting her finger on the weakness in Quinn's analysis.

Getting on the wrong side of casino operators is never a good idea. It was a statement, one that sounded as if it came from experience. Christy looked sharply at the cat, who appeared blissfully uninterested in the conversation.

In the year-and-a-half Frank had been rooming with the cat Christy had learned more about her dead husband than she had in life. It was disconcerting—no, it made her sad to realize just how much they had lived on the surface, with little real communication between them.

She glanced at Quinn, who raised his brows. He must have realized the cat had said something from her expression. She was about to relay the comment when Sledge spoke.

He'd slouched deeper into the sofa and stretched out his legs, crossing them at the ankles. "Frank figures that if Byrne was in hock to the casino, he'd be desperate to get money to repay them, in any way possible."

Not quite what I said, but close enough.

Sledge waved his hand, dismissing this as a triviality. "How might he do that, then? Let me count the ways." He held up his hand to tick off the items on his fingers. Kim chuckled and Ellen rolled her eyes. His father sighed.

Sledge grinned, enjoying himself. "One, he touches that grandparent

Justina mentioned for a loan, which Justina says he doesn't do anymore. Two, he embezzles whatever he needs from his employer, Dunnville Investments, which sounds like a bad idea to me, but who am I to judge? Three, he does some snooping into Clayton Green's life and discovers his bribery scheme, which he uses to blackmail Green."

There was a yawn. *Pretty good suggestions, except the last one. If he was blackmailing Green, why kill him? He'd be more useful alive.*

"Good point. It's the same problem as identifying a motive for Lloyd. There is none." Roy looked gloomy. It was clear the inability to establish a motive for Lloyd, or to shake his alibi was an ongoing disappointment.

Sledge, it seemed, was ready to defend his theory. "Green wouldn't give in easily to blackmail. Maybe he fought back, found out stuff about Byrne and used it against him. Byrne figured his only way out was to eliminate Green, so he gained access to the building and killed Green in the display suite."

Roy's expression brightened. "Blackmailer versus blackmailer. I like it." There was enthusiasm in his voice. He was always up for a complicated plot.

Quinn wasn't. "Embezzling from his employers is a risky thing to do, but it sounds more likely than double blackmail."

"You still have to tie it back to Clayton Green and that brings in blackmail again," Roy said. His eyes gleamed as Quinn grimaced, a silent acknowledgement of his comment.

"We've raised questions and created theories, but we don't have enough information to take any of our ideas beyond speculation," Ellen said.

"Then we must find more." Kim looked at each of them. Her face was lit with enthusiasm and there was mischief in her eyes. "Let's invite them to the party."

They all stared at her, not quite comprehending. Then Sledge laughed. "Absolutely. You have my vote." Amusement danced in his eyes. "Hey! Invite Patterson and her husband too. Maybe one of our bad guys will confess and she can make an arrest in the middle of the party. What better way to introduce SledgeHammer's new management?"

After a moment Roy laughed too. "Mitch's convergence empire taken one step further."

Quinn snorted. "One step further than even Mitch would find acceptable. We'd be inviting a killer into our midst and asking him or her to confess."

"A publicist's dream," Sledge said with some cynicism. He lifted his arm in a sweeping gesture. "I can see the headline—SledgeHammer, Canada's premier rock band, instrumental in capturing killer!—Mitch will be delighted."

"What will I be delighted about?" Mitch ambled over, having emerged from a doorway further down the terrace. Morgan Causton, a tall man with dark hair, ambled along behind him. Both men were carrying highball glasses filled with what appeared to be Scotch.

Kim turned and smiled at him. "I'm adding to the guest list for the party, darling. We're going to catch a killer."

Morgan blinked rather owlishly from behind thick, black-framed glasses. "Why?"

"Because it's the right thing to do, of course," Kim said. She smiled at him in a rather maternal manner and Causton blinked again. Christy doubted he'd ever had a beautiful woman like Kim Crosier smile at him in quite that way.

Stormy sat up, then hopped off Kim's lap. He stretched lazily before he sauntered over to Morgan and Mitch. *Hi, I'm Frank. We haven't been introduced.*

Morgan looked down. The amber liquid in his glass sloshed gently as his hand shook.

"Uh-oh," Quinn said. "The second time today."

The cat stood on his hind legs and put his front paws on Morgan's thigh. He reached higher with one paw and tapped gently. *Sorry, I can't shake hands. This is the best I can do.*

Morgan's eyes widened as they met Stormy's intense green gaze. He gulped down the Scotch that remained in the glass, then drew a deep breath. Patting Stormy's head, he looked over at Mitch. "Nice cat. What's its name?"

"That's the stray Kim likes," Mitch said. "I don't know if it has a name."

The cat dropped down onto his haunches. *Another one who won't listen. And I am not a stray.* Tail disdainfully high, he trotted over to the seating area. *Let's ignore these two bozos and plan a party.*

CHAPTER 29

The ballroom at the Hotel Vancouver was a flexible space, designed to be enlarged or made smaller as event planners required. It opened into a roomy foyer that could be, and often did become, part of the entertainment space for a large event. Like the rest of the hotel, the area was beautifully decorated in a traditional manner that recalled the elegance of years gone by.

On this evening the festivity being held in the spacious ballroom was a large one, with over five hundred people invited to mingle and schmooze. They were here to celebrate Canada's rock band, SledgeHammer, and to hear the announcement of their new management and plans. At first glance, the location might seem an odd contradiction—the traditional space filled with people gathering to enjoy an evening with a modern rock band, but the contrast was exactly what Kim Crosier wanted. It made people think, perhaps unsettled them, and that always made for a more interesting evening.

The event was already under way, the large space filling rapidly, when the Jamieson women and the Armstrong men, along with Trevor McCullagh, arrived. Kim had warned them that half the politicians in the Lower Mainland had been invited, and had accepted, and that there were a couple of federal government ministers planning to attend.

She also expected luminaries and executives from the music and entertainment industry, as well members of the monied set. Officially, there was no dress code, but Kim was quite certain everyone would be showing off. With that in mind, Christy and Ellen were both garbed in expensive and exquisite evening gowns. Quinn, Roy, and Trevor wore tuxes. The only oddity in their dress was the rather large tote bag Christy carried over her shoulder.

Quinn looked around as they exited the elevators and entered the foyer. Now he said, "Kim and Mitch are over there, along with Sledge, Hammer, and their new managers." He pointed to an area near the wide doors leading into the ballroom. There were a cluster of people lined up, waiting to speak to the stars of the evening. A backdrop featuring the SledgeHammer logo had been set up behind them and photographers snapped pictures of the rich and famous shaking hands, slapping backs, kissing cheeks.

"Heavens, it's a receiving line," Christy said. She looked at Quinn and the others. "I think we can skip that part of the event and slip into the ballroom, don't you?"

The bag on Christy's shoulder began to squirm. *I want out!*

"Not yet," Christy said. "Wait till we're in the ballroom."

At least open the damn bag and let me see! The voice was a bellow of frustration.

Christy jumped. Across the foyer Kim looked up, waved, and beckoned them over. Christy sighed. "I guess we're stuck. Kim must have heard Frank's shout."

The squirming in the tote bag became a frantic writhe as Stormy's head butted against the closed top of the bag. Christy opened the zipper halfway, and his head popped out. *That's better.*

They joined the line snaking its way toward the stars of the evening. It took several minutes, and Frank chattered enthusiastically the whole time. Kim was the first in the line and she hugged Christy with her usual enthusiasm, then she reached into the tote and drew out Stormy, who she cradled in her arms. Cameras clicked; flashes went off.

Christy blushed. Stormy preened.

"Can the kitty stay with me? Do you mind?" she asked, rubbing her face in Stormy's soft fur. The voice sighed.

Helplessly, Christy shook her head as she surrendered the tote to a hotel employee who was collecting wraps. "If he becomes a nuisance, Kim, just put him down. He can manage fine on his own, even in a crowd."

Kim nodded, smiling happily. Christy proceeded down the line. She had a hug from Hammer, shared a kiss with Sledge, spoke a polite word with Justina, and ground to a stop at Morgan and Mitch, who anchored the line.

"You brought that cat to a party?" Morgan said incredulously.

"The cat goes pretty much everywhere," Mitch said. "Kim likes him. She probably invited him."

Morgan looked at Mitch in amazement. Mitch, who was fine with whatever Kim chose to do, didn't notice.

"You should take it away," Morgan said firmly. "This is no place for a cat."

By this time Quinn had joined Christy and he caught Morgan's comment. "I understand where you're coming from. I could use a little less of the cat in my life, too."

Mitch brightened. "Kim will adopt him. Just let her know."

Roy wandered up at this point. "You and Kim are adopting? Mitch, I had no idea you were planning a family."

Mitch's eyes widened. He opened his mouth, closed it, then opened it again. "Not a family. The cat."

Christy tugged at Quinn's arm. "We're clogging the line. We'd better move on."

Quinn nodded. He was struggling to control a laugh, but he managed. With only a slight quiver in his voice, he said, "Come on, Dad."

They moved away, followed a few moments later by Ellen and Trevor. Out of earshot of Mitch and Morgan, Roy said indignantly, "Adopt the cat. As if he could!"

Christy looked back at the receiving line. Stormy was basking in all the attention, clearly enjoying himself. Cameras were flashing as people petted him, some gingerly, some enthusiastically. Frank's mumbled commentary was a low rumble in her mind as he exclaimed over this one or that. "Frank's having a great time. Let's leave him to it. Kim mentioned there would be food stations in the ballroom. Let's go in and see what's up."

The ballroom was draped in midnight blue cloth in which holes had been cut in the shape of stars. Light shone through the gaps, providing dim illumination in the darkened room, and giving an impression of starlight twinkling down from above. Here and there a mirror ball rotated, providing further gleaming light. The food stations were situated periodically along the walls, with small intimate round tables set in between. This left the central area open for guests to move about or pause and chatter.

In the middle of the long wall opposite the entryway a stage had been set up. A drum set, several guitars and an electric organ were ready for any musicians who might discover an urge to jam together. Remembering Kim's disapproval over Mitch's desire to have Sledge do an impromptu concert at another party Christy had attended, she wondered if this was, again, Mitch's doing.

As they advanced into the room, exclaiming at the way it had been transformed, Trevor and Ellen made it through the receiving line and joined them.

"Quite impressive," Trevor said, looking around.

"Theatrical." There was the tiniest hint of a sniff in Ellen's voice.

Christy laughed. She agreed the décor was over the top, but she thought it looked great. She pointed to a Black woman standing by one of the food stations. The woman was scrutinizing the room with a satisfied expression on her face as she absentmindedly consumed something from a small bone china bowl. "I wonder if Marenda Riddle had anything to do with the design?"

"She certainly looks as if she did," Roy said. "Let's go over and say hello."

Marenda, a television and video producer they'd met when searching for Pam Muir's killer, had indeed been instrumental in creating the look. She was pleased at their appreciation and volunteered the information that the macaroni bar behind her had the most delicious food. Christy and Quinn decided to give it a try, while Roy, Trevor, and Ellen opted for the seafood booth nearby.

The ballroom continued to fill as they wandered from station to station. Christy saw the provincial minister of tourism and culture and the federal heritage minister chatting together near a mimosa bar. Not far away, Jeff Darling was standing with Portia Quance.

Christy felt a little thrill of excitement. The players in tonight's drama were beginning to assemble. She scanned the room to see who else had arrived and her gaze caught on a familiar profile. Wasn't that Greg Farnsworth, Detective Patterson's husband? The woman beside him had her back towards Christy, so it was hard to tell if it was Patterson. She was wearing a gorgeous gown that emphasized her slim figure and her dark hair was piled up in a combination of braids and twists. A moment later, she turned to say something to Greg and Christy saw that it was indeed Detective Patterson.

She turned to Quinn who had just finished a skewer of chicken bites. "Patterson's here. Let's go over and say hi."

He nodded agreement as he wiped his fingers on a napkin. After he deposited his china plate and the napkin on a small table designated for used dishes they headed across the room.

Greg grinned at them when he caught sight of them. "Hello there! Good to see you." His enthusiasm wasn't surprising. Christy and Quinn, along with Sledge, Trevor and Ellen had been instrumental in exposing the real killer when Greg's brother had been accused of murder the previous summer.

Patterson turned as he spoke and smiled rather ironically. "Quite a party."

Christy laughed. "It's a Kim Crosier party, created with the help of Marenda Riddle, the television producer. It was bound to be spectacular."

Patterson nodded, her smile amused now. Greg laughed. "When Billie came home and told me Sledge had invited us to this event, I couldn't believe it. A personal invitation! Who would miss it?"

Patterson shot him an affectionate glance. "Sledge came down to the station to deliver the invitation in person. I was the butt of some serious teasing over it. I'll never live this down."

Greg grinned. "Yeah, and then when we went through the receiving line Sledge made sure Billie was facing the photographers, then he leaned in for a kiss and they snapped the picture."

"There goes my credibility."

Amused, Quinn said, "At the moment, Kim is presiding over the receiving line holding Christy's cat. No one will live down this party."

Patterson laughed. She shot Christy and Quinn a shrewd glance. "I saw Jeff Darling and Portia Quance earlier and just a few minutes ago I caught sight of Harvey Wrenn, who appeared to be with Roberta Green." She raised her brows. "Was that planned or...accidental?"

Christy could feel a blush rising. At the same time, she wanted to pump her fist and shout, yes!

Quinn said smoothly, "With Kim anything is possible."

"Hmmm," said Patterson skeptically. Her gaze was pointed and serious. "I'm off duty. I would like to stay that way."

"Of course," Christy said. She hoped for a breakthrough tonight, but she wasn't expecting that Patterson would need to make an arrest.

After what appeared to be some sort of internal struggle, Patterson said, "We've ruled out Howard Stoke for the murder. One of the construction crew saw him coming out of the suite where he and Amie Foran had their love nest. The time was ten twenty-five. They went down the elevator together and exited the building." She shot Christy a direct look that said she knew exactly what they were up to. "I hope Stoke wasn't one of the suspects invited tonight."

At that Christy laughed. "Absolutely not. Kim refused to have him anywhere near her or her friends."

"Good to hear." Patterson's mouth lifted in a half smile. "I suppose the rest of them are coming?"

Caught, Christy looked to Quinn for support. He shrugged. "Well... um...Yes."

His expression intrigued, his eyes bright, Greg said, "Oh man, you mean we might have some fireworks tonight?"

Patterson sighed. "I hope not."

"The idea is to put the players together in a situation where they're not on their guard and see what comes of it," Quinn said. "No fireworks, but hopefully some clarity."

Greg slipped his hand around his wife's waist. "Probably for the best."

"Absolutely," she said fervently.

They chatted for a few minutes longer before Christy and Quinn moved on. They reconnected with Trevor and Ellen by a food station featuring tandoori chicken. While they all munched the spicy dish, Ellen said, "How interesting."

"What was that?" Trevor asked.

"I just saw Ruby Cronin. She's wearing an off the shoulder dress in the most gorgeous blue. The same color as my favorite ink, in fact. Quite lovely. She was talking with Harvey Wrenn. They appeared very...friendly."

"How friendly?" Quinn asked.

Ellen frowned. "Lover friendly. But that's so odd. Ruby and Harvey have worked together on the committee for a couple of years and even recently, at the last meeting, they appeared to be nothing more than casual acquaintances."

Trevor looked over at the couple. "Definitely interesting."

"Ruby has an alibi," Christy said, scrutinizing the pair.

"Harvey doesn't." Quinn said.

"No," Christy agreed thoughtfully. "I wonder what they're talking about so intently."

"Could be anything," Trevor said.

"Could be Kim and the damned cat," Quinn said, surprising a laugh from Christy.

Roy found them at that point. He was looking harried. "Evelyn arrived, with Jodie. Seems she managed to convince Lloyd he should let the house be used as collateral for Jodie's bail." He paused, grinned, and added, "Lloyd has also moved out, apparently also at Evelyn's suggestion, and Jodie's back home. He's living in a hotel."

"He won't like that," Quinn said.

Roy nodded. "Evelyn and Jodie arrived about the same time as Lloyd. They met up in line. There was...a bit of a confrontation. Lloyd apparently wants Jodie back. Or maybe he wants to be back home. Jodie's thinking about it and Evelyn doesn't approve."

Quinn's eyes widened. "Uh-oh."

"Precisely," Roy said. "And, unfortunately, Frank doesn't approve either and he didn't keep quiet about it. Kim...ah...realized they all could hear Frank but wouldn't acknowledge him so she had some fun."

"Oh, wow," Christy said, drawing out the words. "What happened?"

Roy shook his head. "Frank taunted Lloyd, saying he was only here to find new donors, so Kim told him that wasn't allowed. He looked absolutely flabbergasted and hurried through the line. Then Frank said Evelyn needed to behave and not cause a scene, so Kim asked what kind of scenes she usually made. While Evelyn was sputtering, Frank suggested Jodie enjoy herself tonight, which Kim said was a great idea. Then, when they got to Sledge, he leaned over and kissed Jodie on the cheek and told her to enjoy the party using the same words Frank did. That freaked her out."

Quinn groaned. Trevor laughed.

Gloom entered Roy's voice. "Evelyn saw me hovering just inside the ballroom. She wagged her finger at me, so I took off." He looked sideways, then at the floor, then up again in the other direction, never meeting anyone's gaze. "And now," he said darkly, "they're headed this way."

He jerked his head to the side, and they all followed the direction of his gesture. Sure enough, Evelyn, dragging Jodie behind her, was bearing down on them.

Suddenly Jodie stopped. She stared across the ballroom. The expression on her face was first astonished, then worried.

Something was wrong.

CHAPTER 30

Realizing her daughter wasn't following her, Evelyn stopped. Turning around, she spoke to Jodie, who shrugged and shook her head. Evelyn pursed her lips, clearly annoyed.

"Quinn Armstrong!" an unfamiliar voice said heartily.

Christy turned to see a good-looking man around Quinn's age. He was impeccably dressed in a black tux that fit him perfectly. He had his hand out in greeting.

Quinn reached out and the two men shook, then Quinn introduced the others. The man, who turned out to be Ethan Byrne, smiled with smooth social precision and said, "This is quite the party, isn't it? I'm delighted Justina Strong passed my name along to the Crosiers."

Sledge must have asked his new manager to invite Byrne, Christy thought.

"I have to admit I'm not a huge fan of rock music—opera and classical compositions are more my style—but I do admire men like Sledge who are successful in what I believe is a highly competitive field."

Christy blinked. She thought there was a put-down in the statement, but it was framed positively, so she couldn't tell.

An edge of ice in his voice, Trevor said, "Sledge is a talented musician. He deserves the success he's had."

"Yes, of course!" Byrne said. "I agree. It's fascinating how creative talented people gather." He smiled warmly, focusing on Roy. "I am right, am I not, that you are Roy Armstrong the novelist?"

Roy nodded warily.

"There, you see? Not just tremendous musical talent in this room, but other types of creativity."

"Right," Roy said. He was watching Byrne with the fascinated dismay of a man who had just discovered that the black cat on his back porch was really a half-grown panther cub, young enough to be cute, old enough to be lethal.

Byrne didn't notice. He looked over Roy's shoulder and smiled. Christy saw that his smile was for a middle-aged man of Chinese extraction who was moving toward them. Like Byrne, his tux was flawless, and he had an air of indefinable wealth about him.

When he neared, Byrne said, "Mr. Lau, let me introduce you to one of our finest Canadian novelists, Roy Armstrong."

Lau bowed. Roy nodded and said, "A pleasure."

Byrne continued, his voice enthusiastic. "His son, Quinn Armstrong, the journalist." More nodding and bowing. "Trevor McCullagh, who is, I believe, Sledge's father."

"Indeed?" said Mr. Lau, looking interested.

"I am," Trevor said, reserving judgment.

"And these ladies are Christy and Ellen Jamieson, of the Vancouver Jamiesons."

Ellen raised her brows and became very much a Jamieson. Christy smiled and held out her hand. "How do you do, Mr. Lau?"

He took it and said, "It is my pleasure, Mrs. Jamieson."

Well, Christy thought as they shook, that was interesting. Ethan hadn't specified that she was Mrs. and Ellen was Miss Jamieson. Lau must be knowledgeable about Vancouver's wealthy.

"Mr. Lau is one of the principals in Dunnville Investments. He's here in Vancouver to finalize the arrangements for a new project we've been working on."

"Ah," said Ellen. "The hotel and luxury apartment complex in the West End."

Lau smiled at her. "As the CEO of Dunnville Investments, Ethan has the details of the project at his fingertips, but I believe the new complex will revitalize a neighborhood that has become sadly shabby in recent years."

Ellen's Jamieson persona deepened as she said in cool tones, "Or it will destroy an iconic Vancouver neighborhood and replace it with one that is nothing more than international slick."

Mr. Lau raised his brows. His expression was impassive, but there was a cold edge to his words as he said, "Hardly that, Miss Jamieson."

Before Ellen could craft a retort, Ethan jumped in. "Clayton Green's company will be managing the project. He was planning to work with the architectural firm, Wright and Associates. I'm sure you know Daryl Wright has a fine reputation for innovation and style."

Trevor said, "Green's company is still involved, despite Clayton Green's murder?"

"Yes, of course," Byrne said. "Harvey Wrenn is on top of all the details. He's worked with Clayton for years. In fact, I think he knew more about the company's projects than Clayton did, so there will be no problem with transition."

"I hadn't heard that the redevelopment has been authorized by city council," Ellen said, her voice as cool as Lau's had been.

"We're hopeful it will be," Ethan said enthusiastically. He reminded Christy of a puppy working very hard to please his new master. "Initial indications are extremely promising. We're pleased with the response the city has given to our proposal and we look forward to receiving a positive result to our petition." His gaze shifted between Ellen and Mr. Lau, then sharpened as he saw someone over Ellen's shoulder. "Ah, there's Councilor Darling. I must have a word with him. If you'll excuse me?" He hurried off without waiting for an answer.

Lau's gaze followed him for a moment before it returned to the group he was with. "He is a remarkably industrious young man and loyal to a fault. I value the work he does for Dunnville Investments." He nodded to Ellen and then to Christy. "His family is old Canadian stock, much like yours, Miss Jamieson. He has always been most generous, opening doors for newcomers like myself and my associates that ordinarily would be closed to us." He bent in a slight bow. "It has been a pleasure meeting each of you." He moved away, following Byrne to where he stood chatting with Jeff Darling.

"Translation," Quinn said, "Byrne uses his family contacts to lobby governments and smooth the process."

Trevor nodded. "That's his big draw and why the wealthy members of Dunnville Investments hired him. He can talk to the right people in the right way. Smooth operation." He nodded again, noting success, but not necessarily approving of it.

"Lau owns the biggest casino in Vancouver. It's where Byrne gambles when he's in town. He's lost a lot of money there," Quinn said.

"Lau may encourage it," Trevor said thoughtfully. "If Byrne's in debt to him, Lau can ensure he does what he's told."

"Lobbies the right people, pushes hard for the concessions Dunnville Investments wants. Uses his family's name and influence on projects or causes other members of his family perhaps wouldn't approve of," Quinn said. "A useful fellow to have around."

Watching Byrne, and now Lau, talk with Jeff Darling, Trevor nodded. Animated and smiling, Byrne touched Darling on the shoulder and moved just a little closer. Lau's smile was less revealing, but he nodded agreement to something suggested by his CEO. Whatever they were saying, the conversation was going well.

Portia Quance glided over to them. "My dear!" She took Ellen's hands, and they exchanged air kisses. "I saw you talking to Lau and Byrne. Were they trying to win you over?"

Ellen nodded. "They didn't, but it looks as if Jeff is falling into their toils." She shook her head. "Portia, you know my niece, Christy? And Roy Armstrong and his son, Quinn? And Trevor McCullagh, of course."

Portia nodded and said hello. Christy was as amazed at Ellen's introduction as she had been when she first described her as a niece, not a niece by marriage, or as her nephew Frank's wife. It sounded so strange, and yet, so very welcoming.

"Portia, if we don't do something, the West End project will go through."

Portia nodded. She looked around the room. "I saw Lloyd Webster earlier. Is Eugene here tonight? We should do a bit of strategic lobbying of our own."

"Excellent idea," Ellen said.

Portia's eyes gleamed. "After our conversation the other day, I had a friend of mine do some research. I think dear Jeff should hear some of the details."

Ellen raised her brows. "Are they juicy?"

"Very," Portia said.

Ellen's gaze lit up. Her enthusiasm transformed her expression and wiped years from her features. "Terrific." She looked over at Byrne and Lau schmoozing with Jeff Darling. "We must also speak with Roberta Green. She's the owner of Clayton's company. If she decides she doesn't want to do business with Dunnville Investments, they'll have to find a new construction team. That will slow them down."

"Excellent idea," Portia said. She linked her arm with Ellen's. "Roberta's over by that mac and cheese station."

"And Harvey isn't with her. Let's do an end around." Ellen nodded decisively and Portia laughed. They went off together, focused on their target.

"Well," Trevor said. He was watching Ellen progress with an almost besotted expression on his face. "I wouldn't want to be Ethan Byrne with those two on my tail."

No indeed, Christy thought. Aloud she said, "If the men behind Dunnville Investments know about Ethan Byrne's gambling, they probably know he spends all his money on flash cars and high living."

"And they don't care," Quinn said.

"In fact, it sounds like it suits their purposes to have him in debt generally, and in debt to them specifically," Roy said.

Grimly, Quinn nodded. "Which means Byrne has nothing to hide. Clayton Green wouldn't have anything to blackmail him with."

"And so Byrne had no reason to kill Green," Christy said.

"Which doesn't mean he didn't," Trevor said crisply. "All Jodie's defense team has to do is throw reasonable doubt on the prosecution's assertion that she's the only one with motive and opportunity. Byrne doesn't have anyone to corroborate his assertion he was in his home office on the morning of the murder, and he has a rather murky private life. We can work with that."

"But it doesn't absolve Jodie and Evelyn won't like that," Roy said gloomily. He looked around. "Where did she and Jodie disappear to anyway?"

"They were headed this way when Jodie saw someone and stopped abruptly. I didn't notice what happened to them after that," Christy said. She scanned the room. The number of people entering the ballroom had settled into a slow trickle and as she watched she saw Mitch and Morgan wander in together. They appeared to be in deep conversation, Mitch's hands moving expressively as he talked. Morgan listened intently, nodding from time to time. A moment later, Sledge and Hammer sauntered in, along with several big-name artists.

As she watched, Christy saw Sledge grin and wave someone over. It was Greg Farnsworth, Patterson's husband. Sledge put his hand on Greg's shoulder and gestured to the men surrounding him. Greg's face lit up as he was introduced to some of the biggest names in the music business. Justina Strong, who had paused when Sledge did, nodded and smiled, then moved away. The quiet woman employed as Sledge's new assistant remained nearby, clearly on call.

Kim followed the rest of the receiving line into the ballroom, rather like a beautiful highland collie herding her charges before her. Stormy was still in her arms, perched contentedly, watching the action with smug satisfaction.

Christy continued to scan the room, looking for Jodie and Evelyn initially, but also trying to see where all the players they'd invited were located. Roberta Green had disappeared but having captured Lloyd Webster, Portia and Ellen were bearing down on Jeff Darling. Ethan and Lau had buttonholed the provincial minister, whose expression was that of a woman who was putting up with one of the nasty side effects of being a public person.

She spotted Amie Foran who was standing not far away from Sledge and the musicians. She looked nervous, out of place and uncomfortable. As Christy watched, Sledge spotted her. He said something to Greg, who nodded, then went over to Amie. As he approached, her eyes widened with surprise. Sledge smiled his laid-back sexy smile, playing to an audience, and she relaxed, smiling back in an almost besotted way.

Christy shook her head.

"One day, that lazy charm of his will get him into a heap of trouble."

Looking over she saw that Patterson had come up beside her and was watching Sledge as Christy was.

She laughed. "Maybe. Maybe not. There's a lot more depth to Sledge than meets the eye."

Patterson thought about that for a moment then nodded. "I saw you talking to Henry Lau. Not someone you want to be friends with."

Raising her brows, Christy said, "So I've been told."

Patterson nodded. She was watching Lau and Ethan Byrne who were chatting with the federal minister now. "It's rumored money is being laundered through his casinos. Lau denies it, but..."

There was probably an active investigation going on, which meant Patterson could only hint and hope Christy would understand the implication. "Quinn discovered Byrne is a gambler and that he's deep in debt to Lau's casino. I suspect that's why he works so hard smoothing Mr. Lau's path."

Patterson's mouth curled into a small smile. "And his momma, the Ontario Supreme Court judge, isn't at all happy about it."

"No? It seems Ethan Byrne has dug himself a deep hole it's going to take some effort to get out of. It would be a terrific motive for murder." Christy grimaced, then sighed. "Unfortunately, it was Clayton Green who was killed, not Lau."

Patterson nodded, her gaze on her husband who was grinning widely as he chatted with Hammer and the other musicians.

Around them the crowd shifted and moved. Christy caught sight of Kim headed their way. So, apparently, did Patterson. She turned to Christy. "Why is your cat here?"

Christy shot her a sideways look. "Kim invited him."

Patterson blinked at her, then she burst out laughing. "Of course, she did. What was I thinking?"

At that point Kim joined them. Her eyes were bright, and energy bubbled out of her. "What a wonderful turn out. I hope you're having a lovely evening."

What's the plan? Have you figured out who the murderer is yet?

Patterson, one of those who couldn't hear Frank's voice, smiled at Kim. "I am. Thank you so much for inviting my husband and me."

"Of course. My pleasure," Kim said. She turned to Christy. "Everyone is here. Have you eliminated any of the suspects yet?"

Patterson groaned. "Not you too?"

Kim flashed her a mischievous look and winked.

Christy said, "We've pretty much crossed Ethan Byrne off the list. He has no motive."

"Who does that leave us with?" Kim wrinkled her brow. "Lloyd Webster? Harvey Wrenn?"

"Ladies! Leave the detecting to the professionals," Patterson said with some asperity.

Why? Christy's pretty good at catching criminals. Besides, you've got it all wrong. Jodie isn't the killer. You're focused on the wrong person.

"Are you seriously looking at anyone other than Jodie Webster?" Christy asked politely.

Patterson sent her a long, uninformative look.

"I didn't think so. Detective, Jodie swears she isn't guilty and I—we—believe her."

For a long moment Patterson was silent, then she shook her head. "All the evidence points to a woman as the killer. If not Jodie, then who? Amie Foran? Ruby Cronin? Shelly Kippen? They're all long shots."

"Perhaps," Christy said. "But—"

At that point Roy joined them. He reached for the cat. "Here, let me take Stormy, Kim. He's got to be feeling pretty heavy by now."

Hey! I'm happy where I am!

Kim surrendered the cat, despite his protests. She sighed, then tickled Stormy under his chin. "You're right, Roy, though I do like cuddling this sweet little kitty. He's so much fun to have around. Particularly when people get stuffy."

Stormy's eyes slitted closed and he purred. Frank might want to stay with Kim, but Stormy was happy being held by Roy, and being the center of attention.

Christy felt her eyes widen as she looked over Roy's shoulder. Evelyn was bearing down on them, dragging a mutinous looking Jodie behind her. "Roy," Christy said, "behind you."

He looked around and blanched. "Uh-oh."

Quinn appeared holding two plates of assorted items from a food station serving dim sum. He handed one to Christy, smiled at Patterson and said, "What's up, Dad?" Then answered his own question. "Oh. Evelyn."

Evelyn stopped abruptly beside Roy, but she pointed to Patterson. "You. My daughter says she doesn't want to talk to you."

Patterson raised her brows, her expression cool. "She doesn't have to."

"Yes, she does." Evelyn turned to Jodie. "Tell her."

"Mom! I'm not sure. It's just...I thought...It may be nothing."

"It may be something," Evelyn said. "Tell her."

Patterson listened to this silently, her cool expression never wavering, but her gaze probed Jodie's unhappy features.

"Mom." This time the word was more whine than exclamation.

Honestly, stop being coy and spit it out. What's the big deal?

Kim cocked her head and studied Jodie. Christy shook her head. Jodie reddened. Evelyn pursed her lips. Quinn ate a dumpling.

Roy said in an encouraging way, "You've got me intrigued, Jodie. What's up?"

Jodie cast him a grateful look. "Well, I..." She drew a deep breath. "You see I saw them together on the day Clayton was killed."

"Who?" Patterson snapped out.

"I don't know!" Jodie's voice rose. "Her face is familiar, so I've probably met her sometime, at an event like this, I think. When I saw her at the Seymour View, she looked different, though. Her hair was down, and she was wearing a business suit in a dark color. Navy blue, I think. But tonight...Well, tonight I realized I'd met her before because I'd admired her dress. She's wearing it again, you see, and I recognized it."

"Which dress?" Patterson asked. "Describe it."

"It's the most gorgeous peacock blue. It looks fabulous on her, with her dark hair and creamy skin. So elegant."

"Ruby Cronin," Christy said slowly. "I admired the color too. Jodie must have met her at one of the beautification committee's Christmas parties."

Jodie brightened. "Yes, that's it! I saw her last Christmas. She and Lloyd were arguing about something, so I avoided them." She blushed, her gaze skittering away. "That's when I started talking to Clayton and, well, you know."

Patterson nodded. Her gaze skewered Jodie. "On the day of the murder where did you see her?"

"I was on my way to the suite to talk to Clayton and they were on the landing when I got out of the elevator. They were standing close together and the man was touching her face. It looked to me as if they'd been kissing or were just about to kiss. He glanced at me when the doors opened. Just a quick look, but I could tell he was annoyed. I...I was embarrassed that I'd interrupted them, so I looked away. I didn't think any more of it. I was focused on what I wanted to say to Clayton. I think they slipped into the stairwell, but I can't be sure."

Patterson tapped her chin. "Ruby Cronin and who?"

"Harvey Wrenn," Quinn said. "We saw them together earlier tonight."

Jodie nodded. "Yes. The same man was with her tonight when I saw them."

Trevor, also holding a plate, joined them in time to hear the last exchange. "No one corroborates his alibi. He says he was out and about, but he could have entered the building with the work crew, hidden in one of the suites until ten o'clock, when he met up with his accomplice and they were both seen by Jodie. Then all he had to do was wait in the stairwell for Jodie to leave before he went into the display suite and killed Clayton Green."

I like it. Let's go arrest the pair of them.

"Impatient kitty," Kim said.

Roy shifted Stormy in his arms to make it look as if the cat had begun to squirm.

Patterson said, "Nice speculating, counselor, but there is no evidence to support it."

"There's my daughter's word!" Evelyn said hotly.

"Not enough," Patterson retorted briskly.

Trevor's plate was full of sushi. He picked up a piece, liberally spread with wasabi, and pointed it at Patterson. "I don't need proof. That's your problem. I just need reasonable doubt and with Jodie's evidence, I'm sure I have it. You won't get a conviction." He popped the sushi into his mouth and chewed. His cheeks turned red, his eyes popped, and his mouth stopped moving. For just a moment, Christy wondered if he was having a heart attack, then he breathed deep, finished chewing and swallowed. He smiled at them all. "Wonderful."

Stormy wriggled in Roy's arms. Roy tightened his grip. The cat nipped his hand. "Hey!" Roy said and shifted his grip reflexively.

Stormy twisted out of his hands, leaping down to the floor. *Gotta go, old man. We've got a murderer to catch!*

CHAPTER 31

The cat's progress through the crowd was neither swift, nor a straight line. He tended to pause regularly to accept pats and occasionally to twine around some lucky person's legs. That often resulted in a human stumble and a bolt in another direction by the cat.

He did progress, though, slowly closing in on his quarry. Kim followed, chatting with her guests, catching the odd person before he or she toppled over, making sure no one stepped on fragile cat paws.

Scanning the room to see where everyone was, Christy caught sight of Sledge. He and Hammer were still standing with the group of musicians. They were all holding glasses, which were moving erratically as their hands waved emphatically. Even from where she stood some distance away, she could feel the positive energy radiating from them. Greg Farnsworth hovered at the edge of the group, his expression besotted. Beside him was Alice Griffiths, Sledge's new personal assistant. Though she appeared to be a quiet woman Christy judged she was a determined one. She was eying Sledge and the other musicians with silent approbation. Whatever they were talking about, she approved.

Sledge lifted his glass to his lips, about to drink, but he hesitated. He looked around, then focused on the wavering path being carved by the cat. For a moment he was very still, then he turned to Greg Farnsworth, pointed to the cat, and said something. His expression startled, Greg nodded, then pulled out his phone as he scanned the room. Sledge turned back to the other musicians, spoke again, raised his glass in salute, then moved away—toward Harvey Wrenn and Ruby Cronin.

Frank was coordinating an entrapment.

Wondering what else he might have planned, Christy shifted her gaze. She caught sight of Ellen and Portia. They were now talking to Roberta Green, whom Quinn had pointed out earlier. Amie Foran hovered nearby, part of the conversation, but from her body language, trying to distance herself from it. Ellen and Portia knew nothing about the latest developments. They were probably trying to persuade Roberta not to work with Dunnville Investments on the West End project. Amie, who had allowed herself to be used by Clayton Green, had her own motives for wanting to see the project go ahead. She would be against holding back, but she was also a living embodiment of Green's perfidy. She wouldn't have a lot of persuasive power with Roberta.

As Christy watched, Portia pointed to Wrenn, bobbed her head several times, then made a series of hand gestures that clearly said they should go over and talk to him. Roberta nodded. She glanced at Ellen, who also nodded, and the three women set off. Amie trailed behind them, her shoulders slumped, her head down. Whatever her position, she was no match for the three older women.

"I think we should follow Kim and the cat," Christy said to no one in particular.

Quinn, who had been scanning the room as she had, nodded. "With Sledge in the mix, Wrenn and Cronin are going to be the center of attention pretty soon."

Patterson swore.

"Is that Sledge's assistant following him?" Roy asked as they all began to move.

Christy looked that way. Sure enough, Alice Griffiths was marching after Sledge. She didn't look pleased.

"Sledge isn't sure he can work with her," Quinn said.

Trevor, his proud father, said, "The sooner he realizes he's the one giving the orders, the better. Maybe he can make that point tonight."

"I expect she's only trying to help," Christy said.

"As long as that's all she's up to," Trevor said darkly.

Quinn said, "Sledge tends to rebel against authority figures."

Patterson swore again.

Sledge's advance was a slow progression that included a quick, social exchange with each of his fans that was a handshake or a slap on the back with the men, a hug, and a kiss on the cheek for the women. There were smiles and laughter, but he never stayed long in one place. Gradually he moved forward.

Battling through the crowd, Alice caught up to him, tapped him on the shoulder, shouted something in his ear, and gestured in the direction of the group of musicians he'd left. Sledge shook his head and pointed toward Harvey Wrenn. Her expression baffled, Alice again waved at the musicians, who had now been joined by Justina and Morgan.

Sledge shook his head, then turned his back on her. She pulled out her cell. Seconds later Justina put her phone to her ear. Frowning, she listened. Finally, she nodded and slipped her phone back into her purse. She turned to Morgan Causton. A minute later, they were on their way toward Sledge.

"Oh my," Christy said. "Looks like there's a posse after Sledge."

This time Trevor swore. So did Patterson.

The crowd at this end of the room was beginning to coalesce, curious to find out what Sledge was doing, while the rest of the hall started to notice something interesting was going on. That made travel difficult. Quinn deposited their plates on a nearby table and caught Christy's hand so they'd stay together. Trevor dumped his plate too, and followed, but, somehow, they were separated. Out of the corner of her eye Christy saw Greg come up to Patterson, holding his phone. He pointed at Sledge, then at the phone. Patterson was frowning, but she nodded and took the phone.

The others, she knew, were interspersed about the room. Roy had connected with Evelyn and Jodie. Trevor would be making his way toward the unfolding drama, but whether he'd get there in time to intervene or not, she couldn't be sure. The whole room was surging toward that one small area, clumping together, making movement difficult.

Out of the corner of her eye, Christy caught sight of Roy easing through the crowd with Evelyn behind, determinedly herding Jodie before her. Patterson and Greg had disappeared, Christy wasn't sure where.

Blissfully unaware of the forces converging on them, Harvey and Ruby drifted to one of the food stations. They were deep in conversation, with Harvey doing the talking and Ruby shaking her head as they collected their food. They continued to talk as they moved away from the booth. Finding one of the little tables free, they sat down and nibbled their refreshments, still talking intently.

Kim had finally scooped up Stormy and was once again holding him cradled in her arms, so she and the cat got to them first. Smiling brightly, she spoke to the now cornered Harvey and Ruby. Both smiled and nodded. Kim was playing hostess, biding time, keeping them busy until reinforcements arrived.

Sledge reached them first, but Quinn and Christy weren't far behind.

Ruby and Harvey stared as Sledge kissed Kim's cheek, then he shoved out his hand and said, "Hi. I'm Sledge. Thanks for coming tonight."

Harvey jumped to his feet. "Sledge. Wow. This is amazing." He shook Sledge's hand, pumping it energetically. "I'm Harvey Wrenn."

Sledge acknowledged that, retrieved his hand, and turned his megawatt smile on Ruby. He repeated his self-introduction and offered his hand.

Ruby was made of tougher stuff than Harvey. She looked up at him coolly. "Ruby Cronin," she said as she accepted his handshake.

By that time, Christy and Quinn had reached the table. Kim shot them a relieved look.

Frank was more critical. *Took you long enough. I thought they were going to escape before you got here.*

"Me too," Kim said.

Quinn didn't hear the cat, of course, but he did hear Kim and could figure out that Frank had said something caustic. He rolled his eyes, but smiled at the couple and said, "Hello, Harvey. I didn't know you were a SledgeHammer fan."

Harvey laughed and said, "I am tonight."

Sledge pulled a chair from one of the other little tables and set it up between Harvey and Ruby.

Alice the assistant tapped him on the shoulder in a deliberate attempt to capture his attention. "Sledge, you need to see more of your guests. Do come." She held out her hand, urging him forward.

Sledge straddled the chair. It was a small wrought iron piece, painted white with a plain latticework seat. The back was also latticework, bowed in an arch. He crossed his arms over the top and grinned at Harvey. It was as if Alice hadn't spoken, didn't exist. "Tell me about yourself. I'm always interested to meet SledgeHammer fans and find out all about them."

Ruby's eyes narrowed. Harvey's cheeks flooded with pleased color. "I'm a vice president with a Vancouver based construction company. We develop large properties and revitalize decaying urban centers."

"Wow," Sledge said, looking impressed. "That must be an interesting job."

"Sledge, please." Alice was sounding irritated now. Christy could see her foot tapping impatiently.

Harvey glanced uneasily at her. Sledge turned to her and said, "Go away." Then he resumed his conversation with Harvey. "What kind of buildings has your company built? Would I know any of them?"

Harvey nodded. Inevitably, he included the Seymour View Hotel and Tower where the murder took place.

Ruby said, "Harvey, darling, don't bore Sledge with picky details."

That gave Sledge the opportunity to flash his trademark smile at her and say cheerfully, "Thanks, Ruby. But I'm never bored by details." He widened his eyes and managed an intrigued expression. His tone was avid. "Hey, wasn't that last building the one where Clayton Green was murdered?"

Ruby and Harvey stiffened.

Quinn moved smoothly into the opening. "It was."

Christy added, "Unfortunately, I was one of the people who found his body."

Harvey looked at her blankly. "You were? That must have been horrible."

"It was," Christy said, and shuddered realistically. "I'm still having trouble sleeping and when I do I have nightmares about it."

Harvey stared at her, his eyes wide and fixed on her face. "I had no idea. I'm so sorry," he muttered.

Milk it, Chris. He never thought about how his killing would affect others. Lay it on him. Make him feel. Make him suffer.

"Harvey," Ruby said in an authoritative way.

He looked away from Christy, over at Ruby, whose firm expression seemed to give him strength. He swallowed. "I'm sure it was very difficult."

Christy shuddered. "It was. I've never seen the body of someone who was the victim of a brutal assault before. There was blood...everywhere. So much blood. And his face..." She paused to shake her head, aware that Harvey's blank expression had been replaced by one of shocked consternation. "Well, there was a lot of damage." She swallowed hard, coming aware that Quinn's hand was holding hers in a secure grasp that was tremendously comforting.

She shook her head, then managed to smile at the dismayed Harvey. When she glanced at Ruby, she saw the woman was watching her narrow-eyed. A telling expression? She thought it might be. "Of course, if it was bad for me, it was worse for my aunt, Ellen Jamieson. I didn't know the man. Ellen did. That makes it so much more difficult, don't you think?"

Harvey looked away.

Christy allowed her eyes to widen. "Oh, I am sorry! Ellen says you were Clayton's assistant. It must be devastating for you to lose your employer that way."

Harvey gulped, then nodded. "Clayton and I worked together for nearly ten years. It was tough."

"And now the company is going to fold." Christy touched her cheek with her fingertips in a gesture of sympathy. "That must be really hard."

"The company is folding?" Ruby said. "Harvey, have you heard anything of this?"

Harvey frowned and shook his head. "I'm sure you must be mistaken."

Though Christy's comment had been an unscripted, spur-of-the-moment idea, Quinn leapt in, holding up his end admirably. "I interviewed Roberta Green a couple of days ago. She told me she intended to wind down the business by not taking on new commissions. She'd operate it only until those projects currently in progress were completed."

"That's not possible," Ruby said. Her expression was stiff, as if she'd been hit with a blow so unexpected, she couldn't react.

Harvey looked bewildered. "Closing the company would be foolish and Roberta isn't a foolish woman. I'm sure you're wrong, Armstrong."

Quinn shrugged as he shook his head. "When the sexual bribery scheme we talked about is exposed, FGC's reputation will be badly damaged. The company may not even have the option of declining new projects. Roberta feels it's better to close, rather than be shut down."

From his deepening frown, Harvey was sucking this in and accepting it without a quibble, but there were some big holes in Quinn's fabrication, and the largest one was headed their way. Ellen, along with Portia and Roberta, had almost reached their little group.

Aunt Ellen! We have Harvey and Ruby on the run. Make sure Roberta doesn't disagree with what Quinn's saying!

Ellen, who was beside Portia and Roberta, but a little ahead of them, leaned toward the other two and said something. They looked at the group around Harvey and Ruby, then stopped. There they huddled, listening to the conversation, glancing at each other every now and then.

They were nearing the climax of this little stage play, Christy was certain. She looked around, searching for Patterson who should be on the scene, hearing everything that was being said. She couldn't see either Greg or Patterson, though she did spot Trevor, caught in the crowd, which was bunched together in a half circle watching and listening.

"That damned scheme," Harvey said bitterly. "Clayton didn't see anything wrong in it, but I knew it would come back to bite us."

"Harvey!" Ruby's voice was a whiplash. Harvey paled.

"When did you find out about it?" Quinn asked mildly.

Harvey wouldn't meet his eyes. He shrugged.

"Was it at the beginning, when Clayton was making his way up, building bigger and bigger projects and discovering new ways to cut corners?" Quinn's voice didn't sound accusing, but his words were.

Harvey flushed. "No, hardly. It was a disgusting scheme, using women, making them give themselves to that corrupt little worm Stoke. I wouldn't have any part of it. If I'd known earlier—"

"Harvey!" Ruby's voice was now a shriek. "Stop!"

"What would you have done? Would you have stopped him? Would you have left the company?" Quinn's gaze bored into him. Harvey must have felt it, for he briefly met Quinn's eyes, before he looked away.

"I tried. I told him it had to stop. Stoke was getting cocky. That's how I found out. Stoke bragged about the damn scheme, how he always enjoyed working on an FGC project because Clayton knew what mattered to a man." Harvey's hands closed into fists. "He clapped me on the shoulder and winked and said we were brothers now, weren't we? I didn't know what he meant, but I knew I had to get Clayton to stop, or I'd have to leave the company."

Quinn nodded. He said thoughtfully, "You told me you used a head-hunter's interest to advance your position in the company. But you invented that story, didn't you? You weren't trying to get a better deal with Green. You wanted to escape him."

"When I went to him, he told me to mind my own business and shut up. I told him fine, but I was leaving. And that's when he told me Ruby was one of his women." His eyes locked with Ruby's. "I didn't believe him. We'd been dating for almost a year, and we were close. We loved each other! There was no way she was involved with that vile project. I told him that. He laughed and said I was a naïve idiot."

"Harvey! You know how I feel. You don't have to say anything more," Ruby said. There was an edge of panic in her voice and a whole lot of command.

"You were caught up with some unscrupulous people, Harvey," Sledge said, shaking his head. "I guess Ruby and Clayton were in cahoots and they were both trying to drag you down with them."

Frowning, Harvey shook his head. "No. Ruby is a victim, one of women he gave to men to influence them. But..." He lowered his head, lifted his hand to his forehead, closed his eyes. Then he sighed as he lowered his hand and raised his head. "The worst of it was, he told me she'd been dating me because he'd ordered her to. That she didn't love me. Then he said I was tainted the same way Howard Stoke was—that I'd accepted sexual services in payment for my silence. If I quit, he'd make sure my next employer knew what I'd done. And when I was fired from that job, he'd tell my next employer too. And he'd keep doing that forever."

Ruby stared at him. "Oh, Harvey." There was sadness in her voice, but there was disappointment too.

Harvey glanced at her, then looked back at Quinn. His voice was quiet now, as if the energy had leached out of him. "So, I stayed. What else could I do?"

"Inform on him to the police?" Sledge suggested.

Alice, a disapproving shadow hovering beside him tugged at his elbow. "We really do need to go, Sledge."

He shook her off.

Harvey gazed at him, his expression pleading for understanding. "I couldn't! Ruby would have been finished. No one would do business with her. She wouldn't have been able to get any listings. All her agents would leave her."

Ruby groaned. "Don't try to pin this on me, Harvey."

Sledge ignored her. He smiled at Harvey in a sympathetic way. "You love her. You'd do anything for her."

Harvey nodded.

"You sacrificed yourself."

Briefly, Harvey closed his eyes. When he opened them again, he nodded, a man who knew he'd sinned, but whose compulsion couldn't be denied.

Justina and Morgan had finally managed to make their way through the crowd to the little table area. "Justina!" Alice said, sounding both relieved and annoyed. "I tried to get Sledge to come back to the musicians for a jam session, but he's refusing to move. Please help."

You, Justina! And you, Morgan! I know you can hear me. Make this stupid woman shut up or go away.

Morgan stiffened and his eyes widened. Justina, equally shocked, looked over at him. Their eyes met, the expressions on their faces horrified and not a little frightened. Almost immediately they each looked away, pretending their names hadn't been linked by an elusive voice in their minds.

Frowning, Alice looked from one to the other. "Justina? Morgan? Is anything wrong?"

Do. It. Now! The cat's green eyes glared at them.

Justina shuddered.

Kim, still cuddling the glaring cat, said, "You really should divert her. It's important."

Morgan whitened, but he said, "It's okay, Alice. We'll wait a moment. No need to rush."

"But—"

Justina put her finger to her lips. "Shhh."

Alice drew back, offended. Or perhaps merely bewildered.

While his management team diverted Sledge, Quinn kept the conversation rolling. "Green still controlled Ruby, though, didn't he?"

"He made her do vile things," Harvey bit out. "And he taunted me about it. He said she was his little assistant, like I was. She did his dirty work for him, and I made his company run. Every time there was a new woman, every time Ruby arranged a room for Stoke's clandestine meetings, Clayton told me about it. Said that I knew how the company really worked and condoned it. Told me I was part of it now. That I could never leave."

"That went on for years. Why kill him now?" There was a gasp from behind him. Quinn looked around and saw that Roberta Green had her hand over her mouth. Her eyes were wide with shock.

Harvey saw too. Quinn sensed that it was Roberta he was replying to when he said, "I met one of the girls he was using. All the others, they were impersonal. Clayton told me their names, but I didn't know them. I never talked to them. They didn't seem real. But Amie…She was different. We worked together on the beautification committee Clayton was trying to control. I discovered she was sweet and kind—a lovely person. She didn't deserve to be degraded this way. I tried to get Clayton to stop, but he just sneered and told me to stop whining. It haunted me, what he was making her do."

Amie made a small whimpering sound and put her hands to her cheeks. Maybe it hadn't been Roberta Harvey was talking to, but Amie herself.

Ruby groaned.

Kim was studying Ruby thoughtfully. Then she turned to Harvey. Widening her eyes, she smiled at him. Her voice begged him to confide in her. "You didn't plan Clayton's death alone, did you? Ruby helped."

Harvey glanced at Ruby, but he shook his head.

"Ooooh." Kim's expression was a miracle of approval. "You're such a chivalrous man, protecting your woman, taking all the blame on yourself." She dipped her head in a little nod. "But Ruby made the plan, didn't she? You put it into action."

Nodding, smiling that understanding smile, she glanced from one to the other. Mesmerized, they stared back.

When neither seemed inclined to confess, Quinn took up the story in that matter-of-fact tone he used when interviewing a subject. "Ruby wanted out, too. She scheduled the rooms. She knew Clayton would be in the building that morning because he asked her if anyone was booked to view the display suite. He wanted a place to talk to Jodie—"

"He wanted to have sex with me, the awful man!" Jodie's voice burst into the conversation. "He said now that Lloyd knew about our affair, it was over. But we could have one last romp together, he said. Because I was good in bed. As if that was a compliment. He didn't care about me as a person, just as a fun bedmate. I thought he liked me, that he felt something for me. He didn't."

"Oh, honey," Evelyn said, maternal anguish in her words.

"And you destroyed our family for that." Drawn to the group by the crowd, or perhaps because he'd been tailing his wife and mother-in-law, Lloyd Webster joined the conversation. It seemed he couldn't resist a dig.

Oh, for heaven's sake. Like I told the other two idiots, shut up! Don't look so affronted. I know you can hear me.

Jodie emitted a weak giggle. Lloyd glared at her.

Quinn shot Lloyd a disapproving look as he continued. "Ruby knew

Jodie would be in the building that morning, Amie too. Either woman would be a good scapegoat when Clayton's body was found. Both had excellent reasons for wanting him dead and neither would have a good alibi. It was the perfect time to get away with murder."

Harvey opened his mouth, but whether to confirm or deny Quinn's story, was impossible to know as Ruby snapped out, "Don't say another word, Harvey."

He shut his mouth and looked away from Quinn.

"I would like him to speak. I wish to know the kind of man I have been doing business with for the last several years," said Mr. Lau. He looked at Ethan Byrne who stood beside him. His expression was neutral, but his eyes were hard. "Did you know what sort of man this Green was?"

Ethan swallowed. "Well, I—"

"You did," Lau said, cutting him off. His mouth pursed into a thin tight line and his eyes narrowed. "I can see changes will have to be made."

Harvey snorted, apparently willing to talk when the spotlight was off him. "Ethan was clueless. He never knew Clayton was bribing Stoke to okay shoddy workmanship and second-rate materials. He didn't even notice Clayton was coming in way under budget and charging you full price, while keeping the difference for himself. All Ethan cared about was his gambling and having a good time."

"I see," said Lau. His tone of voice indicated he was not at all happy with his employee's performance.

Red faced, Byrne said, "Mr. Lau, I can explain—"

Lau silenced him with a flick of his wrist. "Enough."

We're off topic. Someone needs to drag these people back on track, because no one is listening to me!

Sledge did the honors. Smiling pleasantly, he said, "Ruby may have planned it, but you did the murder, didn't you, Harvey? You lurked in the building like a hired killer until you could scuttle out and do the job."

The goad worked. "I'm not a hired killer! I shot Clayton because it was the right thing to do. He had to be stopped. He was never going to change."

Quinn, who had more details than Sledge did, took over. "You hid in the stairwell until Jodie left, then you crept into the suite. I bet Clayton mocked you. Made fun of the fact you were dressed in a workman's clothes. Did he say they suited you? That you were just one of his hired men yourself?"

Harvey jumped up. "He was a vile man. Arrogant. Sarcastic. Full of himself. I told him it was his time to go, and he laughed. Laughed! I had a gun on him. He said I didn't have the guts to kill him. He said even if I shot the damned gun, I wouldn't be able to hit him. So I proved I could do it. I pulled the trigger and fired the gun. Over and over and over until he was lying on the bed, dead."

"Then you ran away and left an innocent woman to take the blame!" That was Evelyn, contempt and fury shivering through her voice. "You call Clayton Green vile. Look in the mirror."

Horror had Harvey straightening. "I'm nothing like Clayton!"

Evelyn snorted. "Sure. Believe what you want to believe."

He jabbed his finger at her. "You don't understand."

She curled her lip and turned away without replying. Harvey was left quivering with outrage as he glared at her back. His gaze moved away from her, and he suddenly seemed to become aware of the avid stares of the crowd that was packed into a semi-circle around the area. He paled.

From behind her Christy heard someone say in an astonished voice, "That guy just confessed to murder. Can you believe it?"

Someone else said eagerly, "This is the most amazing party I've ever been to!"

And finally, the comment that capped them both. "I got it all on my phone! I uploaded the video. #SledgeUnmasksKiller. It's already trending!"

CHAPTER 32

S ledge slowly rose from the little chair. He swung his leg over as he pivoted so he was staring at the crowd. He scanned their faces. "Whoever uploaded the video, take it down and send it to the police instead."

"Too late," Alice the assistant said. She was working her phone, frowning as she peered at the screen. "It's been up less than a minute and it's already gone viral."

Sledge's mouth tightened with annoyance. "Take it down, anyway, and delete the hashtag. This is a police matter."

Ruby stood up. Taking a step forward, she pointed at the man who had uploaded the post. "You should listen to him. Delete it immediately or you can expect to hear from my lawyers in the morning."

"Yeah, sure," the man said.

Harvey said, "Mine too."

"Shut up, Harvey." Ruby didn't even bother looking at him. He shrank back down onto his chair.

Ruby shot Kim an imperious stare. "I'm leaving now. Thank you for the invitation. I can't say it's been a lovely evening." She picked up her bag and took a step forward.

"Not so fast," Sledge said. He held out his hand to stop her. The crowd remained in a tight arc, a wall of bodies that would only open to allow her to exit if Sledge okayed it. He shook his head. "You need to stay here and talk to the cops when they come."

"Nonsense," Ruby said briskly. "I have nothing to say to them."

Sledge smiled grimly. "You may not want to talk to them, but I'm sure they will want to talk to you." His hand remained out, keeping her from moving forward, creating a barrier she could not pass. "Please sit down."

There was an eddy in the crowd as Mitch pushed his way to the front. "That police detective you hang out with has called for backup," he said to Sledge. "Seems she doesn't carry handcuffs with her when she goes to parties."

Sledge raised his brows. "Not surprising."

Mitch nodded. He viewed the two culprits dispassionately and being Mitch narrowed the focus to align with his own interests. "You thought you could steal SledgeHammer's thunder, didn't you? Coming to their party and co-opting it so you could make a big splash when you confessed. Well, the laugh's on you. The comments coming in from the video are not complementary. You'd have been better shutting up and hoping the cops never figured it out."

Ruby made a rude sound between a snort and an exasperated sigh. Harvey put his head in his hands and groaned.

Behind Mitch, Morgan and Justina had been conferring, while Alice worked her phone collecting data and muttering as she did.

A few moments later she looked up and said with some surprise, "Sledge is a hero." She waved her hand at her screen. "People are applauding the subtle way he convinced two hardened criminals to confess—"

"I'm not a hardened criminal!" Ruby said, outraged.

Alice grimaced. "Sorry, but the jury's out on that one."

Justina was working her phone too. "I've already had several requests for interviews." She switched apps. "SledgeHammer's latest album is number one on iTunes."

Sledge said loudly and with great firmness, "Whoever the idiot was who uploaded the video, take it down. Now."

A look at his expression would have told anyone he was serious.

There was some grumbling, but the enterprising man who had filmed the entire conversation deleted the post. He'd had help in making his decision, since Mitch recognized him as being one of the executives in his company and made a point of reinforcing Sledge's demand. Whatever the fellow's personal viewpoint, he wasn't going to risk his job by falling afoul of both the company's leading moneymaker and his ultimate boss.

The police arrived, beating a path through the close packed crowd. Patterson in her figure-hugging evening gown was a stark contrast to the uniformed constables. "Transport them to the station and book them. Then take them down to the cells. They can spend the night. We'll interview them in the morning."

"What?" Harvey said. "You can't do that!"

When one of the cops put his hand on her shoulder, Ruby shrugged him off. She pointed at Harvey. "I'm not the killer, he is!"

"Hands behind your back please, ma'am." The constable took her wrist.

"This is outrageous!" Though she protested and put up a struggle, moments later the handcuffs were on.

Patterson turned to the other players in the drama. "I'll be talking to you tomorrow. Make yourselves available."

Christy nodded. Quinn smiled. Evelyn said imperiously, "Jodie will expect an apology, Detective."

"Mom," Jodie said, high color in her cheeks.

Ellen, who had stayed out of the interview, said, "I would not expect anything of the sort, Evelyn. The detective has yet to apologize to me for a wrongful arrest over a year ago." Disdain dripped from her voice.

Patterson cast her gaze up to the glittery ceiling with the faux starlight. "Oh, for heaven's sake." She followed the constables through the makeshift pathway and out.

After their departure there was an uneasy quiet, the aftermath of high drama and surging emotions. Greg Farnsworth wandered over to say good night. "I'll meet Billie at the station to take her home. Otherwise, she'll end up being there all night." He turned to Sledge with a smile. "Great work. Sorry I can't stay any longer."

"You did fantastic," Sledge said. He shot out his hand to shake Greg's.

"I figured something was going to happen and the police needed to be here. I thought if you phoned them, you'd have more pull than I would."

Greg laughed. "The best I could do was get them on the line then have Billie authorize."

"Whatever you did, it worked. Nice going."

Smiling with pleasure, Greg gave them all a wave then turned to leave.

Justina cleared her throat and said to Sledge, "Your participation in this evening's events was...very...um, civic-minded of you."

"Civic-minded?" Christy repeated sotto voce to Quinn, who laughed.

"But I don't recommend that you do it again. There are elements of SledgeHammer's audience that might not approve of such...er...proactive behavior."

Sledge stared at Justina narrow-eyed. Christy was reminded of a comment Quinn had made, that Sledge did not react well to being ordered around. He certainly looked ready to blow now.

There was a yawn, then, *Stand down, man. She's bossy, for sure, but she's just doing her job.*

Justina colored.

Yeah, pretend all you want, but you can hear me.

The tension eased in Sledge's shoulders, and he grinned. "Hey!" he shouted. "Who's ready to party?"

The crowd roared.

"Then let's make some music!"

An alley opened through the wall of people so Sledge could saunter to the stage that had been set up, ready for just such a circumstance.

As the crowd shifted, moving toward the stage, making way for other musicians to join Sledge, Mitch wove through the mass of people to Kim. He scratched behind Stormy's ears and looked hopefully at his wife. "Why don't you let the cat's owners hold him so you and I can dance?"

"Oh, Mitch," Kim said blissfully as she passed Stormy to Christy.

I've told you before. Nobody owns the cat!

WHEN THE CAT'S AWAY

THE 9 LIVES COZY MYSTERY SERIES, BOOK 9

"My father needs your help!" Tamara turned wide, pleading eyes to Quinn.

Christy tightened her hand on the glass of lemonade she was holding. She, and the other members of the Jamieson-Armstrong group, were visiting Christy's parents in Ontario. They had been enjoying a lazy afternoon on the deck at the back of the Yeager's gracious limestone home when Tamara arrived fifteen minutes ago, distraught and on the edge of panic.

She glanced at her parents, only to see them both staring fascinated at Tamara. They knew Christy and the others had investigated several mysteries back home in Vancouver, but the Yeagers had never been involved in one of their cases. Somewhat reassured they were interested rather than horrified, Christy looked over at Quinn. He appeared to be as tense as Tamara was.

He shifted uneasily. "Look, Tamara, I understand, but I don't think—"

She rounded on him. "No, you don't understand. A man is dead. A man my father had an argument with the day before he was killed. That horrible cop Inspector Fortier, the one who investigated Frederick Jarvis' murder in Vancouver, is involved in this case. In Vancouver he decided I was the killer and wouldn't consider anyone else. Now he believes my dad killed this poor man in Ottawa. He's going to arrest my father, just like he arrested me. And Dad's done nothing wrong! His only crime is caring about people and helping them live better lives." As she spoke her voice rose almost to a shout that ended on a choked back sob.

One of the other occupants of the deck, Rob McCullagh, better known as Sledge the lead singer in the Canadian rock group SledgeHammer, stirred in his seat. "What's the harm in taking a couple of days and checking into it?"

Quinn sent him a smoldering look, but Tamara paused to stare at him hopefully.

Sledge grinned at Quinn, unintimidated by his glare. "Come on," he said. "You've got to admit it would be fun to take on Inspector do-it-by-the-book Fortier again. We showed him up before. We can do it again."

"We're not in Vancouver this time," his father, Trevor McCullagh the third, said, sending him a repressive look. "We don't know the territory and we don't have any contacts."

Sledge shook his head. His phone rang. He denied the call without even identifying who was trying to contact him. "We've got Quinn's investigative skills, Christy's charm—"

Christy made a small sound of suppressed amusement. Her mother beamed while her father eyed Sledge thoughtfully.

With a wicked grin, Sledge continued, "Roy already has a pal in Fortier's sidekick, Sargent Doucet. With a little work, I bet he'd spill all the details. My dad can defend Mr. Ahern if he needs it and Ellen will keep us all organized with her magic pens and perfect paper."

"I'm not licensed in Ontario," Trevor said.

Sledge waved this away as a minor glitch.

"I left my pens and letterhead at home," Ellen said.

"You could buy a new one," Rachael Yeager said helpfully. "There's a lovely pen shop in Ottawa."

"Is there?" Ellen said. She sounded interested. Her expression turned thoughtful.

Sledge's phone rang again and once more he denied the call without checking. "Great. Ellen can add to her collection and my dad can give excellent advice, even if he can't represent."

"Why don't you answer the phone?" Roy asked.

Tension etched Sledge's features for a moment then was smoothed away. "Because it's Justina Strong and she wants me to do some media gigs while I'm here in Ontario."

Trevor raised his brows. "And you don't want to?"

Sledge shrugged.

Roy's eyes gleamed. "Why not do some joint interviews?" A multi-published author, Roy had a new mystery series to promote. He lifted his hands with enthusiasm. "Hey, we could include Quinn. His new book is coming out in the fall. He could use the air time too."

"Dad," Quinn said, sounding disapproving.

Stormy the Cat, with his roommate the late Frank Jamieson, galloped up onto the deck. He'd been playing in the garden, terrorizing the local chipmunks, before the discussion began. Enough about interviews and book promotion. What about me? What's my assignment?

Sledge's eyes gleamed and he grinned with unrepentant devilry. "Your job is to cause mayhem."

The cat sat in his neat and tidy way, back straight, tail wrapped around his front paws. *Awesome. I'm in. When do we start?*

～

Available in Paperback and eBook from Your Favorite Bookstore or Online Retailer

ABOUT THE AUTHOR

The author of the 9 Lives Cozy Mystery Series, Louise Clark has been the adopted mom of a number of cats with big personalities. The feline who inspired Stormy, the cat in the 9 Lives books, dominated her household for twenty loving years. During that time he created a family pecking order that left Louise on top and her youngest child on the bottom (just below the guinea pig), regularly tried to eat all his sister's food (he was a very large cat), and learned the joys of travel through a cross-continent road trip.

The 9 Lives Cozy Mystery Series—*The Cat Came Back, The Cat's Paw, Cat Got Your Tongue, Let Sleeping Cats Lie, Cat Among the Fishes, Cat in the Limelight, Fleece the Cat,* and *Listen To the Cat!*—as well as the single title mystery, *A Recipe For Trouble*, are all set in Louise's home town of Vancouver, British Columbia. For more information, please sign up for her newsletter at http://eepurl.com/bomHNb. Or follow her below.

www.louiseclarkauthor.com

 facebook.com/LouiseClarkAuthor